ACKNOWL

`C000151508`

Thank you so much to everyone at 5 Prince Publishing. I always knew I had one book in me, and if it were not for Bernadette Soehner, my first book, The Perfect Mrs. Claus, would still be handwritten pages in an old steno book. And because of 5 Prince, I am now the proud author of book #2, Beach Rose Path. This also would not have been possible without the eagle-eyed editor Cate Byers who always made me laugh about any misspellings which always meant something totally opposite than what I wanted to say. Thank you, Cate, for your patience and professionalism--I have learned so much from you. Thank you all at 5 Prince for making my publishing dreams a reality!

ALSO BY BARBARA MATTESON

The Perfect Mrs. Claus

Beach Rose Path

BEACH ROSE PATH

CHAPTER ONE

"I'VE JUST BEEN TOLD, CHAR, WHEN THE NEW OWNER AND GENERAL Manager comes later in the spring, he's cleanin' house. Bringin' his own crew with him from some swanky golf club in Georgia."

Hamish Falconer sat in his worn leather chair in the executive office at Castle Loch Country and Golf Club where he had been the General Manager for forty years. Even at age 73, he still maintained as much of his effervescence, energy, and Scottish accent as when he started as the assistant manager so many decades ago. His coal black hair had only a few threads of alabaster running through it, and it was still thick as when he was a young man, and combed neatly away from his face. His large, blueberry eyes were framed by heavy, dark eyebrows. Although still handsome, deep lines now crossed over his forehead and under his eyes, while a coarse salt-and-pepper mustache and beard covered his strong upper lip and jawline. Hamish continued to maintain a trim figure thanks to the many rounds of golf he loved to play each week, and at six and a half feet tall, he cut a most formidable figure.

Charlotte Templeton, Hamish's long-time employee and

friend, sat in a similar wing-backed chair on the opposite side of his desk. Charlotte couldn't believe it had been over two decades since she had graduated from Boston's Calloway Junior College with her fashion merchandising degree, and that Hamish Falconer, the revered General Manager of the Castle Loch Golf and Country Club had offered her a job as the ladies members pro shop buyer. In the twenty-five years they had worked together, Charlotte had come to consider Hamish more of a father figure than her boss.

Although her own brown hair was becoming more pearlescent, she felt she still maintained the enthusiasm of her younger self that had first interviewed to be the ladies' golf wear buyer all those years ago. Her eyes were just as brown and bright, even though tiny lines now creased at the edges and upon her upper lip. She kept busy and took care of herself, and her 5'2" frame was still slender and athletic, due to being so busy and enjoying an occasional round of golf herself.

"I can't say I'm surprised," continued Hamish. "I hoped it wouldn't happen, but I'd heard rumblings of the club going under new management. Rumors like that popped up here and there over my years here, but nothing ever came of it. Until now."

Charlotte felt as if her heart would drop right out of her chest and through the floor of Hamish's office. She had taken the ladies' pro shop from a dusty basement to its own homey shed that she'd converted into the Loch Ladies' Pro Shop. Charlotte's merchandise was very popular, as she consistently consulted golf magazines and updated the wardrobe options from drab and functional to performance pretty. Her inventory always sold out, and the ladies constantly clamored for the newest arrivals, always praising Charlotte for her insights in not only functionality, but in clothes that made the ladies feel and look good. Pastel golf bags, gloves, cleats, and hats completed the ladies' stylish ensembles.

A sharp needling of tears pierced Charlotte's brown eyes. The news was ghastly and devastating. Not only was she losing her job, she was losing her home.

"I know it's shocking, especially with what you've been through for the last few years. I know you have a lot of memories of your boys here."

Your boys. Charlotte's eyes could no longer hold back the tears at Hamish's mention of her boys. Although they were no longer physically here, she felt them with her every moment in her little bungalow, a perk of the job, in which she had lived for over two decades. How was she supposed to leave her home?

"I'm sorry, Hamish. I don't mean..." She wiped the tears from her eyes with the sleeve of her emerald green pullover, a gift from her boys.

Charlotte inhaled deeply, trying to compose herself, knowing that there was nothing she could do about the new management.

"So, when is our little world coming to an end?"

Hamish leaned back in his leather chair, its well-worn springs squeaking with his every movement. Charlotte could smell the comforting hint of the honey and lemon cleaner Hamish used daily on his beloved chair. His entire office was so very reminiscent of a den in a Scottish castle, with its highly polished woodwork shimmering in the rays of the sun that streamed through the floor-to-ceiling windows. The walls were lined with shelves of books, all golf tomes, and where there were not bookshelves, the walls were adorned with paintings of famous golfers from various periods of time. His desk was masculine and large—a behemoth of a mahogany escritoire. Castle Loch was the sister golf club and course to Castle Inverness in the Scottish Highlands, and the sights and sounds of Scotland were clearly evident in this Massachusetts golf club.

"From what I hear, the new GM will start right before Memorial Day weekend, which is in about seven weeks. I just wanted to prepare you, Char. It's better to know than not, and this way we can figure out a plan. Together. I will not be leaving you in any kind of lurch."

"Well, I know what your plan is," Charlotte said, her tears abating. Hamish had spoken often of returning to his beloved Scotland, and Charlotte knew this was his chance, especially because it was where Colin, Hamish's son and daughter-in-law lived.

"Oh, you know me too well, Char," he laughed, settling back into his old leather chair.

"I have missed Colin and now that he and Haleigh have given me a grandson, well, yes, it's time for me to go home. For good," he sighed.

"I'm so happy for you Hamish. Your heart has always truly been in Scotland." Charlotte realized one day her beloved friend would return to his roots, and now that day was here.

Hamish rose from his chair and sat in the one next to Charlotte.

"I know that this is difficult for you. You've always been like a daughter to me, and I am going to make sure you're taken care of as well. It's my responsibility."

"It's no such thing, Hamish," Charlotte replied solemnly. She took hold of his large and calloused hands.

"I made the decision to stay here. I could have left at any time, and I probably should have, but I was never ready. I have no choice now, and maybe this is actually a blessing in disguise. Things happen for a reason. I remember you telling me so many years ago when I did not get the buyer position at Howardson's Emporium, which brought me to you, that when one door closes—"

"Another one opens," he finished, and Charlotte felt his hands clasp tighter about hers.

"I think I might have a door that's about to open for you, Char," said Hamish, still holding onto Charlotte's hands.

"I'd be the proverbial fish out of water in Scotland, if that's what you're thinking," she said, smiling at her old friend. *He would come up with an idea like that*, she thought, watching the mischievous twinkle in his dark blue eyes.

"Aye, I'd love to take you with me, but I know America is your home, especially New England. So..." Hamish rose from the wing-back chair and returned to his old leather one on the opposite side of the desk. He slowly opened a drawer directly under the top of his desk and pulled out a green folder with the Castle Loch logo imprinted on it. He handed it across the desk to Charlotte.

"What's this?" she asked, taking the folder.

"Your next challenge."

"What are you talking about?" Charlotte could not imagine what the folder could possibly contain.

Hamish shut the desk drawer. "Charlotte, what you've done with Loch Ladies was nothing short of brilliant. Remember when it was a tiny corner in that dusty old basement of the men's pro shop? In less than two years, not only did you update the inventory, but you also cleaned that old shed next to the clubhouse and created a paradise for the female members here. And you did it on your own. The success of Loch Ladies is all due to you. And I think you are up to the challenge of tackling something similar again. It's all in that green folder."

Charlotte opened the folder and found a tourist brochure. It had a huge lobster claw superimposed over views of the ocean.

"Lobster Claw, Maine? Are you sending me on that long-needed vacation?" She laughed at the name on the brochure, wondering how in the world a town had such a ridiculous name.

"An absolutely gorgeous place, if I do say so myself. Very reminiscent of Scotland, but that's my humble opinion. My old friend Rory Ruskin ran a place up there, but his heart's not it in any longer, and he's returned to Nova Scotia to be back with his family."

"Heart's not in what, Hamish?" Charlotte asked, as this was sounding more cryptic by the moment. What in the world did Hamish have in mind for her? She suddenly noticed a roguish twinkle in his blueberry eyes.

"A store. A souvenir sort of place. Did very well at one time, but when Rory's wife passed, ah, well, you know, I think she was the true heart and soul of the place, and he just couldn't be there without her any longer."

"So the place is empty? Why doesn't he just sell it?" Charlotte asked.

"Can't say I know, lass. All I do know is that it would be great to have the place occupied, and maybe get the store back up and running. Might be something you'd be interested in." This was a statement, not a question.

"Hamish, I—I don't know what to think. So much has happened so quickly." Her little cottage on the green, the home she made with her boys, was no longer hers, and neither was Loch Ladies. Castle Loch held all of her beloved memories and now Hamish was talking about moving her to some crazy-sounding town in Maine.

"Char, I know it's a lot. But the club as we know it is coming to an end, and we both must move on." Hamish's words were gentle but true. "Take home the folder and think it over, and we can talk again tomorrow. How's that?"

"Thanks, Hamish. I promise I'll read every word tonight." Charlotte put the brochure back into the folder and let it rest on Hamish's desk.

"Good girl." She then chuckled to his reference of "girl," as she was officially now a fifty-two-year-old woman.

Whether a situation was dire or delightful, Hamish Falconer could always bring optimism and a generous smile, which eased Charlotte tremendously.

Charlotte rose from her wing back chair, tucking the folder under her arm.

"Looks like you're going to keep me busy this evening." Charlotte walked to the other side of Hamish's desk and placed a daughterly kiss on his bearded cheek. She could see the blush rise on his ruddy face which made her love him all the more.

CHAPTER TWO

Steam floated from the spout of the stainless-steel electric tea kettle. Instead of heading to her cottage, Charlotte had decided to return to Loch Ladies after her meeting with Hamish, wanting to spend as much time in the pro shop as possible before the new management descended upon it. She poured the scalding water into her favorite teacup that she kept in the shop—a delicate bone china cup painted with red and pink roses. It was part of her parents' wedding china that Charlotte inherited and had planned to use for her own wedding someday. Every time she sipped tea from the cup, thoughts of what might have been flooded her mind, but especially today.

While Charlotte let her favorite peppermint green tea steep, she took a small key from the inside of a slim golf glove that she kept in a basket of miscellaneous junk under her computer. She pulled a small cedar box from under the counter, one she received from a local furniture store when she graduated from high school, a type of miniature hope chest. Charlotte inserted the little key into the lock. She opened the box and sorted through some of her life's keepsakes—the tassels from the graduation hats from her high school and Calloway, a yellowed

8

newspaper article detailing Princess Diana's wedding dress, and a small black velvet box. She took the velvet box, cradled it in her hands, and gently pulled the lid open. Inside of the soft box sat a ring—her engagement ring. It was a beautiful two-carat, oval-cut emerald that shone like newly sprouted spring grass. The emerald was surrounded by twelve diamonds that twinkled like stars in a summer sky. It was breathtaking and stunning, but Charlotte felt the velvet box was a better place for it than her left ring finger. Landon and Peppe were no longer here, and this was a symbol of their future.

Charlotte's cherished memories no longer brought deep heart-rending sorrow. She now basked in the comfort and contentment of knowing that even though she suffered tremendous losses, she also experienced great love. She was aware she could live in her happy and safe past, fantasizing about what life could have been like with Landon as her husband, but also very mindful that Landon and Peppe, their dog, were no longer in her life.

Charlotte gazed at the ring. The diamonds surrounding the emerald seemed to have an extra sparkle in the late afternoon sunshine that streamed through the shop's windows. She watched the diamonds twinkle and wink in the sunshine, and she couldn't help but smile at its beauty. It was too exquisite to be kept inside of the box, so Charlotte put the emerald on the fourth finger of her right hand, feeling she was ready to wear it, for a little while at least.

"Gorgeous" she said, extending her arm, admiring her ring. Charlotte looked around the shop; her shop. It was small, and she was proud of all the work she put into it and of its success. Her eye then caught a deep nick in the old wooden floorboards, and a smile graced Charlotte's face as she let her mind wander back to the day when she met the love of her life.

~

"Char, I can get someone to lift those boxes for you."

Hamish Falconer had just signed off on five boxes of new women's apparel for Loch Ladies Pro Shop. Charlotte reviewed the bill of goods to ensure all the items had arrived, and according to the paperwork, everything was in order.

"I'm good, Hamish. I'm going to open and unpack everything now instead of storing them. If you don't mind handing me the box cutter, I can start getting things unpacked." Charlotte loved nothing more than unboxing new items. Even though she had been at Castle Loch for twenty years, the excitement of the arrival of a new shipment never got old.

"Here you go."

Charlotte turned to an unfamiliar voice and was met with the most penetrating russet-colored eyes she had ever seen. They were the color of autumn chestnuts with slight flecks of amber, making them seem as if they were lit by candlelight from within. His eyes sat in a bronzed face. His thick hair was the color of charcoal with a few silver strands threaded throughout. He was slightly taller than Charlotte with a slim but muscular build. Her heart quickened and she felt her hands begin to shake.

"Can I help you?" she asked. She then realized she was alone with this stranger in her shop.

"I hope so," he said softly, handing her the box cutter. His hand slightly brushed hers, and, distracted, she fumbled it, causing a loud clanking sound when the knife hit the floor, creating a very visible notch in the pristine hardwood floor.

"I'm sorry," he said, retrieving the box cutter and laying it on the counter. "First day jitters, I guess. I'm Landon Harvey, the new golf pro. Hamish Falconer asked me to meet him in the ladies' pro shop." He turned, looking for the General Manager. "I'm not sure why," he laughed. "I don't think anything in here will fit me."

That Hamish, thought Charlotte. She knew exactly why he told this new golf pro to come to Loch Ladies. He was up to no good again with his matchmaking skills. *The next time I see him...*

"Oh, there you are, Landon!" Hamish appeared from out of what seemed like thin air, his blueberry eyes twinkling playfully and his cheeks looking more pink than usual. Charlotte knew he realized she had caught onto his little matchmaking scheme and narrowed her own brown eyes at him. She couldn't be mad at him, this time, thinking that Landon Harvey would make a nice addition to the club. And, more importantly, she knew the ladies would swoon over him, which would get them right into Loch Ladies for the newest apparel.

"So, I see you two have met!" Hamish heartily laughed, extending his hand to Landon.

"Hamish, great to see you again!" Landon not only took Hamish's burly hand, but Hamish's arms engulfed him in a bear hug.

"Aye, Land, it's been so long. Too long." Charlotte thought she heard a note of regret in Hamish's voice, making her wonder how long the two of them had known each other.

"I know my father is smiling down upon us right now, Hamish. It's no coincidence that I'm here." Landon then turned to Charlotte, his smile brighter than a midsummer sun.

"Miss Charlotte Templeton, let me introduce you to Landon Harvey, our new golf pro. Charlotte is our ladies' pro shop buyer extraordinaire," Hamish said, flourishing his arms in admiration for the light-filled and colorful store.

Charlotte felt a warm blush creep into her own cheeks now, and she didn't know if it was from Hamish's acclaim or from Landon's thousand-watt smile.

"Pleased to officially meet you, Miss Templeton." Landon offered his hand to hers, which she accepted, and the blush in her own cheeks seemed to feel hotter from his touch.

"Nice to meet you as well. And please, it's Charlotte."

"Or Char if she gives you permission!" Hamish laughed, walking toward the front door.

"I'll let you two get acquainted. Landon, you can find me in my office when you're ready." He winked at the new golf pro and exited through the shop's door into the warm spring light.

"Hamish is not one for subtleties, is he?" Landon said smiling, watching Hamish leave the shop.

"He tends to be like that with me, too," she smiled. Landon was handsome, and a golf pro, which would make him the prey of many of the members who had eligible daughters, or perhaps even for themselves. Charlotte would not compete with the wealthy members of Castle Loch for the new golf pro's attentions.

An awkward silence permeated Loch Ladies.

"I'm happy to show you the way to the clubhouse, if you'd like," Charlotte said breaking the uncomfortable silence. She found something immensely attractive about Landon, and she wasn't ready to see him leave.

"I'd like that," Landon said, opening the door for her to exit. She looked at Landon and saw sincerity in his soft brown eyes. They were only going two minutes to the clubhouse; no harm in that.

"Great," she smiled, walking through the door with Landon close behind her.

A warm breeze blew through the newly sprouted leaves on the oaks and maples that lined the walkway from the pro shop to the clubhouse. The scent of lily-of-the-valley perfumed the spring air, as this May had been one of the most beautiful after a long and snowy winter. Following a very rainy April, it seemed as if almost on cue, at midnight on April 30, the rain ceased and the golf course was one of the most brilliant shades of emerald green Charlotte had ever seen. Everything seemed to bloom almost overnight, from the red and orange tulips to the sherbet and lavender phlox to the brilliant purple lilacs. The potency of

Mother Nature's fragrances that blended together was heady and exhilarating, leading Charlotte to believe that anything was possible on this beautiful spring day. The sky was a spectacular blue with cottony clouds floating through the sky. She could hear the songs of the cardinals, blue jays and mourning doves cooing, along with the chirping of the fast and fleeting chipmunks, giving her the sense that she had suddenly entered into some sort of magical wonderland. She half expected a deer to appear to escort them both to Hamish's office. She laughed at the silly thought, thinking she was far as could be from Snow White.

"What are you laughing at?" Landon innocently asked as they approached the imposing castle-like doors of the clubhouse.

"It's just such a beautiful day," she said, as he opened the heavy medieval-styled door and let her enter before him. "It's just one of those days where you feel so alive and that possibilities are endless."

"Charlotte," he said, closing the door behind him. "I know we just met, but could I invite you to join me for coffee later this afternoon, when I'm done with Hamish?"

Landon's brilliant smile melted her heart.

"I'd like that," she said, surprising herself. *What's one more heartbreak*, she thought, almost giddy with anticipation of having a coffee date with Landon, promising herself that it would be nothing more than that, and this was just a case of spring fever.

In the months that followed, Charlotte and Landon saw each other exclusively, and then Christmas Eve was upon them. Hamish had left for Scotland the day before and wouldn't return until after the first of the year, and Loch Ladies was closed from Christmas to New Year's. Landon's schedule was sparse as well, as many members of his Castle Loch fan club were off to the sunny climes of the Bahamas or skiing in Europe.

Charlotte stood in front of the bay window in her cottage on the green. It could not have been more perfect—a fire blazing in the fireplace; the tree alight with what seemed like hundreds of glowing fairy lights, and a perfect winter wonderland right outside of her window.

"Merry Christmas, Charlotte." Charlotte turned to Landon's quiet voice, and gasped in astonishment.

He was standing in front of her and cradled in his arms was the blackest little puppy she had ever seen. The puppy had a bright green bow around his neck with a tag attached. Charlotte gently stroked the dog's head and grasped the tag.

Merry Christmas, Mommy. All my love, Peppercorn.

"WHAT YOU ALWAYS WANTED," LANDON SAID SOFTLY AS HE PLACED the dog into Charlotte's arms. Suddenly she was filled with feelings she had never experienced—rushes of immense joy soared within her, and an innate feeling of great protection. *This is what it must feel like when a mother holds her baby for the first time,* she thought. *Motherly love.*

"Landon," she whispered, cuddling the puppy tighter, and gently kissing Landon's lips.

"We're a family now," he said, taking Charlotte and their little one in his arms, and although Peppercorn wasn't human, it didn't matter to Charlotte; she was totally in love with Landon and her new puppy—her perfect little family.

∾

"C'MON, PEPPE, LET'S GET OUTTA HERE!"

Landon gently secured the harness around Peppe's muscular two-year-old body. Charlotte watched as her boys were about to head out on one of their weekly adventures. Landon had planned to drive up to Lighthouse Harbor on the coast of Maine, about a ninety-minute drive north, as it was just after Labor Day and dogs were allowed on the beach all day.

"I'm sorry I'm going to miss out on this," Charlotte said, taking Peppe's soft face into her hands and kissing him gently on his muzzle. He reciprocated with a large kiss of his own.

"Oh, I love you, too, Peppe," she said, kissing the top of his soft shiny head.

Landon bent down and whispered something into Peppe's ear.

"What are you two up to?" she laughed, wrapping her arms around Landon's muscular body. They had been together for almost two and a half years, living happily together on the grounds of Castle Loch and enjoying each day as a small family of three.

"Good things come to those who wait," Landon said, kissing Charlotte, who still thrilled at the feel of his lips upon hers. Two years still felt like two minutes when she was with him, and their dog completed the happiness she felt.

"Well, you two have a good time while I toil away in the shop." Her part-time college student called in sick, leaving Charlotte on her own for the premiere of the new line of ladies clothing from The Fancy Firefly, a popular brand of women's clothing that branched into the women's sports arena. One of The Fancy Firefly's reps was coming to Loch Ladies to help introduce the brand, and the members were already clamoring for their intricately designed apparel.

"Oh, you'll have fun," Landon said, kissing Charlotte on the cheek and heading toward the car with Peppe. "You love these exhibits," he said, opening the back of car, enabling Peppe to hop in. "I'll text plenty of pictures."

Charlotte blew Peppe a kiss and tightly hugged Landon before he got into the driver's seat of their SUV.

"Careful driving," she whispered. "I love you."

"Love you, too," Landon said, kissing Charlotte deeply. He smiled that wistful smile that always sent her heart racing as he got into the car. He started the engine, put the car in reverse and beeped the horn and waved. Charlotte threw kisses to her two boys and headed back into Loch Ladies.

The day flew and Charlotte barely had a chance to check her phone for texts. When things settled down she eagerly grabbed her phone, but saw there was nothing from Landon. She called him, but he did not answer.

"Wow, they must be having a ball," she said to herself, putting the phone down, and going back to the few customers that lingered.

After an extraordinarily busy and profitable day, Charlotte officially closed the shop at six o'clock. She was exhausted, but thrilled that The Fancy Firefly line sold out and she would place an order for more merchandise tomorrow. She noticed her phone flashing near the cash register and ran to grab it thinking it was Landon calling to say they were still at the beach, but an unfamiliar number beamed on her screen.

"Hello?" answered Charlotte.

And then her world turned as dark as a stormy and starless night.

Landon and Peppe were headed back home when a truck swerved onto the wrong side of the road and into Landon's SUV. According to the officer who called her after she closed the shop, they were killed instantly. A velvet black box containing an emerald ring locked in the glove compartment was untouched. Charlotte was given the ring at the police station in some town she couldn't even remember the name of. Hamish had been with her. When Charlotte opened the box and saw the ring, she went into shock.

"Landon told me so many times he was a fool for not asking

you sooner, but you both were so content with your life the way it was," Hamish had told her a few days after the accident.

Charlotte shrugged, still in shock and not caring about anything. Her beloved Landon and Peppe were gone.

"Marriage didn't matter to me," she said, feeling the ever-present tears well up. "I know he loved me and I loved him, and Peppe. That was all that mattered. But this ring... We had seen it when we were in Lighthouse Harbor. I admired it in a jeweler's window. I thought it was so stunning and I had no idea he was even thinking of buying this ring for me," she said closing the velvet box, and with it, the brilliance of Landon's love which was gone forever.

"BUT YOU DID BUY IT, SWEETHEART," CHARLOTTE MURMURED. HER tea was now cold, and she no longer wanted it as the setting sun darkened her shop. She had no idea if Loch Ladies would remain as it was under the new management, but there wasn't anything she could do.

"I hope you live on somehow, Loch Ladies," she whispered. "You'll forever be with me no matter where I go." Charlotte straightened the expertly folded golf shirts into a neat pile, and picked up the odd golf ball that had fallen from a basket near the door. Loch Ladies for officially closed for the day, and Charlotte headed home to contemplate life without Castle Loch.

CHAPTER THREE

DAY JUST STARTED TO BREAK AS CHARLOTTE FUMBLED FOR HER cell phone, the alarm loudly beeping. She stumbled out of bed, stubbing her toe on one of the many cardboard boxes that littered the cottage.

"Ouch," she yelped as she hopped into the bathroom. She had showered and packed all of her toiletries the night before, along with her other valuables and non-perishables that she planned to take in the car with her.

Charlotte leaned over her bathroom sink and splashed her face with ice cold water. She looked up into the mirror and saw the droplets of water beading on her face and thought she noticed a change. Gone were the dark rings of exhaustion underneath her eyes. The whites of her eyes were no longer red and tired—they were clear and brown. She also detected a hint of pink in her cheeks and her lips were not as dry and cracked as they had been the last few days.

"Amazing what a good night's sleep can do for you," she said, shaking her head back and forth to dry to her face, as she had packed the towels. She felt the weight of the last couple years had been lifted, and Charlotte felt it had to do with being forced to leave Castle Loch. If not for the new management, it would have been so easy to have stayed, continuing to go through the motions of life detached and dispassionate. She had been on her own for two years and now she was being pushed from her old life and into a new one. Charlotte no longer felt the dread of leaving. Hamish was moving on in life, and she knew she had to as well.

She and Hamish said their goodbyes last week, but he FaceTimed her and texted constantly, again, never truly leaving her. She texted him that she was about to get on the road and he responded with an angel emoji and 'Safe travels, Char.' Text when you arrive.'

Charlotte heard the moving van arrive outside and she gave the movers her instructions on what needed to be loaded. She had packed her own valuables. Her eye then caught the glinting of her emerald in the early morning sunlight and felt Landon and Peppe with her.

The knots of stress had vanished and a calmness blanketed her. She looked at her home one last time.

"Goodbye little cottage on the green," she whispered, blowing a kiss to not only the bungalow, but to her life at Castle Loch. She closed the door, walking out of her old life and into a new one.

CHARLOTTE WAS ENTERING HER SECOND HOUR OF DRIVING WHEN the iconic blue sign stating *Welcome to Maine—The Way Life Should Be* appeared on the highway. Charlotte rolled down the window of her car and inhaled the salty air that truly said welcome to Maine. The landscape changed sharply as she crossed the New Hampshire border lined with majestic pine trees, now passing small channels and inlets where docked sailboats bobbed on the calm waves, and the landscape was now dotted with fishing boats, trawlers and buoys. Charlotte stopped for a quick lunch at a roadside burger joint, stretching her legs and walking down a dock to a small harbor. She watched more sailboats lazily slide over the gentle waves of the harbor, and the smell of brine and sea salt was tangible and distinct. Her hair felt damp and her skin moist.

It's true, Charlotte thought feeling, seeing and smelling all the aspects of the Atlantic Ocean. *There is something about the seaside that is calming and serene. It's almost as if all my troubles can be washed away with the tide. I hope Lobster Claw can do that for me.*

She hopped back into the car and drove for another hour and then saw a large wooden sign in the shape of a huge red lobster: *Welcome to Lobster Claw, Maine. Get caught in our claws and stay a while.*

"I think I'll do just that," Charlotte murmured, as a smile of happiness spread across her face upon seeing the absurd sign.

"Now I just have to find my way to Beach Rose Path." Her GPS told her take the next left, so she did.

"This can't be right," she said, as she turned her car onto a bumpy and unpaved road.

She reset the GPS, but the automated voice said, "Travel five miles down Sand Dollar Drive and take the first right onto Beach Rose Path."

"If you say so," she said, as the road suddenly turned smooth and paved again. The two-lane path was lined by wild sea grass dancing in the mild ocean breeze. Charlotte heard the swoosh of the ocean waves as she drove. It was a beautiful sound, comforting and soothing. She had never lived this close to the ocean and was used to the rolling of golf carts and the *thwack* of strong and hard golf swings. This was so distinctive. Not only did everything sound different, but the scents were distinct, too. Where Charlotte was used to the smell of freshly-cut grass and cool, woodsy fragrances, she could now smell the salt in the air on the sea breeze. She rolled all of her windows down to let in the fresh air of the coast. It was the scent of summer, although summer didn't officially start for a little more than a month. She continued to drive further down Sand Dollar Drive, and she swore she could feel the spirits of mermaids, sea sprites and pirates the closer she got to Beach Rose Path. It was exhilarating and so brand new, that Charlotte felt a happy anticipation and excitement course through her body.

"In 50 yards, turn right onto Beach Rose Path." Her romantic thoughts of legends of the sea were interrupted by the robotic voice from her GPS.

"Almost there," she said, as the road suddenly became unpaved once again. She slowed, not wanting to hit anything sharp to cause a flat tire or worse. A jagged driftwood sign suddenly came into view proclaiming Beach Rose Path. Charlotte took the right slowly and then abruptly stopped the car and stared at what stood before her.

"This can't be it," she said, getting out of her car.

Charlotte stood before a small weather-worn, gray-shingled cottage. A wooden dock-like structure led from where she parked her car up to the painted-chipped steps to the porch of the cottage. A white balustrade was supported by two wooden beams with a small roof over the porch. A garland of seashells was strung underneath the low-hanging roof and tinkled softly in the ocean breeze. A picture window took up most of the front of the house, framed by very weathered white shutters in much need of paint. In fact, everything that Charlotte could see was in need of a new coat of paint. She grabbed the folder Hamish had given her from the front seat of the car and quickly opened it. What was standing before her and what was in the folder were two completely different things.

"Dear Lord," Charlotte said, grabbing her phone from the car. "What in the world have I gotten myself into?"

Charlotte stood stock still looking at the house. She noticed a worn looking hammock strung to the side of the porch and a smattering of seashells lying on the floor of the porch. Not ready to venture inside yet, she decided to walk around the property.

The house was surrounded by a fence made from weathered birch wood logs which gave the place an extra sense of beachyness. Around the fence she also saw green bushes that contained the first tiny blooms of a pretty pink rose-type flower, which perked up her spirits. She rounded the house from the right and noticed a second set of steps leading to a separate entrance.

That must be the apartment, or it could be the store area, she thought. Tufts of tall silver grass surrounded the house and a sandy path led down to the beach. The water was blue as a sapphire with white caps that looked like whipped cream on top of a scoop of blue ocean. Billowy clouds scudded through the clear sky as the mewing of snow-white seagulls filled the air. Charlotte could make out tiny sailboats in the bay, as well as several larger boats, perhaps ferries or pleasure boats jouncing on the waves. She kicked off her sneakers and decided to take a walk down to the water. As it was still May, the sand was not the burning hot grains of summer that quickly toasted the soles of bare feet. It was soft and not too pebbly. She saw further down the beach a small strip of structures, perhaps stores or restaurants painted in cheery pastels. Charlotte decided not to venture further, as she had now mustered the courage to go inside the house. Walking back, she noticed that the back of the house had a sign and an entrance way simply marked *Beach Rose Path*.

"Oh, I see. I think," Charlotte said, closely examining the front of the structure. It looked like the house was split in half—the front of the house actually being the store entrance, and the back, where she drove in from, was the house entrance. Or vice versa.

"Let's see if I'm right." She dug into her bag for the set of keys Hamish had given to her, latched onto a key ring with a plastic red lobster. The keys were identical, as they obviously opened both the store door and the house entrance.

Charlotte inserted the key in the lock and turned it slowly, hearing it click into place. The doorknob was a beautiful decorative one—solid brass with a chrome finish with carved roses on both the baseplate and the handle.

"That's beautiful," she whispered, turning the knob. It was heavy and it felt very secure.

It was dark inside, and Charlotte could see that the shades were pulled. She fumbled for the light switch on the wall to the right of the door and flicked the switch.

"Let there be light. Thank you!"

The area in which she stood was the shape of a perfect square. Built-in shelves stood on each side of the store, with a counter and cash register. It was totally empty, save for a few old mason jars and dust rags. The floor was blonde oak with huge planks. Two floor-to-ceiling windows each sat on either side of the front door. Rory had left no clues as to what was sold in this store. Not one T-shirt, tote bag, or even keychain. Nothing except the dusty mason jars.

"Thanks, Rory," Charlotte said, actually laughing. "At least you cleaned up—literally—which I guess I appreciate." Charlotte was no stranger to starting up a store from scratch—as long as it had to do with golf. And from what she could tell, there did not seem to be a golf course in the vicinity. She could be wrong, but she doubted it.

"I'll have to do a little reconnaissance later," she said as she let herself out the door and ventured around the back.

"Now for the real test," she said, taking the key and inserting it into the lock with a door exactly the same as the storefront's. "Hamish said it was partially furnished," she murmured.

Thinking about her own furniture, earlier Charlotte received a text from her movers saying they were delayed due to bad traffic on I-95. Charlotte had taken a more circuitous route as she hated nothing more than getting stuck in terrible traffic.

"Oh my," whispered Charlotte upon entering the doorway. The place was immaculate and much bigger than it appeared from the outside. She stood inside of a small living area, containing a couch with a coffee table in the shape of a compass. The right wall had the same type of shelving as the store, but was filled with books and nautical knick-knacks. Behind the couch, Charlotte saw a modest dining area with a small, round dining table and chairs. Her eyes made their way toward the left, and she saw a ship lapped wall on which nautical paintings hung. She climbed the staircase to the left of the couch and found herself in a large loft. This was empty but had an enormous picture window with the most incredible view of the sea. She scanned the coast and noticed a craggy rock formation on which sat a black and white lighthouse.

"How beautiful!" she exclaimed, watching the waves crash upon the rocky shoreline.

She went back down the stairs, around the staircase and found herself in a small but functional kitchen with an apartment-sized stainless-steel stove and refrigerator. There didn't appear to be a dishwasher, but that was no matter as Charlotte never used the one in her golf club cottage anyway, actually enjoying the chore of washing dishes.

"Waste of water anyway," she laughed, as she ran her hand over the small granite countertop.

"Oh, thank goodness!" Charlotte proclaimed, noticing the most important gadget in the kitchen—the coffee maker.

Just need to get some coffee, she thought as she remembered the bags of non-perishables in her car. She opened the cabinets and found a mug, but nothing else.

"Just as well," she said, closing the door, making a mental note to grab her bag from the car. She opened what she thought was a closet door, but found a stacked washer and dryer.

"Wow, Rory, you did all right here!" She was thrilled, since she was actually terrified that she would find an absolute mess. Yes, the store needed work, but not her living area, and she was beyond grateful for that.

> All good here, Hamish. Will text if I need anything!

"There," Charlotte said, tossing the phone onto the coffee table. Lately she found herself constantly looking for texts, at the news, anything to distract her from worries over her new living situation, but now a feeling of calm unexpectedly descended upon her. She stood still in the small living room and all she could hear was the soft rhythms of the rolling sea and the caw of the seagulls. It was peaceful and tranquil, and exactly what Charlotte needed in her life.

Charlotte kept herself busy the rest of the day unpacking what she brought with her in her car—changes of clothes, toiletries, and non-perishables. She was putting the last of her cans of beef and barley soup away when the ping of her cell phone punctuated the silence in the cottage.

"What!" She exclaimed looking at the text.

> Sorry—hit two car accidents and now the truck has a flat. Traffic terrible too. We will be there sometime tomorrow morning.

"Okay," she said tossing the phone on the couch. She knew there was nothing she could do about this. It was just her furniture, although it would have been nice to have her own bed. As Rory's cottage was furnished, she wasn't even sure what she would do with it.

"Tomorrow is another day." Charlotte sighed.

Charlotte went to her car and grabbed the blue down comforter she had brought with her. She laid her weary body on the couch and wrapped the comforter about her, falling asleep in this new house and new town.

CHAPTER FOUR

CHARLOTTE AWOKE FROM A DEEP AND DREAMLESS SLEEP. SHE FELT amazingly energized and relaxed as she made coffee and toast. With her beloved caffeine now in her system, she was ready to tackle the day and decided to explore her new surroundings.

The morning could not have been more perfect for May. The sun rose high in the clear blue sky. Charlotte opened the front door, stepped outside and savored the sunny rays beaming on her cheeks.

"Ah, summer, you're almost here," she said smiling, feeling the heat of the sun warming her body. Charlotte closed her eyes, letting the sun gleam upon her cheeks. A breeze carried the scent of some flower or plant she was not familiar with, sweet, yet vaguely familiar, and she made a mental note to find out what it was.

Charlotte proceeded to walk along the long driftwood dock. It was a weathered gray, very similar to the one outside her new home, and she wondered if they were built at the same time. White, grainy sand bordered the dock on each side, along with green bushes with the same pink flowers near her cottage. She then noticed a hand-painted sign with a bird on it near clumps of grass closer to the shore. Charlotte kicked off her sneakers and carefully walked on the sand.

"Ouch!" she yelled as the gritty sand pierced her bare feet. She brushed the soles of her feet and walked more slowly, eyeing the sign:

DO NOT ENTER
THIS IS A RESTRICTED NESTING SITE FOR
PIPING PLOVERS
THEIR NESTS AND EGGS ARE PROTECTED UNDER STATE
AND FEDERAL LAW

THE SIGN ITSELF LOOKED THREATENING, WITH ITS LARGE RED DO-not-enter lettering. There was a picture of a little tiny bird that reminded Charlotte of a mini seagull.

"Cute," she said, vowing not to go any closer to the cordoned-off area, fearful that the piping plover police were in close proximity.

"No worries, little chickies," she laughed, heading back to the dock, "you won't have any trouble from this newcomer."

Charlotte sat on the dock, wiping away the sand from her feet, and she put her shoes back on. She surveyed her surroundings—she guessed she was about halfway from her house and halfway from the bank of buildings that she was heading toward before going off course to check on the plight of the piping plovers. She then looked straight ahead, out to the sea, waves gently rolling in and out, like the comfort of an old rocking chair—lulling back and forth, back and forth. The color of the ocean today was a clear blue, with caps as white as bouncy clouds in a summer sky, churning into milky pools when they crashed upon the shore. Charlotte watched green strands of seaweed ride onto the shore with the tide, reminiscent of stories from her childhood of mermaids' hair flowing in from sea to shore.

Charlotte let her mind wander at the vastness of the majestic ocean, so tremendous and deep—the home of enormous creatures such as whales, sharks, and loggerhead turtles—it seemed almost too incredible to believe, but here she was, now a neighbor of this colossal sea. She felt herself tearing up at the sheer beauty of what lay before her. Charlotte had an extraordinary respect for the sea, never being one to venture too far out, as when she was a teenager, she once became caught in a whirlpool and almost drowned. It didn't stopped her from summer beach trips, but Charlotte never waded further than her knees, and she was always astounded at Peppe's fearlessness of swimming out into the endless ocean waves. The beach was one of Peppe's favorite places, and it was near to impossible to pull him out of the water after a day of swimming and running.

"You'd love it here, guys," she whispered, thinking of her boys, and if they were with her now, Landon would be pulling large pieces of driftwood from the dunes and throwing them with all of his might into the waves for Peppe to retrieve. Then like a movie playing in her mind, she found herself lost in a fantasy of walking along this beautiful stretch of beach, the man she loved by her side, and their dog frolicking and splashing with pure delight in the surf.

"From the look on your face, seems like a nice daydream you're having."

Charlotte was swiftly snapped from her mind's movie and back into the present. She found herself so lost in her daydream, she had almost forgotten where she was when the unfamiliar sound of a woman's voice jolted her back into reality.

"Just a beautiful day at the beach," Charlotte said, getting up and whisking the sand from her legs.

"It certainly is. And early in the season, too. I think we're going to have a good season here. Are you visiting for the summer?"

This woman is talking too much, Charlotte thought, trying as hard as she could to disguise her annoyance. She was in such a lovely place a few moments ago, and now this woman made Landon and Peppe disappear from her fantasy world simply by speaking.

"You could say that," Charlotte said, turning back toward the cottage. "I'm staying back there," she said pointing in the breeze. "At Rory Ruskin's place. He's gone back to Canada, but he still wanted the store up and running, and I was hired to take care of it."

"Yes, poor Rory," the woman said. She had very long pewter hair pulled back in a thick ponytail and tied with a bright blue scarf. She had large, round, blue eyes and almost invisibly light eyebrows, which gave her a bit of an exotic look for some reason. Her complexion was golden tan and she was the picture of health and elegance. She was thin and was dressed in a pair of light-yellow linen pants and a long white button-down shirt with tiny pink flamingos embroidered on it. Pink seashells made into earrings hung from her ears, and beaded sandals covered her tanned, pedicured feet. She was older and still very pretty.

The woman extended her hand, bedecked with jingling bracelets.

"I'm Tatiana Dulka. I'm a lifelong Lobster Clawer, and I own The Blue Hydrangea, the blue building in that row of stores down there." Tatiana pointed to the row of colorfully painted buildings down on the opposite end of the dock from Rory's.

"I'm sorry," Charlotte said, accepting Tatiana's hand. "I've forgotten my manners. I'm Charlotte Templeton. I'm a new Lobster Clawer."

Tatiana laughed and Charlotte felt the woman's grip tighten slightly before she released Charlotte's hand.

"Well, you seem like you have a great sense of humor, and I

think you'll fit in here just nicely. I'm heading back down to my place—would you like to come with? I can show you around and introduce you to all the shop keeps."

"I was actually heading that way," Charlotte said. "I got waylaid with the predicament of the piping plover, and then the sea just drew me in. Not literally, of course, but, it's just so beautiful here. And peaceful. Something I think I need."

"It is truly beautiful, Charlotte." Tatiana's voice was soothing and serene, like the ocean. It was pleasing to Charlotte's ear.

"And watch out for those piping plover people. You wander one hair over that piece of string, and they'll have your head! Just kidding. There's a group here who takes good care of them, but they can be a bit over-protective, so be warned." Tatiana smiled, putting Charlotte immediately at ease.

"I haven't been a newcomer anywhere in a very long time, so I wouldn't dream of upsetting the birds or their defenders. I totally respect their wanting to protect such a cute little bird," Charlotte said.

"Cute? HA!" exclaimed Tatiana. "They can be a bit pesky, but, well, who can't? Shall we go? I have a class later this afternoon, and I'd love to show you around. I know everyone is at work, so now's a great time."

"Lead the way!" said Charlotte, and she and Tatiana made their way to the bustling hub of Lobster Claw Central.

CHAPTER FIVE

CHARLOTTE AND TATIANA WALKED DOWN THE BEACH END OF THE dock, reaching the little shopping area. The sea spray felt cool on Charlotte's now sunburned face, and she was grateful for the occasional splash of mist hitting her hot cheeks and forehead.

"Feels good, doesn't it?" Tatiana asked, pointing her face toward the ocean. "Nothing better for your complexion like a natural blast of salt water on a warm day." Charlotte smiled at Tatiana as they came upon the buildings that Charlotte saw from her new home.

"We call this the Beach Block." There were four Italianate buildings, each two stories high. They were made of brick, and Charlotte could see every one had a large bay window on the first floor. The buildings had three wide granite steps that led to the front doors of each establishment.

The first building was painted sky blue with a white awning.

"This blue one is mine," Tatiana said, escorting Charlotte to the front door. "The Blue Hydrangea. The most magnificent blue hydrangeas blossom every July around the Beach Block, hence the name. Back in the early 1900s this was a bustling beachfront, but after the depression, so many people left for the cities. These buildings remained, however, because they are historical and very fortunately cannot be torn down. C'mon inside."

Charlotte watched as Tatiana unlocked the snow-white door. A giant blue hydrangea was painted on it, giving the already beautiful building a cozy atmosphere.

"The structures are small, but we make do." Tatiana opened the blinds to let in the light, and Charlotte was delighted to see she was now inside of an art gallery. Paintings and photographs hung on the walls featuring sailboats on ice blue water, brightly painted lighthouses beaming out to sea, and several old photographs depicting joyous beachcombers in their 18th century swimsuits.

"It's beautiful," Charlotte said, delightedly looking at the old artwork and photographs.

"When I took over this building, I found these photographs in a box in the basement. I thought they were too beautiful to be hidden away, so I made copies of the originals and not only do they adorn these walls, but they sell really well, too. People are still nostalgic for the good old days."

"I don't blame them." Charlotte moved on to a beautiful painting of a lighthouse. The picture took up at least half the wall. The lighthouse was the center of the painting—a white structure with a black door, black window, and black lantern cap. It was surrounded by sailboats, with sails the colors of the rainbow skimming on an inky blue ocean, silhouetted by a pale blue summer sky.

"I just love this," Charlotte said, admiring not only the painting itself but the size.

"That's one of my favorites as well. Painted by a local," Tatiana said, as she straightened it on the wall. Charlotte admired a portrait of a group of women with long white summer dresses, wide-brimmed straw hats upon their heads of flowing brown, blonde and ginger hair. She looked more closely at the painting and noticed what she thought was the buildings of the Beach Block.

"You said you teach a class—do you paint?" asked Charlotte.

"Oh, no," laughed Tatiana. "As much as I love art and its history, my artistic skills only stretch as far as stick people. I teach yoga on the beach. I started the summer beach classes last week, and I have a few students. By Memorial Day it gets pretty busy with vacationers still wanting to stretch. My classes are at sunrise and at midday, right now. Once the busy season picks up, I can only offer the sunrise classes. Feel free to join anytime you like."

"That's kind of you," Charlotte said, suddenly feeling tired and in need of a nap. "I'm more of a walker than a stretcher."

"Well, if you change your mind, you can find us right down on the beach. C'mon, I'll introduce you to the rest of the Beach Block."

The building next to The Blue Hydrangea was a bright daffodil yellow.

"This is Take the Cake. Betsy—the owner—is not here this week—drove to somewhere near the Canadian border to visit family, but you're in for a treat with her Maine Blueberry pies—I can guarantee you they will be the best you've ever tasted. This green building is The Lobster Claw Ice Cream Parlour. Priscilla and Niklaus Kotz run this little gem. Best ice cream here too. Especially good with blueberry pie. They keep me stocked up for my daily scoop of ice cream," smiled Tatiana.

"Daily scoop of ice cream?" laughed Charlotte. "I think if I had a daily scoop, I'd be as big as a house."

Tatiana shook her head, her long silver ponytail waving in the breeze. "No, not at all. Everything in moderation. Plus, my yoga helps, too. Some people like an evening drink, I like a scoop of butter cream chocolate chip as I watch the sun set. I can also guarantee you've never tasted anything like that as well. Oh, the last building in our Beach Block is Harry's Surf and Turf."

Tatiana and Charlotte stood in front of the storefront painted bright purple.

"Oh, a little restaurant, how nice," Charlotte said, thinking this would be a great place to grab a bite here and there.

Tatiana shook her head and laughed. "No restaurant. Harry wants you to think that's what it is, so when hungry customers wander in thinking they can get a snack, he ensnares them in his own lobster claws, sells them a boogie board, surfboard, fishing rod, and beach chairs and towels. Then he sends them packing to the bakery or ice cream parlour. He's tricky but he does a mean business. He's good for all of us!"

Charlotte felt the twinges of worry settle over her. These storefronts were beautiful and all had niches that did not cross any territorial lines. An art gallery, bakery, ice cream parlour, and a surf shop did not encroach on any other business. What in the world did Rory sell, and not only that, but how did he even survive?

"Something wrong, Charlotte? You look like you've seen a ghost," Tatiana said as they made their way back to The Blue Hydrangea.

"These are beautiful shops, Tatiana, and you all have your specialties and they don't infringe on each other. I'm sure you all do very well, but what was Rory's specialty? I'm assuming it was T-shirts, key chains and that sort of thing, but it seems that he must have had something special of his own as well?" Simply from all of her years in merchandising, Charlotte knew selling T-shirts was not enough to forge a living from. There had to be something else; something special.

"Well, Charlotte," Tatiana said, "we all sell the obligatory souvenir junk, if you will, but you're right, Rory and Violet did have a specialty, as you put it. Seashells."

"Seashells? But doesn't every beach front store sell seashells?" Charlotte could feel a knot tighten in her stomach and at the back of her neck, and felt stress and tension descend upon her.

She would usually feel this whenever she presented a new line to her Loch Ladies customers or if she tried something entirely new. She had put all doubts and fears into the back of her mind, and ever so slightly, they were starting to emerge.

"Yup!" Tatiana exclaimed. "That string of seashells on your front porch? Violet, made them, and let me tell you, tourists ate them right up. Easy to make, too. I can show you how to do it. All you need is a drill...."

Tatiana's voice became lost in the sea wind. All Charlotte needed to hear was the word "drill" and she knew she'd never be able to make these strings of seashells. She was never any good at crafts, scrapbooking or anything of that nature. She loved fashion and merchandising—that was her talent. But selling seashells on a string? That was beyond preposterous. Right now she just wanted to get back to the cottage.

"I appreciate everything, Tatiana. But if you don't mind, my moving van should be arriving any time now and I should get back to meet them," she said, thankful that this was not a lie, something Charlotte hated to do.

"Of course," Tatiana said gently. "You get back to the cottage, and if you need anything, I'm right here. I'm just like you—I live where I work. You're welcome anytime."

Charlotte got the feeling Tatiana understood Charlotte's apprehension and was nothing but gracious in telling Charlotte to go on home.

"Thanks so much for everything today, Tatiana. I can't tell you how welcome you've made me feel."

Tatiana took Charlotte's hand. "Anything you need just let me know."

Charlotte gently squeezed Tatiana's soft but strong hand.

"I will and thank you again."

Charlotte turned back toward the cottage, just as tears as hot as the early spring sun streamed down her sunburned face.

CHAPTER SIX

THROUGH HER BLINDING TEARS, CHARLOTTE FUMBLED WITH THE unfamiliar key and lock to the cottage. She heard the click of the lock releasing, rushed inside, and felt an instantaneous sense of calm. The warm cedar shiplap and the beamed ceiling somehow felt tranquil, and she plopped herself on the couch and took a deep relaxing breath.

Charlotte busied herself for the next few hours putting away the boxed milk, bread, peanut butter, jam, cereal, tea, honey, and canned goods. She had found a broom and swept out some of the sand she tracked in with her from earlier in the day. She then heard the roar of wheels and the choking of a truck stopping in front of the cottage. She ran outside to greet the movers who were hopping down from the cab.

"Wow, this place is almost impossible to find," one of them said, a heavy-set bald man with a bright red face. He had sweat dripping from the bridge of his nose and onto the clipboard which he shoved at Charlotte for her signature.

"Just tell us where you want it," he said, watching as she scribbled her name on the bill of lading.

"Please put the bed and dresser in the loft upstairs, and I'll show you where to put everything else." The red-faced man grunted and signaled to his partner to start the unloading. Once the bedroom furniture was in place, the man returned to Charlotte.

"Where's the rest go?" he asked, his head and face still red and sweaty.

"It can go in here," Charlotte said, leading the way to the front door of the store. *Thankfully, there's not too much,* she thought. just a couch, loveseat, coffee table and a couple of end tables and lamps.

The men followed Charlotte and she unlocked the front door of the store.

"Just drop it all in here," she said.

They did as she instructed and fifteen minutes later announced their departure. Charlotte tipped each of them, and they grunted their thank yous and hopped back into the truck pulling out of Beach Rose Path and on to Sand Dollar Drive and back to civilization.

"I can deal with this later," she said, closing the door to the store "Time for tea."

She could not find her tea kettle so she poured water into the coffee maker. The heated water filled the carafe and she poured it into her cup and over the tea bag and honey. She took a sip and let the warmth of the ginger tea flow from her throat into her belly, instantly lulling Charlotte into a calmness, and she felt her eyes grow heavy. Settling back into the softness of the sofa, she reflected on the earlier part of the day, meeting Tatiana, whom she truly liked. There was that sudden onset of sadness after shaking Tatiana's hand, a gesture reminiscent of Hamish, who she missed terribly. But there was something also about the cottage that reminded her of him—although it was small and cozy and had feminine touches such as the lace curtains and two chintz accent chairs, the cottage was as masculine as a sea captain —paintings of ships, seashores, and lighthouses adorned the walls and a blue tartan wool blanket covered the back cushions of the couch. She even thought she could smell some kind of scent like a candle—something that was cedar wood and patchouli. The scent and the sounds of the waves breaking on the shore comforted her and she got the feeling that Hamish's presence was in the cottage was with her—watching over her—like a guardian angel.

"Is this where I'm truly supposed to be?" she pondered aloud. Although she had only been in Lobster Claw for twenty-four hours, Charlotte had to admit that she could potentially like it here.

"It's a change for sure," she murmured into her teacup. "But I think it will be a good one. Thank you, Hamish. And thank you, Rory," she smiled, taking another sip. The tea calmed Charlotte's mind and she was clearheaded, feeling a sense of positivity, thinking that perhaps kismet brought her to Beach Rose Path. Her eyes feeling weighted, she put her cup down on the coffee table and wrapped the blue tartan wool blanket about her. It smelled of wood and patchouli. Although it was still early, Charlotte was both mentally and physically exhausted and all she wanted was to sleep. Charlotte's second day in Lobster Claw came to a close as she laid her head upon the couch, letting herself fall into a gentle and tranquil sleep.

CHAPTER SEVEN

"It's okay, Peppe, you're safe."

The soft cries of Peppercorn broke Charlotte's heart. She was trying to comfort her frightened dog, as the poor thing was scared of the sudden outburst of a thunderstorm.

"It's okay" she said again as a loud clap of thunder shook the house. Her dog's cries became louder and more intense, and Charlotte bolted upright, fumbling for her cell phone. The illuminated screen flashed 6:45 a.m.

Pelting rain crashed upon the windows, and Charlotte realized that she was no longer dreaming. Her fantasy and reality merged when the deafening thunderous boom struck, waking her from the dream of Peppe's mournful cries. Charlotte shook the cobwebs from her head and looked out of the bay window, the sky no longer clear and blue as it was when she had laid her head down late yesterday afternoon. Dark clouds now raced across the ocean, as the waves, their white caps higher and more angry, violently slammed onto the shore. Thick rain slashed like daggers falling from the sky, and there was not one seagull to be seen or heard.

Charlotte suddenly felt chilled as she realized that the sun which had warmed the cottage yesterday was somewhere behind today's coal black clouds. She scanned the room for a thermostat and noticed it near the door. She set it to 68 degrees and forced warm air flowed up from the vents, immediately making the cottage toasty.

"Much better," Charlotte said, heading toward the kitchen, as pangs of hunger gnawed in her belly.

"Here we go," she said, pulling a box of granola from the cupboard. Charlotte poured the cereal into a bowl and splashed in a bit of milk. She stood in her kitchen, watching the hard rain batter the window looking out onto the beach. She couldn't believe how dark it was for almost 7:00 am, but the storm was fierce and ferocious. She looked up at the ceiling to see if there could be any leakage, but she saw none.

"You're quite the sturdy little house," she smiled, finishing her cereal. She put the bowl into the kitchen sink and then Charlotte heard a sound that almost stopped her heart.

"I am absolutely awake and not dreaming," she said aloud, trying to convince herself she was truly awake. She reached to turn on the taps to wash the bowl when she heard the noise again, a sound as familiar as the beating of her own heart.

"It can't be," she whispered. She heard it once more.

"Peppe?" The whimpers sounded just like her own beloved dog's.

Charlotte stood stock still in the kitchen waiting for the next whimper, which came almost immediately, from below the kitchen floor.

"There must be a basement," she said, not knowing the layout of the house at all, but the sounds were definitely coming from below the floorboards she stood upon. She saw no doors in the kitchen that could possibly lead to a basement, and she went back to the living room. On the wall of the staircase she saw a door and turned the knob. She flicked on the light switch on the wall and the basement was flooded in golden light. Carefully walking down the stairs, not knowing what might be at the bottom, Charlotte realized that she should have brought a frying pan or rolling pin with her for protection.

"And that is ridiculous," she said, "you have no idea where those even are!" She reached the bottom of the stairs but saw only a few boxes, a lawn mower, and a snow blower. The basement was small but very clean. The whimpering got louder, and Charlotte tracked the sound to the other side of the staircase.

"Oh, dear," she exclaimed, rushing to the sight before her. Laying on the cold cement floor was a dog, about the size of her own Peppercorn. She was barely breathing and her sad eyes looked up at Charlotte.

"Oh you poor thing," Charlotte said, patting the dog's head. The dog lifted its head upon Charlotte's gentle touch. The dog lay her head back on the floor and then pulled herself over slightly. Charlotte heard quiet whimpering and saw a small puppy nursing from its weakening mother. The puppy stopped suckling and looked at Charlotte, its eyes barely open.

"You've had a baby," Charlotte whispered, petting the mother's head. The mother dog looked at Charlotte with large pleading brown eyes. Charlotte knew the dog was in terrible distress, which could put her pup at risk as well.

"I promise I'll be careful," she said, as she gently lifted the pup from its mother. She cradled the puppy in her own arms, making sure it was warm. It looked as if the pup was able to eat, and the pup appeared to be healthy. She held the pup in her arms and watched its eyes close in contentment.

"Now, let's take care of you," she said to the pup's mother. The mother dog looked once more at Charlotte, and then closed her eyes. Charlotte watched as the pup's mother sighed and then her breathing stopped.

"You poor, sweet girl," Charlotte said to the now deceased dog. Charlotte knew there was nothing more she could do for the mother, but she was not going to let anything happen to her puppy.

Cradling the sleeping puppy, Charlotte went back upstairs. She gently placed the pup on the couch and surrounded it with pillows, making a sort of nest. She knew the puppy needed to be kept warm, but more importantly, it needed to be fed. The pup no longer had a mother to depend on for this, so she found her phone quickly looked up what and how orphaned puppies are fed.

"Of course, I have nothing in the house," she said aloud, reading the recipe that consisted of evaporated milk, eggs, and yogurt.

"Okay," Charlotte said to the puppy. "Don't you worry, sweetie. If I have to drive all over this town to find a store, I will. You'll be fine."

Charlotte then looked up the stores in Lobster Claw. The closest one was only a mile down Sand Dollar Drive, Elsie's Everything, and it was claiming to have everything from apples to zucchini.

"I hope you have evaporated milk," said Charlotte. Not wanting to bring the pup with her, she delicately lifted the dog from the couch and went back into the basement. She placed the pup next to its mother. Charlotte felt the dog. She was still warm.

"I'll be back as fast as I can," she promised both of them. Charlotte thought at least this way, the puppy would be warm and could hopefully suckle what little milk was left from its mother.

Charlotte raced upstairs, grabbed her phone and car keys, and jumped quickly into her car.

"Please," she prayed, "let this Elsie have what I need," as thunder rumbled and lightning flashed, she drove down Beach Road Path through her first Maine Nor'easter.

CHAPTER EIGHT

"Shoot!" Duncan Kirk flicked on the light switch in his house. He flicked it furiously up and down several times, but he remained in the dimness of the stormy morning.

"Has to be the Nor'easter," he said, pulling his cell phone from his jeans pocket and turning on the flashlight. He found his way down to the basement and fumbled with the breaker box. He flicked those several times back and forth as well, but to no avail. He knew the house was old, but weren't old houses and their wirings supposed to be better than new ones?

Duncan's sister, Ivy, had been living in the house, until she married the previous year. Ivy had suggested selling the house, but Duncan couldn't pull the plug on it yet. Even though he considered Boston his home, Duncan was not ready to legally part with the house where he and his sister grew up. He also did not want one more thing on his already overloaded plate. He had been extraordinarily busy at work as lead architect at Dane Grayson Kirk, the largest architectural firm in Boston.

Duncan Kirk lived in the fast lane, always juggling clients, projects and city planners. The last thing he wanted to think about was selling the family home. He knew Ivy adored the home as well, but it wasn't big enough to accommodate her veterinary practice, and she and Andy bought their own home last year, one that could accommodate his sister's practice, as well as Andy's equipment being Lobster Claw's jack-of-all trades.

"Nothing like waking up with no electricity," he grumbled, still frantically flipping up and down every light switch in the house.

Duncan had been back in Lobster Claw for a month, staying in his parents' home, a home he had not been in for many years. He returned to his childhood home when he found his fiancée, Melinda, in the arms of his contractor and best friend. After an exhausting day of meetings with city planners, Duncan had arrived home to find Melinda and Eric Duff, his right-hand man, wrapped in a passionate embrace on Duncan's living room couch. Duncan Kirk's life as he knew it came to an abrupt end. The very next day he had packed what he could, and drove the three hours from Boston to Lobster Claw. It was the only place he could go.

Now standing in his lightless kitchen, Duncan recalled the ravaging details that led up to the moment of his leaving Boston: The huge argument after Duncan kicked Eric out of his home with Melinda, with him telling her to leave immediately, which, to his surprise she did. No tears, no begging or pleading; Melinda up and left, right behind Eric.

It was impossible for Duncan to remain in the condo, with memories of he and Melinda planning their future. Nor could he stay after witnessing the two people he trusted the most—his fiancée's body romantically wrapped around his supposedly loyal friend. Duncan was bitter and angry, and needed to get out. He put his firm on notice that he was taking a leave of absence due to a family situation, and decided to sell his condo, furniture, everything. Duncan wanted to be as far away from Boston as possible, and there was no other place to go but Lobster Claw.

"No handy man like at the condo, now is there?" he said,

cursing his former fiancée and her lover, as he tried to find matches for the candles that his mother kept in her china closet.

"Damn," he cursed again. The one thing he could see were the silver sheets of rain pounding into the front yard. He needed some kind of light, and there was no telling when the power would return, and if and when it did, how long it would last. He grabbed his car keys and made a mad dash for his truck and headed toward Sand Dollar Drive and to *Elsie's Everything* for the matches.

"Or maybe I'll just keep on driving back to Boston," he snarled, as the rain poured down upon him.

CHAPTER NINE

"STEADY, GIRL," CHARLOTTE TOLD HERSELF, HER HANDS TREMBLING while gripping the steering wheel tightly. Even though it was just after 7 a.m. it was still dark as midnight, as occasional brilliant flares of lightning briefly brightened the sky. Sand Dollar Drive had no streetlights, and Charlotte made sure her high beams were on, which, along with the lightning, brightened the murky road.

"In fifty feet take a slight right and you will arrive at your destination." Besides her labored breathing, Charlotte's GPS was the only sound in the car. The rain continued to pelt, but the reassuring voice of her GPS calmed her.

Charlotte veered onto the slight right and let out a sigh in tremendous relief. Elsie's Everything was lit up as bright as a Christmas tree. Charlotte smiled at the cheerfulness of the store: A small lighthouse structure, painted red and white was attached to the rectangular store where a large wooden sign hung above the door proclaiming *Elsie's Everything*. Bright white lights not only shone from within, but strings of lights in the shape of miniature lightbulbs welcomingly glowed from over the sign. It was the proverbial lighthouse in a storm to guide all ships, and from the looks of the several cars parked in the parking lot, Charlotte was not the only one who needed something urgently at Elsie's.

Charlotte raced from the car, feeling the hard pellets of rain strike her like tiny daggers storming from the sky. She turned the knob on the red door and a loud jangle of bells shook her eardrums. A plump older woman sat behind a counter that was laden with baked goods wrapped in plastic, along with candy and gum.

"Can I help you, Miss?" The woman's voice had a pretty, musical sound to it, putting Charlotte at ease. She had no idea where to look for the ingredients for the emergency puppy formula, and she quickly consulted her phone.

"Yes, thank you," said Charlotte, tapping her password into her phone.

"I have an emergency at home, and I need some evaporated milk, Karo syrup. Oh, and eggs and pediatric liquid vitamins."

The woman smiled and nodded. She grabbed a basket and proceeded to place everything Charlotte required into the basket wordlessly, for which Charlotte was grateful.

"Oh, and a baby bottle, please," added Charlotte.

The woman smiled, walked around to another aisle and returned with the bottle in the basket.

"Will there be anything else, dear?" the woman kindly asked.

"I'm all set, thank you," said Charlotte, then realizing that she did not bring her bag in the midst of her puppy panic.

"Oh, no, I'm so sorry. I...I just moved here. I'm at Rory Ruskin's place now, and I left my bag there. I'm sorry, but I need this now, and I'm happy to come back later today and pay you then."

Charlotte felt her lashes dampen with tears. She looked pleadingly at the woman who gently smiled at her.

"Elsie, I'll take care of this."

Charlotte turned around toward the voice behind her. A man,

about 6 feet tall with salt and pepper hair was handing the woman his credit card. He smelled of the sea and his hazel eyes twinkled in his ruddy face.

"Consider it a 'welcome to the neighborhood' gift," he said. "Although I have no idea what you'd need with a can of evaporated milk in weather like this. And a baby bottle to boot."

"I don't know what to say. I'm so grateful. I have the money, it's just that, well, it's an emergency of sorts, and I wasn't thinking. I promise, I'll be back here as soon as possible to pay you..."

"No worries," he said. His voice was deep and soothing, and Charlotte felt he meant what he said.

"Here you are, miss," Elsie said, handing a large brown paper bag to Charlotte.

"Thank you," she said to Elsie. "And thank you, but I do promise to pay you back."

Charlotte momentarily forgot why she was even in the store. The man was handsome, that was no doubt, probably about her age, and he had the look of someone who liked to be outdoors by his sunburnt face and expensive-looking outdoor style of clothing. He was wearing a worn, brown leather jacket, plaid shirt, jeans, and work boots.

Stop that! Charlotte reprimanded herself, taking the bag and dashing out of the store straight for her car. She noticed herself trembling again, but she wasn't sure if it was from the storm or from this man. She immediately shook him from her mind, as the puppy sprang into the forefront, and she steered her car down back down Sand Dollar Drive to Beach Rose Path. The rain abated somewhat and Charlotte could see the dark clouds skim through the sky as muted rays of the sun began to brighten the dark morning.

"At least one storm is over," she said, as she put her car in park in front of the cottage. She grabbed the bag and let herself inside, dropping the bag on the kitchen counter. She quietly descended the basement stairs and saw the pup was fast asleep, tucked into its mother's belly. A bit of liquid had leaked from its teat, reassuring Charlotte that the puppy was able to eat.

Not wanting to disturb the puppy from its peaceful slumber, she made her way back to the kitchen and looked up how to mix the emergency puppy formula. She took one of the pots she found earlier, mixed the ingredients, and poured it into the baby bottle. Charlotte tiptoed down the basement stairs once again. She was able to move the mother enough to fit the bottle underneath her body, so that the nipple protruded from under her, resembling one of her own. Just then, the puppy stirred, found the nipple of the bottle, and began nursing. After it was done feeding, the puppy snuggled into its mother again and was fast asleep.

Charlotte looked at the deceased dog and the surviving pup.

"I have no idea how you got in here," she said, petting the mother's soft head, "but I'm glad you did. I promise to take care of your baby."

Charlotte knew she couldn't leave the pup with its mother, so she gently scooped it up, and taking the bottle with her, went upstairs, sat on the couch and gently placed the sleeping puppy in her lap. She strategically placed the bottle in the crook of her arm, with the nipple pointing at the puppy's tiny mouth. She petted the sleeping dog in her lap as those old maternal feelings returned, making Charlotte feel needed and not alone.

CHAPTER TEN

"Peppe, that tickles." Charlotte had dozed off while holding the puppy and was now awakened to the brush of tickling whiskers and sweet tiny kisses on her chin. Every morning before their alarm went off, Peppe used to wake Charlotte and Landon with his gentle and loving kisses. Charlotte reached out to feel for her dog, and then opened her eyes realizing his large body was nowhere near her.

Bright golden sunlight streamed through the front window, and the storm had completely passed.

Through sleepy eyes, Charlotte looked at the puppy who was now intently staring into Charlotte's eyes.

"You certainly are a cutie," Charlotte said, immediately thinking that the dog should be let outside.

"Let's go," she said, holding the puppy in her arms. She opened the door and was greeted by the sweet scent of the ocean—the salt air and sunshine, making Charlotte feel immediately awake. There was a warm ocean breeze while white puffy clouds lazily sailed through the blue spring sky. The pup also seemed to be enamored by the beautiful morning, as its nose wiggled as if smelling the world for the first time, while the slight breeze ruffled its golden fur.

"Perfect!" she exclaimed upon seeing what was probably once a garden with some chicken wire fence securing it. It was a small square of land with a few weeds, and Charlotte gingerly placed the puppy into the enclosed area.

"You're not only adorable, but smart, too," she said to the puppy. The puppy finished its business and looked at Charlotte to be picked up again.

"Okay, now let's get you some breakfast and then we have to make sure you and your mom are properly taken care of." Just the thought the poor deceased dog in the basement broke Charlotte's heart, but she also knew that was the nature of the beast—mothers, fathers, dogs, and fiancés died, leaving the living to grieve and trying to forge a way to live on without them. This was something Charlotte knew all too well. She also knew she needed to get the pup to a vet, so she pulled out her phone and looked up local veterinarians.

"Great, there is one, right next to Elsie's Everything. At least I know how to get there! Ivy Anthony, DVM."

Charlotte bundled the puppy back onto the couch with the bottle close by. She wanted to wrap the puppy into blankets to keep it warm in the car, so she dashed upstairs to the bedroom in which she hadn't yet slept. She grabbed some blankets she had thrown on the bed after the movers left, and ran back down the stairs. She enveloped the puppy into the softness of the blankets, gathered the dog into her arms, and went outside to her car, gently placing the puppy in the back seat.

"There, little lovey, I'll be back in a sec." Charlotte ran back into the house, grabbed her bag, keys, and tossed her phone into her bag.

"Oh!" she exclaimed, making sure her wallet was also in her bag.

"Barely even been here a day and I'm already in debt. Not going to happen again, especially with a vet! Okay, all set."

She raced back to the car and jumped into the driver's seat, looking back to check on her precious cargo. Its tiny eyes were open, intently watching Charlotte, who snuggled the bottle into the blanket next to the dog.

"Okay, little lovey, let's get you checked out." She put the car in drive and once again headed down Sand Dollar Drive, this time to Dr. Ivy Anthony, DVM.

The ride down Sand Dollar Drive was completely different from the one of just a few hours ago. Where hard rain had sluiced, bright rays of sun now shimmered along the road. Charlotte could see the line of land and sea on the passenger side of the car window, as clusters of greenish-blue dune grass lazily swayed in the warm breeze. Seagulls cawed as they glided over the white caps of the waves, dive bombing for their seafood breakfast. Charlotte cracked her window just a bit to get some fresh air into the car and deeply inhaled the invigorating sea air. It was briny, salty, and had a tinge of sweetness to it as well, energizing Charlotte. She felt ready to tackle the day even though she only had one cup of coffee. She then realized she had a mountain of work to do—she had planned to spend the day in the store area cleaning and ordering supplies. Rory had left all of his merchandise ordering information in the green folder, and Charlotte planned to contact companies for merchandise. It was only a few weeks until Memorial Day and she planned to have a soft opening a few days prior.

"Maybe a little tougher with a pup, but I'll manage. I won't let you down, sweetheart," she said to the pup, approaching the end of Sand Dollar Drive. The lighthouse of Elsie's Everything sprang into view, looking very pretty in the bright sunlight of daytime.

"Simply charming," said Charlotte, veering to the left, and pulling into the lot of Dr. Anthony's practice. She noticed she was the only car parked there.

"Shoot," she said, realizing that she should have called before driving here.

"I'm all out of sorts," she sighed, in frustration. She then noticed the shades on the windows of the practice suddenly fly up.

"Oh, someone's in there! C'mon, little lovey, let's go."

Before Charlotte got out of the car, a woman opened the door of the practice. Her long blonde hair was tied in a ponytail and she was wearing a white coat. A bright pink tee shirt peeked from underneath her coat, as did a pair of jeans. She had on pink sneakers that matched her shirt, and appeared to be quite young. She looked at Charlotte and gave a wave and headed down the steps of the porch and walked toward Charlotte's car.

Charlotte rolled down her window.

"Hello! I'm looking for Dr. Ivy Anthony, please."

A brilliant smile illuminated the woman's face. Her hazel eyes were large and round, and her cheeks were as pink as her sneakers.

"I'm Dr. Anthony." Dr. Anthony extended her hand through the car window, which Charlotte accepted.

"Charlotte Templeton. I just moved into Rory Ruskin's place."

"Oh, yes, we've been expecting you. Well, not here, but in Lobster Claw. Welcome! How can I help you?"

"I have a newborn here—a puppy—it must have been born in Rory's basement. I have no idea how the mother got inside, but she did, and well..."

"Where's the mother?" Dr. Anthony's tone became much more serious and professional.

"She's in my basement. She's passed, I'm afraid, and I promised her I'd take care of her pup, who is in the backseat."

Dr. Anthony stepped back as Charlotte opened the driver's door. She quickly opened the back door of her car and carefully pulled out the swaddled pup and handed the bundle to Dr. Anthony's outstretched arms.

"I made an emergency puppy formula, but I wanted to get her to a vet as soon as possible. That's why I'm here."

Dr. Anthony calmly unfolded the blankets and found a perfect little yellow puppy fast asleep.

"Looks to be in pretty good shape. Thanks to you. Let's go inside and I can get a better look."

"Oh, thank you so much," Charlotte said, relief flooding her body, as she followed Dr. Anthony through the doorway and into her veterinary practice.

"It's okay, little lovey," Charlotte lovingly said, as the puppy opened its eyes and let out a high-pitched squeak.

"Pretty vocal, which is great," Dr. Anthony said, laying the pup on an examining table. She felt the puppy's body, looked into its ears, and mouth, and stood her on her four stubby legs, feeling along her spine and underneath her belly.

"She looks to be in excellent shape. She's probably about a week old, so she's been there before you moved in."

Charlotte felt tears stream in her eyes at the thought this poor little dear was born alone in a cold basement.

Dr. Anthony gently touched Charlotte's arm.

"Animals are amazing. That's one of the reasons I chose veterinary medicine over human medicine. They don't need a voice to tell us what they need. This pup's mother knew what she needed to do so her baby could be born in a safe place. And then you came along."

"Timing is everything, right?" Charlotte smiled, feeling her tears dissipate.

"I'll hydrate her and keep her here for a while just to be sure everything is fine. Once my assistant arrives, I can come by your place and take care of her mother."

"Thank you so much." Charlotte took out her wallet and produced her credit card and handed it to Dr. Anthony.

"Oh, no, this one's on the house. You should be paid for what you did for this little one."

Charlotte shook her head in disbelief. "This is the second time today that someone has been so kind and generous to me. And you don't even know me!"

"I may not know you, but I do know that what you did was heroic. You saved this little pup, and now I think you have a friend for life." Dr. Anthony smiled as she began an IV for the puppy. She inserted the catheter and monitored the saline, which flowed from the bag into the little puppy's front leg. Tiny snores escaped from the puppy's open mouth.

"A contented one she is."

A loud jangle of bells made both women turn toward to the front door.

"Oh, good, that's Dina, my assistant. She can monitor the pup while we go back to your place."

Charlotte nodded and gave the pup a gentle kiss on its soft golden head. "Be back soon, little lovey."

"Ivy, you here?" A man's voice boomed from the waiting area of the practice, "Can you believe it, I still have no…. Oh, I'm sorry. I didn't know you had a patient."

Charlotte turned toward the somewhat familiar voice and felt her heart skip a beat.

"Dun, how many times have I told you not to come barging into my practice. I'm a very busy woman!" Dr. Anthony laughed and engulfed the man in a huge bear hug.

"Charlotte, this is my big brother Duncan Kirk. Dun, Charlotte… Oh, I'm sorry, I didn't catch your last name."

"Templeton. Charlotte Templeton." She felt she could barely get the words out as her eyes fell upon the man standing in front of her. The man who was so gracious in Elsie's Everything.

"We've met," Duncan said, extending his hand toward Charlotte.

"What? Charlotte, I thought you just got into Lobster Claw? What's going on?" Ivy asked suspiciously. Charlotte detected a sly smile slide across the veterinarian's face.

Charlotte extended her hand which Duncan firmly grasped. *Darn, I hope he's not noticing this,* she thought as she could feel a warm blush flush in her cheeks. Her hand trembled slightly as he loosened his grip.

"Your brother was my knight in shining armor, graciously taking care of my puppy formula emergency at Elsie's Everything earlier this morning."

Charlotte felt Duncan's gaze hold her eyes a little bit longer than she would have liked, and she pulled her eyes from him back to the puppy.

Duncan walked over to the exam table, a scent of some kind of spicy and peppery fragrance assailing her nostrils, and Charlotte tried to shake off the somewhat intoxicating scent.

"So this little guy here caused all the commotion?" Duncan smiled, petting the puppy who still remained asleep.

"Ah, that's a girl, I will note. And a very pretty one at that." Ivy said, winking at Charlotte.

"That's big brothers for you," Dr. Anthony sighed. "He can design a thirty-story building in a heartbeat, but still can't tell the difference between a boy puppy and a girl puppy."

"Hey, that's not fair," Duncan laughed. "The dog's all wrapped up. How was I supposed to know? That's little sisters for you. They know everything."

"Well, everything about the animal kingdom that is," Dr. Anthony laughed.

"I'd like to pay you back for this morning," Charlotte said, opening her wallet, fingering the twenty-dollar bill she had in her wallet.

"If it helped save this little guy—oh excuse me," he said gallantly bowing toward his sister, "girl—then the pleasure was all mine," Duncan said, stepping closer to Charlotte.

"I do appreciate that, but I can't accept." She looked at both the brother and sister standing before her. Duncan was tall, broad shouldered and masculine with what was probably once hair as dark as pitch, but strands of silver threaded themselves throughout his thick hair. Ivy was tall as well, appeared as lithe as a dancer, and her long sunshine blonde hair was bound tightly in the back of her head. Charlotte now noticed the fine lines around Ivy's eyes and the creases around her mouth, indicating she was older than Charlotte had earlier thought. There was no mistaking they were siblings. They each had the same round hazel-gold eyes, and a single dimple in their right cheeks, as their duplicate endearing smiles lit up their faces.

"Sorry, Charlotte," Ivy said, walking back to the puppy. "If you're going to live in Lobster Claw, you need to know and respect one thing; we help each other in times of need and expect nothing in return. Right, big bro?" she asked, nodding toward Duncan.

"The doctor is right, as she always is." Duncan petted the pup and then looked directly at Charlotte. "It's something I need to remember as well, as I just returned myself. Big city living, business competition, deadlines, well that can make you forget about the simple things in life, and one of those things is helping your neighbor."

"Well, you seemed to remember that over at Elsie's, and I do appreciate it. I appreciate what you both have done." Charlotte ended it there. She was not going to argue and be disrespectful toward the two people who helped her in her direst need. "I hope I can return the favor in the future."

"Oh, I'm sure you will," Ivy smiled, again turning toward the sound of the loud jangling bells.

"That's definitely Dina," Ivy said, buttoning her white lab coat. "I can tell by the bells," she laughed, "always louder when she arrives."

Ivy made the introductions and instructed Dina on what to do so she could go with Charlotte to pick up the mother dog.

"Oh, Dun, I'm sorry, was there something you needed?" Ivy asked turning toward her brother.

Duncan nodded. "No, just my power is still out and I was wondering if Andy could help out."

"Call his cell. Big storm last night, big bro. He's probably up to his ears in calls, but he'll stop by for you." Ivy turned to Charlotte. "My husband, Andy, is Lobster Claw's electrician. Always busy, but more so on post-storm days."

"Good to know," said Charlotte, grabbing her bag and keys from the chair in the exam room. She walked back to the table to pet the pup once again.

"See you soon, little lovey," she whispered to the sleeping puppy. She bent and placed a gentle kiss on the pup's golden head.

"Ready," she said to Ivy.

"Good. I've got everything in my van, so I'll drive that and meet you there." Ivy dashed out of the door and into her veterinary van. Dina was absorbed in the puppy as Duncan held the exam door open for Charlotte.

"Nice to see you again, Charlotte," he said, as they headed into the morning sunshine.

"You as well, Duncan, and thanks so much again. I won't forget it."

Charlotte smiled and waved as she got into her car and followed Ivy's van back to Beach Rose Path.

Duncan watched his sister and Charlotte walk out the front door and into the morning sunlight.

"You need anything else, Duncan, besides your electricity?" Dina's gravelly voice broke the silence in the practice. For some reason seeing Charlotte again made him think of Melinda as ridiculous as that was. Duncan had no idea why Charlotte triggered this memory, but the thought of Melinda's painful betrayal seized his mind for a few short moments. The sound of Dina's scratchy voice, one of having smoked a few too many cigarettes in her lifetime, roused him not from his daydream, but from his nightmare.

"She is a cutie, isn't she?" Dina asked, gently moving the puppy to one of several crates lined up against the exam room wall. Cozy fleece blankets lined each crate, and Dina snuggled the puppy into one, careful not to remove the IV from its tiny leg. She rolled the saline drip up to the crate and the puppy did not wake at all.

"All puppies are cute, Dina," Duncan said, heading out of the exam room. He had a sudden need to escape the now cramped and stifling room.

"That's not what I meant, and you know it." The command in Dina's voice made Duncan turn to face her. "I meant your sister's client. The one who brought in the puppy." Duncan noticed the slight smirk that began to form on Dina's deeply lined face. Not only did her love of cigarettes affect her voice, but the tobacco and nicotine also created long hard creases in her once youthful and pretty face. Although Duncan hadn't seen Dina in years, Lobster Claw ties were tough to break.

"When Ivy bought this practice from my husband, she didn't have to keep me on, but she did. And I knew she would because you and your sister were raised the Lobster Claw way. I know I've had my share of problems since Pauley passed, but just because I haven't seen you in a while doesn't mean I don't know what you may need. And that my dear is a significant other. She would keep you young." Dina winked at Duncan, chuckled loudly and left to return to the front desk.

I don't think so, Duncan thought, thinking that if the electricity wasn't back on in his place, he was going to hightail it out of Lobster Claw and back to Boston. He'd stay in a hotel if he had to as long as it had electricity and hot water.

"I'll see you around, Dina," Duncan said, reaching into his leather jacket to feel for his truck keys. He heard her mutter something, but he was not interested in engaging with her and her ridiculous notions about him needing a significant other.

"Been there, done that," he angrily said, flinging open the

truck door and climbing in behind the leather steering wheel. "It didn't work out the last time, and I'm not getting bitten again."

Duncan slammed the truck door shut and furiously jammed the key into the ignition. He let the car run for a moment as his white-hot blood boiled within him. Melinda. Leaving Boston. Lobster Claw. Thunderstorms. No electricity. Things that normally wouldn't bother him now began to gnaw like an irritated itch that would not go away. Was moving back to Lobster Claw the answer? Or was being here worse?

Duncan loved his job, loved Boston, loved his Seaport condo. But Melinda had destroyed that, and Duncan could no longer fathom living and working in Boston. He knew he would see Melinda in every coffee shop, clothing boutique, bookstore, restaurant, on every street corner of the city. She would be everywhere, and he would not be able escape her presence. Melinda's beautiful green almond-shaped eyes, her bouncy golden-brown hair, her slender figure jogging through the Common. Her signature scent of Coco Chanel permeated his nostrils anywhere he would venture in the city, never mind his condo.

Duncan had to leave, and Lobster Claw was his only option. His intention was to put the condo on the market, and the only escape plan he could think of was to his childhood home in Lobster Claw, Maine.

Still sitting in the parking lot of his sister's veterinary practice, Duncan reached for the key in the ignition and shut off the car. He looked out of his windshield into the bluest sky he had seen in years. He rolled the window down, and instead of the fragrance of Coco Chanel, here he smelled the even more delectable scent of salt and sea. Instead of jackhammers and drills, the call of the seagulls filled his ears. The clean ocean air permeated his lungs instead of diesel and smog, and for the first time in weeks, he felt his heartbeat slow and his body ease.

"Maybe I won't miss you as much as I thought I would,

Boston." He took another deep breath, filling his lungs with the magical and healing Atlantic air.

The healing sea. Duncan heard his father's words inside of his head, remembering how much he and Ivy's father loved going down to the beach and walking for miles.

Anytime I'm troubled, Dun, I head to the beach, and I am instantly at peace.

"I hope you are still at peace, Dad," Duncan said, ruminating on his father's words. His father had worked so hard for his family and he had his own dream that was never fulfilled. Duncan knew that dream was still there, sitting under dusty tarps, waiting to be unwrapped and made a reality.

"Hmmm," said Duncan, restarting his truck. "Maybe I can, Dad." He steered the truck in the direction of home wondering if he could make his father's dream his own reality.

CHAPTER ELEVEN

"She's all set." Ivy wrapped the dog in a soft bed sheet and respectfully placed her in the back of her van.

"Like I said, I'll keep her pup for a while just to make sure there are no complications, but I'm assuming she's all yours once I give the okay?"

The realization hit Charlotte that she would become a dog owner again, and she knew this puppy was meant for her.

"Whenever she's ready to come live with me, I'm all hers." Charlotte watched as Ivy lovingly tucked the sheet tighter around the pup's mother.

"I lost my dog a couple of years ago. I actually lost a lot, and I never thought I'd find another dog like my Peppercorn. But I think I may have," Charlotte quietly said as she watched Ivy.

"Peppercorn? What a great name! Black dog, I'm assuming," Ivy said, securing the rear door of her van.

"A Labrador as black as a shiny piece of obsidian. We called him Peppe for short. He was the best." Charlotte wanted to end it there for fear of starting any waterworks.

"We?" Ivy innocently asked. "Were you married?" Ivy stopped short. "Charlotte, I am so sorry. I think it's my line of work—

always asking questions, and I apologize if I overstepped. Duncan and Andy always tell me that I do that."

"No worries, Ivy," she laughed, delighting in finally telling someone she had a family. Once.

"My fiancé, Landon. He gave me Peppercorn as a Christmas present. My boys. But they were both killed in a car accident down in Lighthouse Harbor two years ago." Charlotte stopped talking, realizing she hadn't used those words "killed in a car accident" before. It was always "I lost" or "passed on" but she had never said those harrowing words until now.

"Oh, Charlotte, I am so sorry to hear that."

Charlotte nodded and smiled at the concerned woman standing next to her. "I appreciate that. I've been through some pretty dark times, but I think I can see the light at the end of that long and gloomy tunnel. It took a long time, but I do know that 'tis better to have loved and lost than never have loved at all. You know what I mean."

"I do, Charlotte. Duncan and I lost our parents just a few years ago, too. It most certainly was the worst of times, but then Duncan and I also know how blessed we were to have such loving parents, and that love will always stay with us. I used to kid Duncan that he had them longer than I did—he's thirteen years older than me—and then he'd jab me back saying how lucky he was to have me."

"That's sweet, Ivy. You are very fortunate."

"So are you, Charlotte. I think you'll be happy in Lobster Claw, and even happier with this dog's puppy. Funny how things work, isn't it? I believe it was fate—all meant to be."

Charlotte smiled at the sweet and kind veterinarian. "I couldn't agree more."

"Well, I'd better get back to the office. I need to make arrangements for momma here, and I have a slate of patients for this afternoon!"

Charlotte extended her hand to Ivy. "Thanks again, Ivy, for

everything. I truly appreciate it. And your brother, too. He played a big part in this little puppy's survival."

"That's Duncan. Always the knight in shining armor. Or worn leather bomber jacket—he's always got that thing on!"

Ivy hopped into the cab of her van and rolled down the window, "Feel free to stop by anytime to check up on the pup."

"I will!" Charlotte enthusiastically said. "But I think you can start calling her Little Lovey. I've been calling her that, and I think it's a good name for her. What do you think?"

"Little Lovey it is! I'll give you an update on Little Lovey later! Talk to you soon, Charlotte."

Ivy pulled out of Beach Rose Path and back onto Sand Dollar Drive, with Charlotte waving as the van drove out of sight.

A fatigue like no other swiftly seized Charlotte. She felt lightheaded and drained and headed into the bungalow. She plopped onto the couch and looked at the bright green folder on the coffee table that contained all the information about the cottage and the store. She leafed through the documents and found merchandising catalogs similar to the ones she'd made orders through at Loch Ladies. She flipped through and saw the various souvenir types of things—T-shirts, sweatshirts, tote bags. All the ordering information was written on a bright orange Post-It note and stuck onto the catalog along with several credit accounts.

"Ruskin Enterprises. PO Box 0607, Halifax, NS. Thanks, Rory," she said. She laughed at his old school way of handwritten notes, and knew she needed to make a more updated inventory on spreadsheets. Charlotte was unimpressed by the paraphernalia in the catalog, but knew stuff like that sold like hotcakes, so she would order what was necessary.

"And something else as well," she mused. "But coffee first. No wonder I'm exhausted."

Charlotte stepped into the kitchen to start a pot of coffee, letting her mind wander back to all those years ago when she had transformed Loch Ladies from a basement on a championship golf course into to a pretty shop, and quite the booming retail business.

"No reason why I can't do that here," she said, taking a freshly brewed cup of coffee back to the couch. "Of course, not with golf attire," she murmured, leafing through the catalogs. Charlotte grabbed her purse and pulled out her trusty notebook and began making notes of what she thought needed to be ordered.

"T-SHIRTS, CHECK. TOTE BAGS, CHECK. SWEATSHIRTS, CHECK. KEY chains, check. I'll need more than that," she said, and texted Hamish.

> Hey, there! Just going through the merch catalogs—usual stuff. With your permission, I'd like to order a few non-traditional items—do you think that would be okay with Rory?

HER TEXT WAS IMMEDIATELY ANSWERED.

> Cart blanche, Charlotte. Hope all is well. All my love.

> All is good. Only been here a day and so much has happened. I'll email you all the details later!

> Looking forward to it!

CHARLOTTE SETTLED BACK INTO THE COUCH SIPPING HER COFFEE. Within 24 hours, she was introduced to the Beach Block, saved a puppy, and a knight in shining armor—or rather, waxed leather —came to her rescue. Not to mention meeting his charming veterinarian sister.

"Like the sign said, I think I'm already caught in the claws of Lobster Claw and may stay for a while after all," she laughed, opening her laptop and began placing orders for what she hoped would be a most successful summer season.

Charlotte's eyes blurred from looking at the computer screen. She had lost track of time, and her tired eyes were telling her to shut it down.

She wearily closed her computer and pushed it aside. She shut her eyes, knowing they needed a respite from the intense gadgets of the 21st century. Charlotte still maintained her own old school approach when working—she liked brick and mortar stores, and found that patrons did as well, and she loved nothing more than finding a thick catalog in the Loch Ladies' mailbox. She used any downtime perusing the pages of these compendiums and could spend hours leafing through the colorful pages of inventory. Landon had been the same as well, browsing and analyzing golf clubs, gloves, cleats, anything that could improve one's game.

Landon. Charlotte was shocked that several hours had passed since her last thought of him. Although he had been gone from her life for two years, he was always in her thoughts, and she found herself wondering what he would think of her new life.

"It's just started," she whispered, "but did I do the right thing? Should I have hung on at Castle Loch? I didn't have a choice, Lan." Feeling more alone than she ever had, Charlotte could not help but think about the once secure love and happiness she had with Landon and Peppe, but especially in times of duress tears, anger, and sadness had overwhelmed her and any positive thoughts for a future were washed away with her tears. *Will I ever be happy again?*

"It's too late," she whispered, closing her eyes. "I'm past my prime," she laughed, musing about the non-probability of a romance in her future.

I am alone, she thought. *Alone in a town where I barely know anyone. Alone to jump start a business.* Suddenly, all the anticipation and expectation she felt moments ago while leafing through the catalogs, vanished like the sun in a stormy sky. Doubt snaked into Charlotte's psyche making her feel she had just made a monumental mistake.

"Stop it!" she shouted, jumping up from the couch. She walked into the kitchen and looked out of the large window facing the beach. She watched as the waves leisurely rolled in and out, a metronome marking the rhythm of the sea, the rhythm of time. Charlotte stared out the window, the waves rolling away her old life at Castle Loch out to sea, and washing a new one onto the shores of Lobster Claw. Simply looking at the waves turning over, their rocking back and forth comforted her, and she felt a shift begin to take place.

"You can do this," she said, and she thought she could almost hear the whisper of the sea encouraging her.

"Time and tide wait for no man," Charlotte whispered. "Or in this case no woman."

With each wave that trundled toward shore, along with each comforting sip of coffee, Charlotte felt her own tide begin to turn, and vowed not to let any negative thoughts block her way.

You did this before—you can do it again. And you will.

"There, how's that for the power of positive thinking," she laughed, pouring another cup. Just as she put the pot back on the burner, a knock on her door startled her so, she almost dropped it. She had spilled a few drops of coffee and wiped them up as the knocking continued.

"Just a sec!" yelled Charlotte, throwing the paper towel into her sink. Charlotte opened the door and saw Tatiana standing before her looking like the quintessential queen of the sea. She was dressed in mermaid-styled leggings, beautiful sparkles and sequins gleaming on her legs, with a matching athletic top, looking as if she had just arisen from the depths of the ocean. Her long silver hair flowed down her back and shoulders, making her look even more mermaid-esque.

"Hello there," she said, a beautiful smile brightening her luminous face.

"It might be presumptuous of me, but I thought you'd like to try my seaside yoga class today. Gearing up for the summer season. What do you say?"

Charlotte took in the glistening creature that stood before her. She was lithe, toned, and looked absolutely magnificent. *And here I am with my stringy mousy brown hair, ripped Castle Loch sweatshirt with an old pair of Landon's gym shorts. Not to mention my unshaved legs and non-pedicured feet.*

"I'm not really the yoga type," Charlotte responded, scrunching her face and feeling like one of Cinderella's ugly stepsisters compared to this shimmering sea goddess.

"Exactly what I said so many years ago," Tatiana smiled. "Might do you a bit of good, sea air, a bit of stretching. Good for the mind and for the soul."

Time and tide wait for no man. The idiom crashed like the waves on the beach and through her head again.

Take any and all opportunities, Char, you never know where they may lead you. Charlotte heard Hamish's voice echo inside her head, and it was the best advice he ever offered as it erased any doubts she had with Landon and finding true love with him.

"You're right," Charlotte said. "It would do me a bit of good, but I'm not exactly dressed for a yoga class, though," she said, now fully embarrassed by her shabby appearance.

"No worries! I've got plenty of gear. I'm sure we can find you something for you."

"All right then," Charlotte chirped, realizing that as time nor tide would wait for her, Charlotte accepted her new friend's offer.

CHAPTER TWELVE

Duncan drove down Sand Dollar Drive and onto Beach Rose Path. He could see from the narrowing road a gray-shingled house with a wooden dock that led to a row of multi-colored buildings.

"I don't recall these," he said, slowing the truck so he could take in the classic views of the Maine coastline.

His memory jogged as he drove closer to the buildings, remembering from childhood the old brick and dusty storefronts. These had obviously been renovated and painted to match the hues of the beach.

"Clever idea, whose ever it was," he said, the design-architectural part of his brain clicking on.

Duncan's curiosity got the better of him, and he steered his truck into the lot behind the storefronts. He got out of the truck and walked around to the front, admiring the simple yet obviously strong architecture of the four buildings.

Duncan noticed a plaque on the first building.

1907. Isaiah Henry House.
Lobster Claw, Maine Historical Society.

"Not ringing any bells," he said to himself, revisiting the summer memories of so long ago. As a kid he couldn't have cared less about the architecture of historical buildings. He was only interested in being at the beach for hours on end, starry-night bonfires, and when he was older, secretly stealing beers from his father's cooler in the garage, and sitting on the dunes of Lobster Claw Beach with his friends, drinking and talking about one day escaping from this little saltwater town.

Admission to Boston State College took him south from Maine, and an elective class in Boston Architecture Through the Centuries, piqued his interest in city planning. It was all up from graduation, being hired by Dane and Grayson, Boston's most prestigious architectural firm, and being made partner by the age of 40, solidifying his success with the firm's name change to Dane Grayson Kirk. Duncan was one of Boston's most eligible bachelors and made the prestigious 'Best of Boston' for *City of Boston* magazine three times in ten years. He had the world in the palm of his hand when he met Melinda Bellini, a former model and absolute knockout who managed a modeling agency. Together, they ruled the Boston social scene like a king and queen, never eating a home-cooked meal, always out at an event, always together... but still so far apart.

Duncan laid his hand upon the blue painted brick of the Isaiah Henry House, feeling the warmth of the sunbaked bricks flow through his hand. He looked out toward the ocean, the same ocean he looked at from the picture window in his 34th floor condo in Boston's Seaport district, a once dilapidated warehouse-laden part of town that he helped magically transform into a shining and glittering city of Oz. Magnificent skyscrapers constructed of glass and condominium towers with terraces that stretched over the Boston Harbor graced the newly paved sidewalks lined with upscale clothing stores, restaurants, and luxury hotels. He and Melinda never wanted to be anywhere else. They were the big wheels that spun the city, and they had their own cogs spiraling and spinning all over town. Duncan Kirk and Melinda Bellini wanted for nothing. Duncan's mind returned to the day when he discovered Melinda with his best friend; how Melinda looked so beautiful in the lemon-colored silk dress wrapped around her perfect body. He was the only one who should have been peeling it from Melinda's voluptuous curves, but instead, the lustrous dress was in the grimy grip of Eric's hands. He had immediately thrown Eric out of the condo and fired him. And then it had been Melinda's turn to be tossed to the curb.

Melinda had blown up his phone with texts but Duncan never responded. He'd sometimes had the sneaking suspicion that there was someone else, but Melinda's overconfidence and cockiness destroyed their relationship—and, to make matters worse, with his best friend. Duncan never imagined that the friend he worked so closely with, drank with, and lamented about the lack of good women available would do this to him. But Eric had betrayed Duncan's friendship in the worst way possible. With his fiancée.

Melinda's presence permeated every room, the bed which they shared, and even the sofa on which he had found the disloyal lovers. There was no escape from Melinda's unfaithfulness in the condo so Duncan had hightailed it to Lobster Claw.

A strong breeze blew the pungent scent of salt air and brought Duncan back to the present. He then noticed two women walking toward a group of three others on the beach. One woman was tall with long silvery hair and the other was shorter and slender, wearing a sweatshirt, long wavy brown hair blowing in the beach breeze.

"Charlotte," he whispered. He watched as the women put down mats on the sand, and then saw Charlotte head up toward Isaiah Henry House.

"Time to go," he muttered aloud. Being lost in thoughts of

Melinda was enough, and as attractive as he thought Charlotte was, he was not in the mood for any small talk. He hopped back into his truck, turning his thoughts toward fulfilling a dream for his father.

CHAPTER THIRTEEN

T<small>ATIANA WAS RIGHT</small>—<small>THE SOULFUL STRETCHING AND MEDITATION</small> of her yoga class had made Charlotte feel more rejuvenated—both physically and mentally. It was nice meeting Betsy's niece from Take the Cake and Priscilla from the Lobster Claw Ice Cream Parlour. They were sweet and very welcoming and made Charlotte feel at ease despite her exhausted appearance.

Tatiana found a pair of comfortable yoga pants and a tank top making Charlotte feel even more self-conscious as she felt absolutely out of shape. She was used to walking miles every day on the golf course, or running back and forth from Loch Ladies to Hamish's office for some sort of business—or personal—advice, but the last few weeks were filled with packing and bad eating habits, and she felt it was a good day if she remembered to wash her face and brush her teeth.

The warm jets of water that streamed from the shower head not only cleansed Charlotte's body, but her mind as well, making her feel refreshed in body and spirit. She hopped out of the shower, cleared the fogged mirror and examined her reflection.

"Yes, you do look better, but..." she said to her reflection. Her shoulder-length brown hair looked more like mousy beige than the shining chestnut-colored hair she was blessed with in her younger years. Charlotte couldn't even remember the last time she had it cut and styled as she noticed more newly sprouted wiry threads of steel-wool gray threaded through her dull hair.

"Arg," she sighed as she painfully yanked one from her scalp with her fingers, watching the coiled strand fall into the sink. She turned the taps on as strong as possible and watched, with satisfaction, the silver strand flush down the drain.

She continued to examine her face, thinking her eyes looked tired, with shadows of dark circles laying beneath her brown eyes, but her cheeks were pink and glowing from sun she got while on the beach.

"A little better, but not much," she said. "Okay, that's enough cross examination, or you'll drive yourself crazy!"

Charlotte wrapped her old but still comforting bathrobe around her relaxed body and sat on her bed looking about the loft. The window on the right looked directly out onto the ocean and she watched sailboats bob steadily on the placid waves. She got up and opened the window and let the sea air breeze in, infusing not only the loft, but her soul with its most magical scent.

"Ah," she said, inhaling the invigorating air. She felt ready to get to work. She needed to do more unpacking and then figure out what to do with her furniture in the store.

"One thing at a time, and that one thing right now is coffee. I don't care what time it is," she said looking at her watch. It was almost 2 p.m. She felt she needed a kick to get herself going, even after the yoga class, and coffee would give her that kick, so she put on a pot of coffee and set to unpacking.

The hours passed quickly for Charlotte getting the bungalow to her satisfaction. All her clothes were put away and her toothbrush was in its holder and she now felt the bungalow was in order.

"Looks good!" she exclaimed, quite pleased with all she accomplished within a few hours.

Charlotte then gave Ivy a quick call to check on Little Lovey.

"She's amazing, Charlotte. Stop by when you can," Ivy sang from the other end of the phone.

"My day just escaped me," she said to Ivy. "I've been ordering merchandise, unpacking, and oh I took an impromptu yoga class on the beach. I'm glad she's doing well, and I'll stop by in the morning if that's okay."

"See you in the a.m. Charlotte," Ivy said and disconnected the call.

"The place absolutely needs a dog," she said looking around, now realizing how alone she was and knowing Little Lovey would be a wonderful companion.

"I think you two may have sent her to me," she murmured, feeling that Peppe and Landon were watching over her.

"Little Lovey and I can figure out our lives together," she said, hunger pains now stabbing the insides of her stomach.

"I'm really not in the mood for a can of soup, that's for sure. Maybe a little drive around the town might do me some good," she said. She put on a pair of jeans, a white cotton blouse, and a pair of blue slip-on shoes. She combed her hair and pulled her bangs down onto her forehead conveniently covering the line that seemed to have deepened over the last few days between her eyes. She threw the rest of her thick hair up into a clip. She rummaged through her bag for her lipstick and put some on, giving her face an instant lift.

"Hmm," she said, "maybe this yoga thing is good for me after all." Then she laughed. "Nah!! Once Little Lovey is older, we will walk, just like I did with you, Peppe."

She smiled at the thought of walking on the beach with Little Lovey, and a feeling of contentment settled over Charlotte. Two days in Lobster Claw and so much had happened. And, finally, for the better.

"Okay! Something to eat. And not out of a can." She did a quick search on her phone and the first thing that came up was Elsie's Everything.

"What?" she said surprised. She scrolled down through the description and found Elsie's also had a diner.

"How do you like that," she laughed, "Well, there's a lot of good things about diner food, and I could use some meatloaf and mashed potatoes, so look out Elsie, here I come again!" Just the thought of comfort food made Charlotte happy and hungrier. She locked up, got into her car and once again, for the second time in twenty-four hours, made her way to Elsie's Everything, and this time she was grateful it was not because of a puppy emergency.

CHAPTER FOURTEEN

CHARLOTTE CHECKED HER REAR-VIEW MIRROR TO ENSURE NO ONE was in back of her, as she didn't want to slow anyone down as she took in some of the most beautiful sea views she had ever seen. Tall, seemingly endless pines reached to the watercolor pale blue sky, branches slowly wavering in the warm spring breeze. Puffs of white clouds sailed leisurely through the late afternoon sky. Mother Nature created a picture-perfect moment.

Charlotte knew Maine was stunning, but she and Landon pretty much kept to their favorite town of Lighthouse Harbor, only 90 minutes from Castle Loch. They needn't go any further, as that was *their* heaven on Earth, and they felt no other town in Maine could give them any more happiness than Lighthouse Harbor. But the views in Lobster Claw were just as spectacular.

Is there a more beautiful town on coastal Maine? she wondered, driving slowly so she could take in the breathtaking views of not only the enormous pines, but the sparkling ocean that flowed beyond them. The shoreline was more rocky in these further reaches of Maine but just as beautiful, in a different, more untamed way.

"What is that?" she questioned, noticing a cluster of pines that appeared to have risen right out of the ocean depths.

Charlotte pulled her car onto the shoulder of the lane, ensuring that she was not parked on the narrow stretch of road. She got out of the car and stood before one of the prettiest sights she had ever seen. A grove of towering pine trees stood on what appeared to be an island in the bay. The island's shoreline was jagged, with small waves clattering over the rocks, creating a fountain of salt-water sprays. The color of the sea between the island and the shore was the most gorgeous hue of blue Charlotte had ever seen, almost indescribable— not the dark blue of a sapphire, nor was it the light blue of a topaz, but almost a perfect combination of both, with the reflection of the waning afternoon sun creating a diamond-white shimmer over the bay. She could feel the mist of the sea salt on her face with the warmth of the setting sun, and Charlotte inhaled as Tatiana had demonstrated earlier, explaining that this breathing technique induced a calming effect. Charlotte concentrated on her breathing, and she felt her spirit lift with the tides, feeling one with the land, sky, and sea. Contentment filled Charlotte's soul, and the beauty of nature at this moment in time was nothing less than perfection. Charlotte knew this could never be captured in a photo, because it was more than that—it was the seeing and it was the feeling— what it meant to be "in the moment."

The loud sound of a truck's mighty motor roar broke the spell.

"I won't forget this," she said, blowing a kiss to her little private island. "I'll be back. Thank you."

Charlotte then saw a lavender streak in the sky and looked at the dashboard clock.

"Oh, boy!" she said, starting up her car. "No wonder I'm now starving, but that was worth the stop. So well worth the stop."

Feeling even more revived and alive, Charlotte proceeded the few miles down Sand Dollar Drive and pulled into the parking lot of Elsie's Everything.

She looked at the layout of this cute little establishment. It was the typical design of the New England Saltbox, with its one-sided steep pitched roof. A large brick chimney climbed up one side of the house, while the small lighthouse graced the other side. The house was painted white with red shutters and a bright red roof that matched the circular stripes painted on the lighthouse, its lantern top also painted bright Christmas red. Charlotte wondered if the lighthouse was in working order or was just ornamental. But it didn't matter; it was charming, and screamed 'coastal Maine'. Imposing pines stood behind the structure, and Charlotte heard a slight roar of the ocean.

"That is adorable," she said, getting out of her car, now even more hungry.

Charlotte walked up the wooden steps and onto the front porch. She opened the door to the loud clanging of cow bells and her mind's eye saw where she had stood the day before, at the register with Duncan paying for her evaporated milk.

Charlotte then heard the clinking of silverware and followed the tinkling sound to the back of the store and found an old-fashioned diner counter. Five red leather bar chairs lined the shining formica counter that sat upon a black and white checkered linoleum floor. It was most definitely dated, but that's what made it so inviting. She noticed coffee makers with pots full of coffee even at this late hour of 6 p.m. along with soda fountains, and a grill. Above the grill, paper plates were taped with today's specials written on them. Charlotte couldn't help but smile, as she felt as if she'd suddenly stepped back in time. She loved everything about Elsie's.

"Well, good to see you again, Miss."

The woman who was behind the cash register yesterday was now behind the diner counter. She had just come out from what Charlotte assumed was the kitchen area, as she was holding a heaping plate of French fries that she poured into a flimsy white carton. "Elsie" was written on her name tag with now smudged magic marker.

"Here's your fries, Chris," Elsie announced to a teenage boy sitting at the other end of the counter.

"Thanks, Elsie," he said, greedily stuffing them into his mouth.

"Looks amazing and smells even better," Charlotte said, already knowing what she was going to order from the paper plate that advertised the daily specials.

"What can I get you, dear?" Elsie asked, wiping down the already spotless counter.

Charlotte nodded her head toward the paper plate above the grill.

"Today's special is exactly what I had in mind—meatloaf with mashed potatoes. And extra gravy, please."

"Coming right up!" Elsie disappeared behind the flapping doors leading back into the kitchen. Charlotte could envision the mouth-watering meatloaf, loaded with ketchup, gravy and mashed potatoes. A sudden and loud jangle of bells musically clamored once again from the front of the store, interrupting Charlotte's thoughts.

Charlotte heard heavy footfalls behind her and a certain scent of pine, pepper, and leather made her heart suddenly quicken.

"So, we meet yet again." Duncan Kirk's voice was smooth and low and she turned to see his handsome smiling face.

"So we do." Charlotte tried to sound as pleasant and nonchalant as Elsie flew from behind the flapping doors with a huge plate heaping with slices of mouth-watering meatloaf and what seemed like a small mountain of mashed potatoes. Charlotte saw that she was about to dig into a dinner fit for a longshoreman.

Elsie also had a grease-stained paper bag in the other hand which she placed on the counter on her way to the table from the kitchen.

"Oh, Dun, just in time," she said, laying the huge plate before Charlotte.

"Here you go, Miss. Enjoy. Duncan, your double cheeseburgers are in the bag, and your fries are right here." Elsie deftly poured the fries into a carton and put it into another paper bag and handed the bags to Duncan.

Charlotte was dying to eat. It smelled heavenly and she could feel her stomach churn from hunger, but decided to wait until Duncan left.

"Here you go, Elsie," he said, handing her a twenty-dollar bill. "And keep the change. Big order."

"You are a doll, Dun," Elsie said, opening the register and depositing the money. The shrill bell of a telephone rang in the kitchen and Elsie ran to answer it.

Duncan nodded toward Charlotte's plate. "I almost ordered the meatloaf, but tonight was more of a cheeseburger night for me."

Charlotte smiled. "Some nights it's meatloaf, others, cheeseburgers. And fries."

Okay, you can go now, Charlotte thought, the only thing on her mind was just wanting to devour this delectable meal in peace, and her first true one in Lobster Claw.

"Dining alone?" he asked, gripping the bags in his large hand.

"That I am," Charlotte replied. *Trying to,* she thought.

"Oh, Dun, could you do me a huge favor?" Elsie jumped from behind the flapping doors, a look of concern crossing her perspiring pink face.

"That was Sam Holley. Unexpected guests dropped in and he just ordered a ton of food, but his truck's broke down. Again. Would you mind waiting and bringing it up to him as he's just down the road from you?"

Duncan smiled flirtatiously at Elsie.

"Anything for you, Elsie. I'll just eat here while I wait."

"You're a lifesaver, Dun! Oh," she exclaimed, bending from

behind the counter. "Here's a plate. Thanks again!" she sang whisking herself back into the kitchen.

"Hope you don't mind some dinner company?" he asked, that flirtatious grin now directed at Charlotte.

"Not at all," she said, feeling a bit captivated by that smile. *Just two patrons in a diner, that's all this is, Charlotte. You didn't come here for romance. You came here to survive.*

"So, what do you think of Lobster Claw?" asked Duncan, sipping on his root beer. He had just finished one of the huge cheeseburgers and fries.

Charlotte wiped her hands on the cloth napkin resting on her lap.

"I like it," she said, hoping mashed potatoes were not smeared on her face. All she wanted to do was to eat alone, but when Duncan sat down beside her, she knew her evening wasn't going to be as solitary as she planned, and she was strangely okay with this.

"I've only just got here, and I still have so much to do. No dull moments for me, that's for sure."

She wasn't going to share her reasons for being in Lobster Claw with him. Nor was Charlotte sure of anything at all, even Lobster Claw. She liked Tatiana and Ivy, and adored Little Lovey, but she had to take things one day at a time. She had to give it a go since she really did not have much of a choice.

"I'm going to revive Rory Ruskin's store and hopefully bring in lots of summer customers. That's my plan. And like I said, I have a lot of work to do in the next couple of weeks." She was hoping he'd somehow get the hint she was trying to throw his way.

Duncan tossed his own napkin on the counter. She noticed he was not wearing a wedding ring—not that it mattered. Her father never did either, as he hated jewelry of any kind. This never seemed to bother her mother, however Charlotte knew it would have upset her if Landon didn't wear his wedding ring. But he never got that chance.

"Same. I just moved back to my old childhood home, and I'm not going to lie, it is not in the pristine condition my sister led me to believe it was in. I hope I didn't make a mistake."

"Where did you move from, if you don't mind me asking?" She took a sip of the ice cold coke she ordered.

"Boston." Charlotte thought she detected a bit of anger in his voice.

He turned to her, his hazel eyes seemed to be tinged with a bit of sadness, which Charlotte totally understood.

"No kidding," she said nonchalantly. "I moved up here from Winchester. I worked at the Castle Loch Golf and Country Club. I managed the ladies pro shop. I lived there as well, but new management took over and cleaned house, so here I am."

"Hmm," Duncan said, twisting on his counter stool, now facing Charlotte. "I never was much of a golfer, but I've heard of the club. Nice out there. Sounds like you had a great gig."

"I did. That's for sure. But you know, all good things come to an end, right? When we found out the club was under new management, my mentor, a friend of Rory, fixed me up with the job here to revitalize the store. But I'm not quite sure..."

Charlotte stopped, suddenly filled with doubt. Her stomach felt like it was flipping like a pancake on a hot griddle and all she wanted to do was get out and fast.

"Order's up, Dun! Thanks for waiting, and oh, your next cheeseburger is on the house since you're doing me a huge favor!" Elsie placed the large paper bag on the counter, grease stains now forming from the inside out. The aroma of the burgers, fries and onion rings made Charlotte queasy and she wanted to get out of Elsie's fast or her dinner would be reappearing on Elsie's pristine formica counter.

Elsie nodded her head toward Charlotte.

"Yours is on the house, Miss. Welcome to Lobster Claw!" Elsie turned and pushed through the flapping doors, disappearing back into the kitchen.

"If you don't mind me saying so, you look a little green. You okay?" asked Duncan, standing up and engulfing the large greasy paper bag into his strong arms.

"I'm okay, thanks. I think I'm just exhausted. It's been a long twenty-four hours. Just need a good night's sleep is all."

Charlotte could feel her body flush, and she wasn't sure if it was the closeness of Duncan or the nauseating scent of Sam Holley's dinner. Or both.

"Well, let me walk you to your car at least. Ivy would disown me as a brother if she knew I left a newcomer in distress. And a client, at that."

Duncan smiled, the deepening lines under his eyes and on his cheeks making him even more handsome. Charlotte took a deep breath and one last sip of her coke.

"Better," she said, placing the cold glass back on the counter.

"Oh," she said, looking into her bag for her change purse. She pulled out a five-dollar bill and left it by the side of her plate.

"That was very sweet of Elsie. She didn't have to do that." Charlotte felt her composure return, the dizziness abating and the nausea waning.

"Elsie gives out so many free meals, I'm amazed she's still in business," Duncan laughed as he followed Charlotte out of the Everything and into the small parking lot in front of the lighthouse. It was balmy for mid-May and the sky was streaked with pink, lavender and mauve, as the sun was setting on another day in Lobster Claw, Maine.

"Sunsets are pretty here," Duncan said as Charlotte pulled her car keys from her pants pocket. "I forget how peaceful these spring evenings are up here."

"Do you miss Boston?" She surprised herself at the words coming from her mouth before she could stop them. *Where did that come from?* she thought as she pressed her keypad to unlock her car.

Duncan shifted the bag from his left arm to his right, still gazing at the paint-brushed sky over the blue-gray ocean.

"Verdict's still out. Never thought I'd leave Boston and never thought I'd come back here. So, never say never, I guess."

"True. One never knows." She suddenly laughed. "Well, I just said never. How about one not ever knows."

Duncan laughed. "Good one. One not ever knows. I most certainly don't, especially these days. But," he said grabbing the handle of Charlotte's car door and opening it deftly still holding the bag, "I'll say good night here and I hope you get a good night's sleep. Better get this dinner over to Sam. He hates cold food."

Charlotte got into her car and rolled down the window.

"Thanks, Duncan. That's exactly what I plan to do."

"Drive safely," he said, as Charlotte started the car and backed out of the parking lot. She could still see him watching her in her rear-view mirror as she headed left onto Sand Dollar Drive.

The ocean breeze was bracing and salty, just what Charlotte needed on her drive back to Beach Rose Path. Having dinner with Duncan was not what she had in mind when she set out for a quiet evening alone, but it turned out to be a pleasant diversion, much to Charlotte's surprise. It was nice to sit with someone and eat and talk, even though she hardly knew him, he at least wasn't a total stranger sitting next to her trying to strike up the odd conversation. He seemed pleasant enough, and thoughtful, especially with running the errand for Elsie. Here he was, just returned from the bright, big city of Boston, and he was acting like he had never left. She inhaled the clean air, her dizziness now totally gone, and she wondered, as she drove down Sand Dollar Drive, if he was like that in Boston as well. Charlotte also wondered what had made him leave Boston and return to Lobster Claw.

"I can't even imagine," she said as she turned into the

driveway in front of the bungalow. The fluorescent green numbers on the car clock flashed 7:35. It was just getting dark as she headed inside and flicked on the lights. The bungalow looked cozy under the inviting glow of the chandelier, but Charlotte felt something was missing. Although she had lived alone for the past two years, she was never lonely but it wasn't lonesomeness she was feeling. She couldn't quite put her finger on it and headed up to the loft to her bed when her phone rang. She fished it out of her bag and saw Ivy's name on her screen.

"Ivy, hi, is everything okay?" She couldn't imagine why Ivy was calling. And then it dawned on her—Duncan must have let his sister know they had dinner together at Elsie's.

"Everything's great," Ivy said enthusiastically.

Oh, boy, she definitely knows about my dinner with Duncan, thought Charlotte.

"Just wanted to give you a Little Lovey update, that's all. She's doing just wonderfully. All of my clients are ready to adopt her, but I told them she already had a great mom waiting for her."

"Don't you dare think about giving that pup to anyone else but me," Charlotte laughed. She needed that puppy as much as the pup needed her.

Ivy laughed. "No way. She's a little pup with a big personality, that's for sure."

"I just walked into the bungalow, Ivy, and felt something was just off, you know, something was missing. I couldn't figure out what it was and now I know. Little Lovey was born here and she belongs here. I think the cottage misses her. And I do, too. When can I pick her up?"

"Let's give her another few days on the IV—just because it's better to be safe than sorry. She's all yours soon enough!"

"Wonderful. Thanks for calling, Ivy. I really appreciate it."

"And, oh, my brother tells me he had dinner with you." Charlotte detected mischievousness in Ivy's voice, and she couldn't help but smile herself.

"Word travels fast in these parts, I see. That we did. You've got yourself a nice brother, Ivy." *And that's all I'm going to say. Actually, that's all there is to say,* Charlotte thought, listening to Ivy's playful giggle.

"Glad you enjoyed your evening. I'll give you a call tomorrow for another update!"

"Sounds good. Thanks so much, Ivy."

"Good night!"

Ivy's words rang through Charlotte's head. *She's all yours.* Another thing Charlotte thought would never happen—owning another dog.

"She's all mine," Charlotte whispered as she pulled the covers down on the bed, putting her head on the soft pillows and falling into a calm and restful sleep.

CHAPTER FIFTEEN

THE SHRILL SOUND OF HER PHONE'S ALARM ROUSED CHARLOTTE from sleep. She grabbed the phone and instantly shut it off, not even remembering setting it.

"Just a habit, I guess," she said. She yawned and stretched as the sunlight glinting off the bay caught her attention. The sky was already a bright blue at 6:30 a.m. with marshmallow-like clouds gently floating through it. The yellow sun beamed brightly, and Charlotte couldn't help but smile.

"Million-dollar view," she said, getting out of bed, walking toward the window to watch the day continue to break. Seagulls cawed and drifted on the warm spring breezes, and the sound of the peaceful lapping of the waves upon the shore completed Charlotte's picture-perfect morning.

"Coffee," she laughed as she threw an old sweater around her shoulders and padded downstairs. She started the coffee and sat on the couch, listening still to Lobster Claw's seagulls, greeters of the new day.

"Okay, day number 3. Or is it just 2? Or even four?" The aroma of the freshly brewed coffee brought back her senses. This was going to be her third day in Lobster Claw, and today was the day she had to start on getting the store into some kind of shape.

"Coffee first," she said, smiling as she savored the rich, black brew.

"Ah, nothing like it." She picked up the cup and opened the door that entered into the store area. The movers did exactly what she told them when she said to dump the furniture anywhere. It was a mess, with couch cushions scattered across the floor, lamps tossed on top of the couch, along with upturned end tables, and her small dining table upside down with its legs sticking up like some kind of stranded animal. Everything was tossed in a heap as if it was trapped within a hurricane.

"Ug," Charlotte said, taking the lamps from the couch and standing them on the floor.

"Say, this may be an idea." She put her coffee mug on the store counter and began to rearrange the furniture the way she had it in her Castle Loch cottage. She discovered the few framed pictures were in a pile under the couch, and she positioned them on the bare walls, making a mental note to find a hammer and nails, or if she went back to Elsie's, that new kind of tape that could be used to hang pictures.

After a couple of hours of arranging and rearranging the furniture, Charlotte was satisfied with the layout.

"A book nook," she said, as she envisioned patrons sitting on the couches reading and drinking coffee, realizing that there would have to be coffee provided, along with cups, and other restaurant-type accoutrements.

"Maybe not such a great idea after all." Charlotte took a sip of the now cold coffee from her mug. She kept looking at the layout imagining this *could* be a possibility. From what she learned from Tatiana, there was an art gallery, ice cream shop, bakery and a surf shop on the Beach Block. No bookstore, however, or cafe, where one could sit and peruse books.

"I have my own books. It's not much, but could work,"

Charlotte muttered as her mind went into the old retail mode it was used to.

"This can be so much more than a souvenir store. I can still sell the T-shirts, key chains, and all that stuff, but why not something else, too?" She walked to the bungalow side and brewed more coffee. She found her notebook and pencil and returned to the store.

"This can be done," she said, determined to make the store more than it was previously.

"I'm definitely up for the challenge," she said, smelling the freshly brewed coffee. She grabbed her mug and flopped down on the couch she and Landon purchased together—just a standard couch with well-worn denim slipcovers. She sat on the center cushion, 'her cushion' as Landon referred to it, as he always sat on her right side, with Peppe spread over their laps. She could almost feel the warmth of Peppe's body over her legs now, along with Landon's strong arm that always reached around her shoulder. Charlotte closed her eyes and for a brief moment, and they were back, sitting peacefully on the couch, happy in each other's company. A gust of wind blew the door separating the bungalow and store to slam against the wall. Charlotte startled and found herself alone on the couch. The silence was deafening and she could feel her heart beat faster and her breathing become a bit ragged, trying to fight off a crying jag.

Charlotte shook her head vehemently.

"No, I won't let it happen. I'm not alone. I have Little Lovey. I can do this. I *have* to do this."

She got up from the couch and stepped outside to watch the waves lap and the seagulls fly. Something caught her eye and she turned toward the cordoned off area of the piping plovers and saw two women measuring and re-securing the roped off area. This immediately put a smile back on Charlotte's face. People care. They care about birds. They care about orphaned dogs and getting dinner to a neighbor. Charlotte's sadness abated as she watched the two women trudge toward the Beach Block, their yellow tape measures blowing like party streamers in the morning breeze. She couldn't imagine what it would be like here in a few short weeks when the tourists began their descent, and this made her realize all the more that she'd better get a move on.

"Got a store to open, Charlotte, lass." She could hear Hamish's voice in her head telling her to get to work.

"Yes, sir," she said, closing the door on the beach, and opening the door and into a store full of possibilities.

CHAPTER SIXTEEN

CHARLOTTE SPENT THE NEXT SEVERAL HOURS CONTACTING catalog companies and ordered the usual souvenir merchandise, but the more Charlotte looked around the bare store, the more she realized she could do more—do better with it.

Charlotte hadn't been in the basement since Ivy took Little Lovey's mother away, and decided to take another look. She flipped on the light and headed down the wooden stairs.

"Poor thing," Charlotte said, turning her head to the area behind the staircase where she'd found the dogs. She heavily sighed and turned to look at the rest of the basement.

She noticed shelving on the back wall. Three storage boxes were perched on the top shelf. They were a thick, clear plastic, and each had a different colored top that snapped to the sides. The boxes also had labels carefully affixed to the front of each box. *Seashells* was labeled on the box with the white top; *Garland* was labeled on the box with the red top; and the last box, with a green top, was labeled *Annabelle*.

"Hmm," Charlotte said, pulling down the seashells box. She pulled the top off and gasped in delight. The box was chock full of the most beautiful seashells Charlotte had ever seen. She then noticed a folded piece of paper nestled within the collection. She unfolded it and in the script of a typewriter was written: fighting conch, melon, king's crown conch, horse conch, cockle, channeled duck clam, calico clam, bittersweet clam, sundial, oyster, whelk, banded tulip, angel wings and sand dollar.

"Someone knew their shells," Charlotte laughed, marveling at the box of precious relics, colored in all shades of pastels—light pinks, lavender, pale yellow, and iridescent blue and white.

"Just gorgeous," she said, carefully inserting the list back into the box and securing the cover.

Charlotte then pulled down the garland box. She carefully removed the top to discover more of the beautiful shells. She reached inside to lift one out, and noticed that several shells were attached on some kind of rope, creating a garland of seashells.

"Just like the one hanging on the front porch," Charlotte said. "I definitely can do something with these." Each garland was carefully coiled and she counted fifteen garlands. She gingerly replaced the garland and secured the top of the box. She then reached for the box labeled *Annabelle.*

"This could be interesting," Charlotte said, removing the lid. Charlotte's hands wafted through mounds of tissue paper, and she was beginning to think that this was the only thing in the container when her hands felt something soft.

"What is this?" she whispered, pulling out what appeared to be an article of clothing from underneath the tissue paper. It was folded neatly and had a pattern of pinecones, red holly berries, and wintergreen sprigs, obviously something for Christmas or winter. Charlotte gently unfolded the garment and saw that it was an apron. Not the run-of-the-mill "kiss the cook" apron, but an apron that was obviously made with the wearer in mind, whoever that could be. Rory's wife?

"What a beautiful print," Charlotte said, now standing and holding up the apron in front of her. Thick light green satin ribbons were sewn to the bib of the apron, while the same ribbons were used for the ties around the waist. There was a patch of silk or satin in the shape of a perfect square that formed a pocket in the front of the apron, which would have fallen right upon the stomach. Charlotte put the top ribboned part over her head, the ribbons now resting on her shoulders. She pulled the ribbons sewn at the sides around her own waist and tied it in a perfect bow.

"Just like a Christmas present," she laughed, wishing she had a mirror. It was a beautiful piece of craftsmanship, the apron itself a soft cotton and the silky ribbons, or ties, made it just the more spectacular.

She carefully removed the apron and put it on top of the other boxes. She dug further into the box and pulled out three additional aprons, all of the same pattern, but with different material: a yellow print with brown and white rabbits with white daisies and pink butterflies, with light yellow silk ties; a white one with delicate blue flowers and blue silk ribbons; a white one with cheery red cherries and pink silk ties; and a rustic one with ruby dahlias and orange pumpkins with light orange silk ties.

The aprons were obviously not purchased in a store, but custom made. Charlotte examined the apron for a tag of some sort, but found nothing. They were in pristine condition and Charlotte wondered if they had even ever been worn. Charlotte was careful in refolding them and putting them back into the box when she noticed another layer of tissue. She removed it and found more aprons.

"What in the world?" She gingerly removed what were the exact prints of the aprons she had just taken out, but smaller. They were the exact replicas of the bigger ones, but for a child.

They were as beautiful as the adult sized ones, maybe even more so as they were made specifically for a certain child.

"I'll have to ask Hamish about these," she said, thoughtfully repacking the aprons. She heard the vibration of her phone and headed upstairs and saw Ivy's name flashing on the screen.

"Ivy, is everything okay?" Charlotte was afraid she was calling with bad news about Little Lovey.

"Everything's fine, except me. Charlotte, I'm so sorry. I wasn't even thinking. I'm going to keep Little Lovey for a while longer. You just moved and have so much to do, the last thing you need is to care for a newborn pup. Let me keep her a while longer while you get the store in order. You two just seemed so perfect for each other, and, well, I tend to get a little overexcited when it comes to people finding animals. And vice versa. You don't even have what you need, but I do, and I can collect everything and bring it next week. Along with Little Lovey."

"Oh, Ivy, that's so thoughtful, but I think I can manage. I feel like she's already a part of my new life here, I'd love to bring her home."

"Well, let's play it by ear. Little Lovey is still very young, and you literally just moved here and have a business to set up. I'll keep her but you can visit anytime you need your Little Lovey fix. It will just be easier for you. Besides, she's got some buddies here already."

Charlotte then recalled Peppercorn's early days, all the late-night trips outside, and other various puppy duties. But she and Landon cared for and trained Peppe together. She was on her own now.

"Well, if the vet thinks it's best, then I won't argue. Even if I did, I don't think I'd win this one."

"Oh, you're a quick learner, Charlotte! I have crates, blankets, toys, food—this way I can also have time to gather everything you need and get it to you. Deal?"

Charlotte smiled at Ivy's thoughtfulness. "Deal. But I will be by later this afternoon for my visit."

"Sounds great. I'm seeing patients until about 5, so anytime after that is great."

"Thanks, Ivy. You've been such a good friend. See you later."

"You're very welcome. Looking forward to it."

Charlotte disconnected the call. She felt a slight flash of disappointment, but she knew Ivy was right. Little Lovey was better off in the care of the veterinarian while Charlotte got the store ready.

"Okay, Charlotte, get to work!" She went back into the store as ideas suddenly began filling her head, along with an excitement she hadn't felt in a long time.

CHAPTER SEVENTEEN

"I SEE YOU STILL HAVE THE PUP." DUNCAN OPENED LITTLE LOVEY'S crate and patted the sleeping dog's soft golden head. He stopped by his sister's practice to see if she had a spare minute, but from the looks of her waiting room, he'd have to make it quick.

Ivy shot her brother a sarcastic smile.

"You of all people know what it's like to relocate and it ain't easy—like my day—ain't easy. I've got a depressed parakeet, a cat who refuses to eat, and a gecko whose shed is caught in his eye. You have no pets—what do you want?"

"Ouch! Your big brother returns to the homestead and this is how you treat him?" He peeked out into the waiting area where the parakeet was being chased by its owner and a cat's high-pitched mewing was about to break a window.

"I know you're busy, Sis. Just a quick question. Do you have the keys to Dad's storage shed? I thought they were in the house, but I can't seem to find them."

"There's only one thing in that storage shed," Ivy said as she ticked off a list on a clipboard, getting ready to call her next patient.

"The keys are where they've always been—open the cellar

door and you'll see the key holder—you know—the wooden one —in the shape of a big key that you made in shop class when you were, what, nine? Oh, it even has the word *keys* wood burned into the top. Try that."

Ivy affectionately winked at her brother. Duncan felt the flush of embarrassment creep into his face. He recalled giving that key holder, a birthday gift to his father that he made with his own hands, and the happiness and surprise his father bestowed upon his son.

Hanging it right here, Dun. Duncan relived the moment his father hammered a small nail into the basement wall, behind the door. *I'll always see them and know where my keys are at all times."*

"Thanks, Ivy. I didn't think—"

"It's okay." Ivy patted Duncan's shoulder as she made her way into the waiting room.

"Call you later," she waved and joined in the game of capture the fleeing parakeet.

Duncan quickly escaped Ivy's waiting room before the parakeet decided to land right on him, and jumped back into his truck and headed toward home. A few minutes later, he found the key. Duncan ran his fingers over the old wooden key holder.

"Still here," he said, taking the shed key from the holder, smiling at the sentimentality of his father. He walked out into the back yard to the storage shed, and Duncan could feel his father near him as he put the key in the lock and opened the doors. The shed was dark, and Duncan was greeted by the smell of must and motor oil as he made his way inside the shadowy enclosure. Bright beams of sunlight began to stream in through the open doors, and Duncan saw the silhouette of his father's happiness, still covered in a dusty blue tarp.

He grabbed one end of the tarp and vigorously tore it away, revealing the boat his father had bought himself for his 70th birthday. Duncan could still remember his father's hope for his newly purchased boat.

. . .

Gonna take this boat, son, and have myself a little business when I officially retire. Going to go up and down the coast from Lobster Claw to Camden, shuttling tourists, or anything else anyone might need. You know, deliveries, whatever. Just want to work for myself on the water. My dream come true.

Duncan had only half listened to his father. He had just come up to Lobster Claw from Boston for the day for his father's birthday and was anxious to get back. He had a big date later that night, and the voluptuous model with long silky black hair was more on his mind than his father's wistful wishes of retirement.

Been up since 3 a.m. Dun. Gonna grab a little shuteye before the barbecue. See you in about an hour. He patted Duncan on the shoulder, strode to his hammock behind the house and never woke up. He suffered a massive heart attack in his sleep and died on the day he was born, seventy years before.

So Duncan never made it back to Boston for his date, nor did his father ever realize his boating dream.

Duncan's mother never ventured into the shed after her husband's death, and she joined her husband fifteen months later. But somewhere in the recesses of his mind, Duncan was listening to his father that day, and he never forgot his father's dream. Living on Boston Harbor, he saw boats every day—sailboats, yachts, ferries, tugboats accompanying imposing ocean tankers— and he would think of his father, wondering if that would ever be enough for him someday—a quiet life back in his hometown. *Maybe someday* he would think. *Someday.* Now someday was here. After all the turmoil in his life these past few months, Duncan was afraid to end up like his father—a man who never fully realized his dreams. Duncan had accomplished so much professionally, but he found himself questioning, especially lately, was it enough? What was his dream?

"Dreams," he snorted as he ran his hands over the Sea Hunt

Victory. It was a pretty little boat that could fit about six people comfortably. When Duncan was growing up, his dad would rent a similar boat for special occasions, and Duncan remembered the feel of the ocean spray on his face and through his hair, the freedom of getting behind the wheel of a boat and soaring over the ocean. And now his father's dream sat in a shed collecting dust.

"Dreams can come true, Dad," he whispered, patting the boat on the side. It was brand new and in pristine condition, and in that moment Duncan was determined to make his father's dream his own reality.

CHAPTER EIGHTEEN

"Amazing!"

It was the week before Memorial Day, and Charlotte worked harder than ever in getting what she now called The Shop at Beach Rose Path up and running, and she looked on with delight around the space. She decided to keep her Castle Loch furniture in the store which gave it a cozy, den-like feel, reminiscent of Hamish's old office. She unpacked her box of favorite books that included beloved classics such as Jane Eyre, Little Women and Gone with the Wind, along with several Daphne Du Maurier novels. She also added the books that she'd cherished from childhood—her collection of Nancy Drews, Bobbsey Twins, and other favorites she purchased at library sales, along with some 21st century paperbacks.

"I can start a little lending library," she mused, thinking to create a spreadsheet of her books in the event customers wanted to borrow them while on vacation.

She sprinkled home decor, lifestyle, and food magazines along the top of the paw-scratched wooden coffee table and added some battery-operated candles on the shelves and counter tops, giving the store a more warm and at-home comfortable feel.

All of the merchandise she ordered was now on full display—T-shirts and sweatshirts on one wall, along with the kitschy trinkets of coasters, keychains, and other tourist ephemera she thought would sell well scattered throughout the store. She set up a mini coffee bar behind the register with two coffee makers —no fancy coffee here—just black, cream and/or sugar. Charlotte created a logo for The Shop at Beach Rose Path—a drawing of the beautiful blossoming beach rose, like the ones that had bloomed all around the cottage, on a single green vine with two unfolding buds. *The Shop at Beach Rose Path* was printed below the rose. She was quite pleased with the results, feeling that she could work her retail magic once again in this sweet Maine tourist town.

The three weeks Charlotte had been in Lobster Claw flew like the Canada geese over the bay every evening—swiftly and quickly. Little Lovey was thriving under Ivy's watchful care, had a sweet disposition, and Charlotte couldn't wait to get her home.

She had seen little of Tatiana these last few days, as she and the others from the Beach Block were all busy getting ready for their own grand re-openings, and Charlotte found that she missed them, especially Tatiana, of whom she had grown especially fond. She, like them, had become consumed with getting her store exactly the way she envisioned, there was no time for loneliness, just work, visiting with Little Lovey and Ivy, and then bed.

Charlotte took another look at the store. It looked like a comfy living room, which was exactly how she wanted it—warm, inviting, and welcoming. The coffee would be ready to pour and books ready to peruse, with merchandise to purchase.

"Oh, one more thing," she said as she jotted down "cookies" on her daily to do list. She planned on having a plate of Take the Cake bakery cookies, free of charge for the first day, as a way to draw in visitors who would hopefully end up purchasing coastal Maine paraphernalia. She also hung two of the seashell garlands on the wall near the door to see if she would get any takers on those. If she did, she had a whole crate of shells she could figure out how to string and eventually sell.

Charlotte had not seen Duncan since their impromptu dinner, but on one of her Little Lovey visits, Ivy mentioned he was busy with a project, but Ivy confessed she knew nothing more.

"No time for that," Charlotte said, taking one more look at the store. Thoroughly satisfied, Charlotte grabbed her bag and headed toward the Beach Block for the cookies.

CHAPTER NINETEEN

THE DAY WAS ABSOLUTELY GLORIOUS WITHOUT A CLOUD IN THE pristine blue sky. Charlotte happily waved at the piping plover ladies who were hard at work with their tape measures, busy calculating and gauging whatever they felt was important in keeping the precious birds safe. The ladies returned her wave and then quickly went back to their work.

Charlotte spotted Tatiana's long silver hair flowing in the breeze, as she set out colorful Adirondack chairs in front of The Blue Hydrangea. A few early-bird tourists were meandering around the Beach Block, strolling in and out of the shops, carrying brightly colored paper shopping bags printed with the stores' names and logos.

Charlotte jumped at the roar of a loud motor and swung her head toward the dock. A man was starting up the engine of a motorboat, but looked to be having a hard time pulling the lines from the dock. Charlotte felt him catch her gaze and she realized it was Duncan. He waved her to come down toward him.

"What is he up to?" she said carefully making her way down the uneven boards of the Lobster Claw dock.

As Charlotte got closer, Duncan elaborately outstretched his arms on the deck of the boat.

"What do you think?" he asked, his smile as bright and broad as his muscular shoulders.

Stop that, Charlotte scolded herself. Yes, he was a handsome guy, but she had no time or interest for romance. Despite the thought, Charlotte couldn't help but smile at Duncan's obvious enthusiasm.

"I didn't know you had a boat." *Now that sounded dumb. Why would you think he would or would not have a boat!* She hoped he didn't notice her silly remark, so she casually swept it away.

"Very pretty!" *There, much better. But what do I know about boats? Nothing!* she thought as she felt a warm blush creep into her cheeks.

"I'm just full of surprises," he said, extending his hand to her, inviting her on board. As she accepted his outstretched hand, she felt her heart quicken, his warm grip tightening about her fingers helping her aboard.

"It's actually my dad's," Duncan said when Charlotte was safely on the deck. "He planned to open a little ferry business after he retired, but life—or death, I should say—had other plans. He passed away shortly after buying the boat and it's been in storage since."

"Oh, Duncan, I'm so sorry to hear that." Charlotte knew all too well how death had a way of destroying life's dreams.

"Thanks. I thought I'd let her see the light of day once again, so I've spent the last couple of weeks making sure she was in good shape, and she most certainly is. I was just about to take her out—interested in coming along?"

Charlotte looked into Duncan's deeply tanned face. His black hair ruffled in the late spring breeze. He was wearing a light gray T-shirt that had some kind of swordfish logo on it, and she could see his strong and lean physique straining against the shirt. He was wearing old, faded jeans and a pair of well-worn deck shoes.

"I was heading to the Beach Block to run some errands—grand openings are tomorrow—and I just wanted to make sure I have everything I need." Charlotte felt awkward in her response, as if her tongue was tied and her words were garbled.

"That's exciting," he said, now successfully pulling the line from the dock.

For some reason, this movement fascinated Charlotte and she unexpectedly said "but I can run the errands later. I haven't been on a boat in a long time. I'd love to come along."

Duncan's broad smile illuminated his face.

"Great. Let's go. Oh, the lifejackets are under the seat there, just in case."

"Oh, oh, okay," Charlotte stammered.

"Just kidding. I'm pretty capable at driving a boat. Besides, we're not going too far. Just out into the bay for a test run."

Charlotte smiled. She needed a bit of adventure in her life, and what better adventure was there than going out on a boat?

"Let's do it," she said, ready to take yet another U-turn in this magical world of Lobster Claw.

CHAPTER TWENTY

THE SALT AIR AND SEA SPRAY THAT MISTED CHARLOTTE'S FACE WAS refreshing and exhilarating. She felt a bit queasy the first moments on the choppy waves, as she was prone to motion sickness, but that queasiness quickly evaporated into the chill sea air. She watched as Duncan expertly maneuvered the boat over the rocky shoals and further out into the harbor.

"Just like riding a bike," he said, driving the boat over the waves in the bay. "Some things, no matter what, you just don't forget. And I guess steering a boat is one of them."

"How did you learn?" Charlotte asked, the wind whipping her wavy brown hair into her face and eyes.

"My dad. He loved it. He taught both me and Ivy. Ivy was only interested in animals, but I took to it like a fish to water—no pun intended. Entered a few races, but then when I left for college, and well, I guess I just sort of forgot about it. One of my regrets. And a big one."

"Because it took time away from you and your dad?"

Charlotte watched as Duncan looked thoughtfully out into the sea, and she wondered if he was thinking of all the missed opportunities he could have had with his father. She knew she had similar thoughts about herself and Landon.

"You could say that," he said, still looking out over the horizon. Charlotte didn't want to press him any further, sensing his hurt may have been too great, and Duncan was perhaps realizing this as he drove his father's boat—that it was him behind the wheel instead of his dad.

"We all have regrets, Duncan. But life goes on too. And now, you're back and I'm sure your father is with you. Right now."

Duncan slowed the boat as he steered it into Lobster Claw Harbor.

"That's pretty perceptive, Charlotte, because that's how I feel. That he's with me. And that I hope he has forgiven me."

"Whatever happened between the two of you, I'm sure has been forgiven." She believed that from her own experiences.

"Ready to head back?" She saw Duncan's hands clench the wheel at her last remark, and Charlotte detected an edge of annoyance in his voice. *He leads me to think he's going to start a conversation about his life, then he abruptly changes the subject,* she thought. While it was true they hadn't known each other for long, Charlotte sensed there was a part of him that wanted to open up, but he shut right down as he maneuvered the boat. The boat bumped the dock, and Charlotte felt herself lose her balance, almost falling.

"Steady there," Duncan said holding onto her shoulders. She looked into his hazel eyes and realized from their boat ride there was a lot to Duncan Kirk—he could be charming and then standoffish as well. Charlotte was not sure if the combination was one she could truly like. But he was also experiencing a life change, and as it was with her, feelings and attitude were all over the place.

"That was incredible!" she said, her stomach lurching just the tiniest bit. Was it because of his nearness? Or the roughness of the waves? Or both?

Duncan climbed out of the boat first and offered his hand to Charlotte. Once again, his grip was tighter than it should be or was it just her ridiculous and wild imagination? It didn't matter. He was clearly a gentleman, something his father obviously had to do with.

"I'm glad you enjoyed it and I hope I didn't keep you too long from the store. How's that coming, by the way?"

Charlotte brushed the wavy wind-blown hair from her face and felt tiny grains of sea salt prickle her skin. The ocean air most certainly agreed with her. Whatever queasiness she had felt moments ago had vanished and she now felt even more invigorated and ready to get back to work.

"I think it's coming along just fine. At least I hope so. We'll see on Saturday when the crowds start to pour in. All the merchandise is ready and so are my coffee makers!"

"Coffee makers?" Duncan finished knotting the ropes on the pilings when he turned to Charlotte. "Are you serving coffee, too?"

"I am. Sort of a little coffee place as well. I was heading to the bakery for some cookies when I was interrupted by a little boat ride." She once again felt a pleasant blush flush her cheeks. If Duncan said anything, she was going to claim it was windburn.

"Hey, why don't I repay you with a cup of coffee and a cookie? Can you meet me at the store in about an hour? That way you can test my coffee, which I think is pretty good, and you can also give me an honest opinion of what you think of the store."

Oh, my gosh—did I really just do that? She couldn't believe she had been so forward, but there was no going back now.

"I'd love a cup of coffee," he smiled, his face lighting up with delight. "But I have to warn you—I am quite the coffee connoisseur. It was only the best coffee houses for me in Boston —so I'm a tough customer."

Charlotte smiled back, relieved that he accepted.

"Well, it just so happens that I have haunted many a fantastic coffee house, in the suburbs of Boston, so I think I can brew a pretty mean cup of coffee."

"I'm sure you can." The way his eyes penetrated hers and his smile brightening made Charlotte's stomach flutter.

"Well, let me run and get the cookies and I'll see you shortly." Charlotte felt the need to escape fast or else his presence might render her mute.

"See you in a bit," he said, now turning his attention back to the boat, for which Charlotte was grateful. She walked up the dock to the Beach Block, and glanced behind her. Duncan was now standing on the bow of the boat watching her. He waved and went back to securing the remainder of the lines.

Charlotte sighed heavily. She could not for the life of her figure out what this man was doing to her, and she could not let him distract her from the task at hand. But he did. And she guiltily admitted she was glad that he had.

CHAPTER TWENTY-ONE

"It truly looks magnificent, Charlotte. You should be very proud of yourself." Charlotte had run into Tatiana on her way from the bakery and Charlotte had also invited Tatiana to come look at the store. She was feeling unsure of herself with her invitation to Duncan, and with Tatiana near, another female presence would be of great reassurance.

"I'm so glad you like it," Charlotte said, pouring Tatiana's coffee into one of her newly printed paper cups.

"And the cups—what a great idea. Very feminine and pretty. And very Maine. You fit in here perfectly, Charlotte. Cheers!"

Tatiana held up her Beach Rose cup toward Charlotte in a toast, and the two women "clinked" their paper cups. Charlotte smiled at Tatiana's kind words.

"That means so much, Tatiana. I have to admit, I do feel comfortable here. Not sure if I can call it home yet, but I do like it. Everyone's been so wonderful."

"Especially that Duncan Kirk, I see." Tatiana gave Charlotte a wink.

"Don't give me that," Charlotte laughed. "Yes, he's been helpful, but his sister Ivy has been quite amazing as well, especially with the puppy. And you. My first Lobster Claw friend." Charlotte quickly changed the subject.

Tatiana put her cup down on the counter and wrapped her slender but strong arms around Charlotte.

"That's one of the nicest things anyone has said to me. I'm proud to be your first friend, and I can tell everyone in Lobster Claw I knew you when. Seriously, Charlotte, the shop looks amazing. Nothing like when Rory ran it. That's not to say it wasn't successful; as far as I know it did well but when his wife passed, a bit of Rory died, too, and his heart wasn't in it. I'm just glad it wasn't demolished and some new out-of-Lobster-Claw-character building was erected. You saved a lot more than the shop, I can tell you that. There was a realtor sniffing around earlier in the spring, and we thought for sure Rory would sell, but he didn't, thank the Lord. And now you're here. We are going to have a great summer, girlfriend!"

"I hope so," Charlotte said wistfully looking over toward the surf gently lapping on the shore. There were already several people on the beach with their blankets and picnic baskets enjoying the sunny warm afternoon. A few brave souls put their toes in the water, but that was all, as everyone still wore light jackets and sweatshirts. The air was mild but there was still a chill down by the water's edge. The sun was shining brilliantly, and the forecast for the holiday weekend was clear skies, and temperatures hovering around 70 degrees. Perfect weather for a summer kick-off.

"You hope so? Am I detecting doubts?" Tatiana gently took Charlotte's hand.

"Charlotte, just remember, you did this before when you started up the golf store you were telling me about, and you can do it again. I know you can." Charlotte smiled at Tatiana's kind-hearted words. The older woman's face was full of concern and friendliness.

"I know, but it's been so long. It's like catching lightning in a bottle. Lightning struck once, but can it strike again?"

"Do you want it again?" asked Tatiana.

Charlotte smiled at Tatiana's kind face.

"I do want it, but I wonder if I deserve it. When I got my pro shop up and running, it was such a different time in my life. I was younger, single. Loch Ladies became my life and not just because it was my job. If it weren't for the pro shop, I never would have met Landon. We never would have had our dog. I never would have had such a wonderful life without that pro shop and that golf club. Then Landon and Peppe were taken from me, and a few years later, so was the store and my home, as well as my friend and mentor. I am alone, starting over. Of course I worry I might not be able to do this again."

The mere mention of Landon and Peppe, and the thought of Hamish, combined with what Charlotte had at Castle Loch suddenly created doubts deeper than the Grand Canyon. She felt all the enthusiasm she had about the opening, also like the Grand Canyon, run dry, and a heavy sense of bereavement now hung over her.

"Oh, sweetie. I'm so sorry for your losses. I truly am, and I do understand. But I also believe we are given second, third, fourth, however many chances in life to start again. We have to. We lose people or pets close to us all the time in this life, and yes, it does feel as if we are left behind, and I suppose we are. But the ones we lose don't want us to die either—I'm sure your Landon is cheering you on from his heavenly seat right now, as is your pup who is right by his side. And don't forget, there's another pup who now needs you too, and I'm sure there will be another man for you to love someday as well. I can tell, Charlotte, you are not meant to be alone."

"But you're alone." The words escaped before Charlotte could stop them, and she instantly regretted opening her mouth.

Tatiana laughed. "'Tis true! I am. But, like you, there was someone extraordinarily special once, a very long time ago. And also like you, I felt this was my one and only true love, and I was filled with a love beyond all measure. But I had to let that person go, and I did that for love. So, yes, I am very bad about taking my own advice, but I just have a feeling about you, Charlotte. I'm just asking you not to shut yourself away from possibilities."

Charlotte wrapped her arms around Tatiana's strong and lithe body, the woman's long thick hair cascaded around Charlotte's neck.

"You're a good friend, Tatiana. Thanks so much for those kind words. I think you're right. Landon is looking down on me, rooting for me. I truly believe that. I just needed someone to tell me."

"Oh, no tears," Tatiana commanded, brushing a tear that had fallen onto Charlotte's cheek.

"You should be very proud of yourself. You are talented and you are strong. I'm sure this store will be just as successful as your pro shop was. Even more so. I can just feel it in these old bones of mine."

Tatiana's smile brightened, her blue eyes glowing in her tanned face. Her smile was beautiful, warm, and encouraging, giving Charlotte the boost of confidence that she needed.

"I can't wait to call Hamish later and give him all the details, and about my new friend. I hope he's not jealous."

"Hamish?" Tatiana asked, her eyes appearing to recognize the name somehow.

"Yes, Hamish Falconer. He was my boss at Castle Loch and Rory's friend. He's the one who set me up here. He's actually more of a father figure and a wonderful friend. You don't happen to know him, do you?"

Charlotte watched Tatiana's tanned face redden a bit, and her eyes grew misty.

Could she possibly know him? Charlotte wondered as Tatiana's reaction to his name was surprising.

"I think I recall meeting a man named Hamish here, a few years back. He was with Rory. A Scottish man. Seemed to be very kind."

"Yes, that would have been him. Hamish would drive up every now and again and play golf with Rory. Funny that you met him. Small world."

"That it is." The slam of a car door made both Tatiana and Charlotte turn toward the road.

"And speaking of small worlds, here comes your knight in shining armor. Oh, and he seems to be bearing gifts as well."

Charlotte watched as Duncan walked toward the two women. He was dressed in jeans, worn leather work boots and his ever-present leather jacket. The collar of a red and blue plaid shirt popped from under his jacket. He was carrying a huge bouquet of spring flowers wrapped in delicate white tissue paper.

"He certainly is a handsome one," Tatiana gently nudged Charlotte as a playful smile formed on Tatiana's face.

"Shhh!" laughed Charlotte, as Duncan approached them.

Charlotte made the introductions, noticing that Duncan was once again a true gentleman in his courteous manner with Tatiana.

"Charlotte, anything else you need, you know where to find me." And with that, Tatiana casually strode down the rickety wooden dock and back to The Blue Hydrangea.

Charlotte felt her face redden. Duncan looked even more handsome than he had on the boat, and the smell of pine and sea salt was heavy in the air. His smile lit up his sunburned face, the deepening lines around his eyes and cheeks making him look even more distinguished.

"For you." Duncan held out the large bouquet to Charlotte, who engulfed the flowers with her own arms.

"They are simply magnificent," she said, as the heady scents of rose, lilac, and lilies assailed her in a strange sort of way, intoxicating her and making her light-headed, almost as she was back on Duncan's boat.

"That was so kind of you." Charlotte was finding that she was having some difficulty with words coming to her. *Why is he making me feel this way? Dizzy. Lightheaded. Nauseous?*

"C'mon inside and I'll get them right into some water," Charlotte said, turning toward the front door.

"Can't wait to see what you've done with the place. Not that I have anything to compare it with, but I'm sure it looks amazing," he said, following Charlotte into the store.

"Well, see for yourself," Charlotte said, almost tripping over the threshold. She wished Tatiana had stayed, as she wasn't trusting of her actions when she was alone with Duncan.

Just don't do or say anything ridiculous, she commanded herself, leading Duncan inside of The Shop at Beach Rose Path.

"Looks great," Duncan enthusiastically said as Charlotte went inside to find a vase. She found one of the large mason jars Rory had left behind, which she filled from the tap, and put right next to the register.

"Well, compared to what it looked like a couple of weeks ago, I have to say I think it doesn't look bad at all."

She watched Duncan for any kind of reaction—she didn't quite know what she was expecting, but he stood near the register taking it all in. Charlotte could feel Duncan looking at her, and he had a sort of quizzical look on his face.

"I hope you don't think I'm prying, but what brought you to Lobster Claw, Charlotte?"

Charlotte was taken aback by his unexpected question, and she thought she detected an odd tone as well. She couldn't put her finger on it; a bit on the gruff side, perhaps.

"I'm sorry, I didn't mean to sound so brusque—my sister constantly tells me it's not a strong point of mine. But what I mean is, the place looks spectacular and you're obviously very talented. Why didn't you stay in the Boston area? Lobster Claw is beautiful, but it can be tourist-trappy, too. You just don't seem the tourist trap type."

Did he just insult or compliment me? Charlotte thought, now very unsure of herself, and actually wishing he would leave. It was the same feeling she had experienced earlier on the boat— one minute he's sweet and the next he's distant. But she had a verbal arrow in her quiver to aim at him, too.

"Well, you're here. Your sister tells me you were Mr. Boston at one point in your career, obviously talented yourself. What's this tourist-trappy town have for you?"

Back at you, she thought.

Duncan uncomfortably scratched his neck and scrunched his face in embarrassment.

Duncan's tone softened. "I had no place else to go, Charlotte. That's why I'm here."

"Well, I had no place else to go either, Duncan. That's why I'm here." Charlotte heard the resignation in Duncan's response, and decided she was not going to argue with him. She was feeling tired and drained, and she thought he could also be feeling the same, as an awkward silence now put a wall between the two of them, making Charlotte uncomfortable in her own home.

"Duncan, maybe someday I'll elaborate, but I can't think of the past, especially right now. This store is my future, at least for the short term. I'll see what happens after the summer. That's what I've given myself. The summer. If things go well, I'll re-evaluate after Labor Day. It all depends on the summer."

Hopefully he won't know I'm lying. This IS it for me. The store HAS to be a success, and I'm determined to make it one, she thought as she searched Duncan's face for any kind of expression.

"Understood." A loud beep echoed from his shirt pocket. He pulled out his cell phone, looked at the screen, and frowned.

"I have to take this call, Charlotte," he said. He started toward to the door and stopped and turned toward her.

"I'm sure you'll have a great opening. I'll see you." He walked out of the store. She watched him as he put the phone to his ear. She couldn't hear him as the crash of the surf was loud, but he appeared agitated by the way he paced back and forth in front of his truck. His free hand angrily raked through his thick black hair. There was no laughing or smiling, just a lot of head nodding and hair raking and pacing. She watched as Duncan finally put the cell back into his pocket, climbed into his truck, and she then heard the loud slam of his car door before he peeled down Sand Dollar Drive.

Charlotte looked at the mason jar of flowers. They were beautiful pink, white and yellow roses surrounded by lilacs, orange lilies, magenta Gerber daisies and purple irises, enveloped by delicate baby's breath. "I'm sure you have a heart under that heavy leather jacket," she said, as she rearranged the beautiful bouquet. Charlotte decided to shrug off Duncan's mood, and blamed it on the stressors of moving and restarting life. But Charlotte also wasn't going to be a doormat for Duncan to trample on either.

"Lord knows I've had my own share of moodiness these last few weeks." Charlotte inhaled the magical scent of the flowers and felt her spirits rise. She also thought she detected the piney scent of Duncan's aftershave hovering over the beautiful blooms.

Duncan, by his own admission, *had* become brusque in their conversation, and Charlotte also noticed a sense of agitation when he received the phone call.

"Maybe he received a similar phone call earlier," she mused, grabbing her feather duster, absentmindedly dusting around the mason jar, wondering what could have upset him. Charlotte could not even begin to guess as her thoughts became occupied now with the store opening. She then eyed the bakery box of cookies behind the register. She untied the red and white bakery string expertly tied around the box and opened it to the most delectable looking cookies imaginable—chocolate chip cookies the size of small plates, although chunk was more an apt description than chip. There were pretty pastel-colored sugar cookies, along with lady fingers, and vanilla and anise biscotti. She took one of the chocolate chip cookies and bit into it, savoring the sweetness of the cookie and the richness of the dark chocolate.

"Absolute heaven," she laughed as the store was now at the forefront of her mind and Duncan Kirk became a faded memory. Charlotte decided to make coffee, and in a few minutes, she was sitting on the couch with another cookie and her coffee, getting an actual feeling of what it might be like to be a customer at The Shop at Beach Rose Path. There were magazines on the coffee table, plenty of coffee and cookies, and two bookshelves of books to peruse. *And while you're at it, pick up a tourist trap key chain or T-shirt!* The delicious snack not only comforted Charlotte, but energized her as she still had more sprucing up to do before tomorrow.

She then heard the wheels of a truck pull into her driveway.

"Oh!" Charlotte gasped, as she watched Ivy climb out of her veterinary van. She watched Ivy walk to the back of the van and open the doors. Cradled within Ivy's arms was Little Lovey, who didn't look so little anymore!

Charlotte ran out of the store, excited to see both Ivy and the pup.

"Oh, Ivy! I'm so glad it's you!" Charlotte raced toward the van and found herself taking Little Lovey from Ivy's arms.

"Who else could it be?" Ivy asked, happily handing over the puppy to its rightful owner.

"Oh, I'm just so busy, I thought it was another delivery, that's all." Charlotte cuddled the puppy. Her eyes were bright and big and brown, and her coat was as yellow as a buttercup and as soft as a lamb's fur. Little Lovey had grown and put on some weight and she looked fantastic.

"I thought I'd bring her by to see her mom before the big day.

She's doing very well. She's so sweet and affectionate. You've got yourself a great dog, Charlotte."

"All thanks to you," Charlotte said, nuzzling Little Lovey's face. "She is awfully sweet, if I do say so myself."

"Well, she said she's really looking forward to coming home. Oh, speaking of which, how about I bring by a crate for you? I've got other supplies as well. You just let me know when you're ready."

"Oh, I will. Hey, come on in and let me know what you think of the place."

"Don't mind if I do!" Charlotte, still holding her puppy, led Ivy into the store.

"Oh, Charlotte!"

Charlotte turned to Ivy as Little Lovey buried her muzzle into Charlotte's neck. Charlotte heard the puppy contentedly sigh into her new momma's arms. A thrill of happiness wrapped around Charlotte as she snuggled the now sleeping puppy into the store.

"I've only been in the shop once or twice, but it didn't look like this! This is so cozy and homey. I'm just afraid if I sit down on that couch that I won't get up!"

"That's exactly how I want it!" Charlotte said as she gently placed the sleeping puppy upon a couch pillow.

"In all honesty, I had no idea of what I was going to do, and when the movers dumped my furniture in here, well, I thought I could be onto something." Charlotte looked around the store and was thrilled with how it turned out. It was warm and inviting, the aroma of freshly brewed coffee filled the air, and a shiver of contentment ran through her body.

This could just work, she thought, as she watched Ivy's face beam in wonder.

"Charlotte, you are a miracle worker, that's for sure. I think Rory's business did okay, but after his wife died, he was never the same, and neither was this place. You have certainly breathed new life into it, that's for sure. Oh, excuse me," Ivy said, pulling her pinging cell from her jeans pocket. A look of consternation gripped Ivy's face.

"Do what you want," she whispered as she texted something quick and put the phone back into her pocket.

"Everything okay?" asked Charlotte, seating herself next to Little Lovey, and gently patting the sleeping puppy.

Ivy sighed. She was obviously frustrated with the text she'd just received.

"Just that bull-headed brother of mine." Ivy plopped down next to Charlotte.

"I wish he'd just make up his mind about what he wants. He thinks for some reason, I have all the answers—and I am the younger one," she winked. "I think I remind him of our mother, because he always says I give great advice like she did, but sometimes I just don't know what to say to him."

"What's going on?" Charlotte's previous thoughts about Duncan being preoccupied with something were now confirmed by his sister. Charlotte didn't want to mention Duncan's strange visit.

"He broke up with his fiancée—that's why he's here. Caught her with his best friend. He couldn't stay in Boston, so he escaped back home. Now he's texting me that he thinks he made a mistake and might head back to Boston. I texted him I'd talk to him later, but he has to give it a chance. I know it's a huge change for him, in more ways than one, but I just don't think it was the break-up—I think something else was going on—he's never said anything, it's just sisterly intuition, but he's frustrated about something here." She shook her head and looked at Charlotte.

"Got any brothers?" she laughed.

"I got nothing," Charlotte said. "Just little old me, and now little old me has this little new sweetie." She lovingly looked at the little dog, a dog who Charlotte knew would be there for her and she silently promised to be there for her as well.

Ivy sighed heavily. "He'll figure it out. He's a big boy." The pinging sound emanated from her phone again.

"So help me, if it's him…" She looked at the text.

"Duty calls—emergency in a cow pasture. Let me take Little Lovey back…"

"Oh, she can stay. I'm just doing some last minute prepping— she might as well start getting used to her new home—even for a little while. Can you come back after the cow pasture?"

Ivy gave the sleeping puppy an affectionate pat on the head.

"Of course. It would be good for the two of you to spend some time together anyway. I'll be back when I'm back!"

"Sounds good!" Charlotte watched as Ivy dashed out the door, into her van, and off to the cow pasture.

Charlotte gently kissed the top of Little Lovey's head.

"You get your rest, little one. I'm just right over here." The puppy slowly opened her tiny eyes and poked her tongue out at Charlotte as if she was returning her kiss. Charlotte's heart swelled with love for the little pup, feeling the spirit of Peppercorn with them.

"I know you two are looking after us," she whispered, going back behind the counter to check on the credit card readers and the register.

"More coffee," Charlotte said scooping dark rich grounds into the coffee maker. The perking was like music to hear ears, as she surveyed the store. What was once empty and barren was now full of life and potential. Merchandise the colors of the pastel Lobster Claw sunrises filled the shelves, and Charlotte strategically draped additional shell garlands over the counter, while her furniture and the bookshelves completed the homey atmosphere. Tomorrow was opening day, and summer would be in full swing. A sudden sense of deja vu filled Charlotte as she recalled her first grand opening so many years ago, and all the wonderful things came along with her success of Loch Ladies. She felt confident and positive that The

Shop at Beach Rose Path would be just as wonderful; if not more so.

Charlotte poured herself coffee and savored her efforts as she looked around the store. A peacefully sleeping puppy. An inviting store full of possibilities. Eye-catching souvenirs as well as the beautiful seashell garlands. Books and magazines. Coffee. Cookies. Duncan Kirk...*What??* *Where did he come from,* Charlotte scolded herself, sipping her coffee, reflecting on their chance meetings.

Do I really want to be involved with someone else? Would I be able to, after having the perfect relationship? Could Tatiana be right?

While Charlotte had romantic opportunities, she could never put her toe back into the romance waters after Landon, as the thought of his sweet disposition, handsome face, and strong loving arms, always pulled her back.

"Better to have loved and lost than not have loved at all," she murmured, listening to the surf gently splash along the shoreline. Could she truly love again? Not that she was in love with Duncan; she hardly knew him, but there most definitely was a spark between them, one he may have arrogantly extinguished.

"You are a fool, Charlotte, to think he'd be interested in you," she reprimanded herself, as she got up and looked out the bay window at the ocean and the sky. It was breathtaking, and this bungalow was now her home, no matter how long—a year, a summer...

"Don't think about him," she commanded. "This store will work. It has to."

But the thought of Duncan still niggled at the back of her mind. He was the only man since Landon who kept returning to her thoughts, and she didn't like it at all, and not only because of his hubris, which secretly hurt her feelings, but because of the simple fact that he was another man other than Landon.

I don't want to cut myself off from the possibility of a relationship, but at the same time, it scares me to be in one, she thought, turning from the window and back into the store.

"I'll call Hamish" she decided, thinking that simply by hearing Hamish's fatherly Scottish burr and parental words of wisdom would put her heart and her mind at rest. Just hearing Hamish's confident and benevolent voice would be just the medicine she needed.

CHAPTER TWENTY-TWO

Hamish Falconer was tired. After a day of playing with his grandson and then hitting nine holes of golf, he looked forward to nothing more than his pot of earl gray tea and cinnamon scones. He was just about to sit down to his favorite afternoon treat, when he saw his phone flash and heard the shrill vibration.

"Oh, not now." He was in mid pour, but he finished pouring the steaming aromatic tea into his old, chipped Castle Loch mug. He reluctantly got up from his chair, and when he saw Charlotte's name flash on the screen, he quickly forgot about the comforting tea and scones.

"Charlotte, lass! So good to hear from you! How have you been?" He sat himself down in his old leather chair and stirred a few drops of cream into his tea.

"Hamish, it's so good to hear your voice. Sounds like you're in the next room instead of on the other side of the Atlantic!"

"So good to hear yours, too, Char," he said tenderly, as he put his cup down onto the saucer.

"I'm sorry I haven't called sooner. I have been so incredibly busy, and well, tomorrow is the grand opening. I guess I just need to hear your voice."

"Oh, Char, I'm sure everything looks wonderful. And just remember, you built a small ladies empire from a musty old basement. I am highly confident that Rory's old store looks just as incredible."

"I'll text you some pictures tomorrow. I have a kind of a party planned here—you know, lots of coffee, cookies, cake—oh, no scones—I'll have to see if the bakery can make those. But it looks pretty inviting and I'm ready to go. Oh, and everyone here has been so kind to me. I've got great neighbors down at what they call the Beach Block, and I've made friends with a woman and she thinks she may know you."

"Know me! Who in that part of the world would know me?" He laughed as he bit into one of his scones.

"Her name is Tatiana Dulka. I mentioned you to her the other day, and it seemed like she knew you, and then she said she remembered you as a friend of Rory's and that you had met once or twice."

The scone fell from Hamish Falconer's trembling hand.

Tatiana Dulka?

"Hamish? Are you still there?" He barely heard Charlotte's voice on the other end of the phone.

"Yes, yes, I am. I'm sorry, Char, but I don't recall a woman named Tatiana. Maybe she has me confused with someone else."

"I don't think so. She described you pretty well, Scottish accent, handsome."

Hamish could hear laughter in Charlotte's voice. He wanted to change the subject. Immediately.

"Well, she probably has me confused with another friend of Rory's. He and Violet always had relatives and friends from Dundee or Glasgow flying up over to Maine."

"I suppose, but she really seemed like she knew you. Anyway, I really wish you could be here for the grand opening...."

Hamish no longer heard Charlotte's chatter about the store. His head was now full of thoughts of Tatiana, from so long ago.

The only other people who knew of what happened between himself and Tatiana were Rory and Violet, and as far as Hamish knew, it went no further. Rory had promised he would take their secret to the grave, as did Violet.

Tatiana. Tati.

"Char, tell you what," Hamish began. He wanted to appease Charlotte, and he truly did wish he could be there.

"I'll try to hop over later in the summer, maybe closer toward September or October. Colin and Haleigh were talking about visiting the States, and well, I am sort of their unofficial babysitter. I'll let you know more as the summer moves along."

"Oh, Hamish, that would be amazing! You could meet Tatiana, my other friend, Ivy, and, you won't believe this, but I have another dog! Her name is Little Lovey!"

"Char! A dog! How wonderful! I'm sure she is an absolute delight." Good. Subject changed.

"She's not quite here with me yet, but that's another story… Oh, Hamish, can I call you back? Someone's knocking at the door. I think it might be the bakery, as I have a huge cookie order being delivered."

"No worries, Char, you give me a call when you can. I'll be thinking of you, and I know it's going to be a smashing success. Text me pictures when you can."

"Oh, Hamish, I miss you so much. I know it hasn't been too long, but I think I'm going to like it here. Thank you for taking care of me."

"Oh, Char, nonsense—you're taking care of yourself. I just gave you a little kick. That's all. You go get those cookies, and I'll speak with you soon."

"Bye, Hamish!"

"Bye, darlin'." The call disconnected.

Hamish no longer wanted the tea or the scones. The mention of Tatiana put a knot the size of a ship inside of his stomach. Tatiana was someone he had put into his locked box of memories and had thrown away the key. It happened so, so long ago. He suddenly felt hot tears at the back of his eyes. The burly and brawny Hamish Falconer slumped back in his aged leather chair, and cried like he had never cried in his life. For his regrets. For Tatiana. For what could have been.

CHAPTER TWENTY-THREE

CHARLOTTE HAD SET HER ALARM FOR 5 A.M. BUT SHE FOUND THAT she didn't need it as a searing headache woke her at 4:30. She lay in bed as the throbbing behind her eyes pulsated and flashes of bright light beamed behind her tightly closed eyes.

"Steady, Charlotte," she told herself. She knew this was a headache related to the stress she was feeling before she went to bed last night. The last time she had experienced a headache like this was when she was told Landon and Peppe were dead, and at that time, the headaches lasted for months.

She had thought the headaches were gone for good, but she was wrong.

"Am I wrong about everything?" she asked, lying with her eyes tightly shut, the flashes of blue and silver exploding like firecrackers behind her closed eyes.

Charlotte took several deep breaths and exhaled slowly with each. She felt her heart slow, and the bright and blinding light flashes dimmed. The pain behind her eyes diminished and she felt her body soften. The relaxation techniques she learned after Landon and Peppe's deaths still worked, and she could feel her body begin to calm and relax.

"Opening day jitters, that's all," she reassured herself. She got out of bed and walked to the window that overlooked the sea. Although it was still dark, she could see the light pink of dawn over the horizon as the beacon of the Sea Star Lighthouse beamed over the bay. The lapping of the ocean upon the rocks and the shore calmed Charlotte even more, and she opened the window and deeply inhaled the salt water, the clean morning air.

"You got this, Char." Hamish's calm and encouraging voice replaced the banging drums of her headache and all she saw now was the expanse of blue ocean and no more zinging bolts of lightning behind her eyes.

"Yes, Hamish, I got this. I can be so silly sometimes, doubting myself."

Ivy had picked up Little Lovey yesterday, and Charlotte felt lonely for her little puppy. She made coffee, sat on her couch and made a last-minute to do list. Before she knew it, it was eight o'clock, as the rays of the morning sun streamed into the bungalow.

The slam of a car door in front of her house startled Charlotte and she jumped from the couch and looked out the window. Duncan's pickup was parked in her driveway.

"What the heck?" she whispered. "He can't see me like this!" Charlotte ran her hands through her wild hair, trying to manage it somewhat, but instead, she grabbed a comb from her bag and pulled her thick, silvering brown locks into a messy bun. She also found a lip balm and smoothed it over her lips for a little shine, but then realized she was still in her pajamas. She quickly ran upstairs, threw on her jeans and sweater, glanced one more time in the mirror as a loud knock on the door jolted her.

I have no idea why he's here, but here goes, she thought as she opened her front door.

"Good morning," she said, trying to sound as unruffled as possible. It was hard not to notice the large box tied with a pink ribbon in his hands.

"I owe you an apology, Charlotte." Duncan handed the pretty box to Charlotte.

"Bridget's Irish Chocolate Box. The best chocolate in Boston," was all Charlotte could think to say. A beautiful scene of the Swan Boats from Boston's Public Garden was handprinted on the box, the chocolatier's signature style. She had never received a gift from this well-known chocolate shop, but she had definitely heard how amazing the candies were, especially due to the artistry of each chocolate—almost like snowflakes—no two were alike.

"Come in," she said, stepping aside and letting Duncan into the living room.

"I'm sorry if you thought I may have insulted you after the boat ride, asking what you're doing here in little old Lobster Claw. I had no right to do that. That's your business. I know I can come across as gruff, and I didn't mean it the way it came out. I have a lot going on myself, but that's no excuse, and I am sorry."

"Charlotte shook her head, recalling the conversation she had with Ivy. Charlotte most certainly knew what it was like to be torn and indecisive about life's directions.

"No apology necessary. We all seem to have a lot weighing on us lately, and I understand. I truly do, since I'm sort of in the same predicament."

"I know it's your opening day, but how about I treat you to dinner when you close?" he asked.

"Dinner would be great." Charlotte responded without hesitation. She liked Duncan, and if he was willing to explain what was going on in his life, she would love to listen. And perhaps she could even be persuaded to share.

Charlotte saw a smile form on Duncan's unshaven face. He looked tired himself, as dark rings shadowed beneath his eyes.

"Great. I was hoping you'd say yes. What time do you think you'll close?"

"Oh," she laughed. "I haven't even thought about that! Probably around 6:00 or so? Is that too late?"

The musical and masculine sound of Duncan's laughter made Charlotte's heart quicken.

"Late? Most of my dinners were eaten after 10 p.m. so this will be an early dinner for me. Sounds good. I'll pick you up closer to 8, if that's okay?"

"Perfect. That will give me time to close down and put things away."

And to figure out what to wear, fix my hair, shoes...

"Okay," Duncan said, nodding his head, still smiling. Charlotte even thought she detected a hint of rosiness under the thick salt and pepper stubble on his cheeks.

"Enjoy the chocolates," he said, and walked out of her front door and hopped back into his truck.

"I will," she whispered, a sudden giddiness overtaking her, feeling a smile form on her own face, one of happiness, anticipation, and possibility.

Charlotte's attention was suddenly caught by the bright pastel buildings that formed the Beach Block. Yesterday there were a few tourists here and there, but now it looked like a stampede of people roaming the streets of Lobster Claw, Maine.

"Oh, my gosh!" Charlotte exclaimed, looking at her watch.

She had one hour before the grand opening of The Shop at Beach Rose Path. She quickly hopped into the shower, blow-dried her hair, and put on a touch of make-up. She wore a new Beach Rose Path T-shirt, a pair of beige cargo pants and black and pink running shoes and she was ready and waiting to greet her first customers of this year's Beach Rose Path summer season.

CHAPTER TWENTY-FOUR

"Tatiana! You are a sight for sore eyes!" Charlotte hugged her friend upon seeing her enter The Shop at Beach Rose Path.

"I wanted to cruise up here earlier, but I didn't even get a break today! All of us were so busy on the Block, and I didn't even have a sec to text! I did notice lots of traffic up this way, though!"

"Traffic, gridlock, bottleneck—you name it! It was amazing! The cookies were gone in the blink of an eye, and I must have brewed gallons of coffee. Everyone loved the seashell garlands, and I'm glad I ordered plenty of inventory—almost sold out of tee shirts and hats!"

"I knew you'd be a smashing success! I hope any doubts you had have been washed out to sea."

"Hamish once told me that having doubts was completely normal and it was actually good to doubt. I decided to just channel all my doubts into positive thinking, and it worked!"

"Hamish is most certainly a wise man indeed, Charlotte. What time are you closing?"

Charlotte glanced at her watch. 5:45.

"I was hoping in about fifteen minutes, since it's slowed down in the last half hour. I'll be opening earlier tomorrow, so if there are any late stragglers, they can come back then."

"Oh, good business sense, there," Tatiana laughed.

"We're having a little celebration at Harry's Surf & Turf, an opening day after-party around 7:00 tonight. Please come."

"Sounds amazing!" Charlotte exclaimed. And then she remembered Duncan.

"Oh, Tatiana, I'm so sorry. I almost forgot about dinner plans I have this evening." The day had been so frantic and frenzied that she had no time to give Duncan's dinner invitation a second thought. Until now.

"Oh, lucky man," Tatiana said with a wink.

"You know what, I'll be there. Let me just close up and quickly change my clothes and I can text Duncan to meet me at the Beach Block. You've all been so wonderful to me and have truly made me feel so welcome, I don't want to miss this."

"Wonderful!" Charlotte felt Tatiana's arms engulf her in a loving embrace.

"We are so glad that you are here, Charlotte. Welcome home."

Charlotte felt tears start to glisten in her eyes at Tatiana's words. Welcome Home. Charlotte was home.

CHAPTER TWENTY-FIVE

For the first time in a long time, Duncan Kirk was a nervous man. He had just received a text from Charlotte asking him to meet her at the Beach Block for a quick appearance for an opening day party, and then they could head to dinner, a dinner he was very much looking forward to.

He should have been exhausted after his round-trip drive from Lobster Claw to Boston the previous day, but any tiredness dissipated into happy anticipation at seeing Charlotte. She looked absolutely stunning this morning when he dropped off the candy, her pretty, thick and wavy brown hair messily gathered upon her head. Her warm honey brown eyes sparkled in the morning sunlight, and her face was as pink as a newly bloomed rose. Her full lips shimmered and he wanted nothing more than to feel those lips upon his, but he knew if he tried, Charlotte would definitely be the type of woman to kick him out of her life permanently. So, he would wait as patiently as he could before doing so. Duncan felt Charlotte would absolutely be worth the wait.

Unlike Melinda.

Her texts had been relentless over the past weeks and when

he blocked them, she called. And then he blocked her calls and when he had done that, she somehow finagled Tom Hudson, a former client, to call him yesterday under false pretenses, asking him to come to the office to discuss some architectural issues with a new building. Duncan reluctantly agreed as Tom refused to speak over the phone or video chat, so he had no choice but to make the long drive to Boston only to be told by the administrative assistant that he was not coming into the office. Duncan angrily punched the buttons of the elevator and when he reached the lobby, there sat Melinda in all her runway model glory. Her long hair cascaded down her shoulders and she was wearing a very form-fitting lavender dress, showing off her suntanned, slender legs and toned arms. She was striking, ravishing, gorgeous. She was the perfect woman on the outside, but cunning and deceitful on the inside.

She stood up at the sight of Duncan and flashed her million-dollar smile—and it literally was, after all her veneers and whitening—her dentist was a very rich man just from Melinda's dental work and maintenance.

"Dunny," she breathed, racing toward him, embracing him within her willowy and soft arms. His nose was buried in her hair which smelled of citrus and mint, and for one quick moment he had forgotten where he was and why, and he was back in his fiancée's loving caress once again.

As Melinda's hug tightened, Duncan lurched back to reality and he roughly pulled away from her.

"You cannot be serious," Duncan said, feeling the heat of his anger course through every cell in his body.

"Dunny, honey, please let me explain. This was the only way I could see you in person. I'm sorry I had to be deceptive, but since you were not answering my texts or calls, I had to do something drastic, and well, I knew Tom would help me. You know how fond he has always been of you and me, of us." She seductively licked her lips into a pout, something that in his previous life

Duncan would have fallen for and amends would have been made with a passionate kiss. But not any longer.

"You're right about one thing you just said, Melinda. You had to be deceptive. And we both know how good you are at that. Get out of my way and don't ever try this with me again."

Duncan shook her off, but Melinda blocked his way.

"Dunny don't. You know I can explain. It was a mistake. A stupid mistake. I want you back, Dunny. Please. I've been miserable…"

"I don't care how miserable you've been, Melinda." He tried to keep his voice low and measured. They were in the lobby of one of Boston's busiest professional buildings and he didn't want to cause a scene. He knew that Melinda concocted this, too, as being in a public place, she knew he'd keep any kind of anger in check.

"And don't call me Dunny. I've always hated it, and you know it."

He watched as Melinda ran her fingers through her hair, another one of her tantalizing ploys. She obviously wasn't aware that she no longer held any beguiling or seductive powers over him, especially not after finding her half-clothed body in the arms of his best friend.

Melinda put her hand on Duncan's chest and pulled herself in closer. Her white teeth glared through her blood-red lipstick and Duncan suddenly felt he was the prey in the jaws of a great white shark.

"Dunny," she murmured, again sidling closer to him. "Please, let's talk about this. You came all the way down here from that silly Maine hick town. This is where you belong, and you know it. You belong in Boston. And with me." She cloyingly caressed his cheek with her manicured hand, her violet-blue eyes looking deeply and pleadingly into his. Duncan instinctively put his hand on hers and whipped it away from his face.

"You made your bed, Melinda. Now go lie in it. With Eric."

Duncan furiously stormed out of the building, his beloved

workbooks thumping with each step. He fiercely shoved himself through the glass revolving doors and out into the busy city street. He didn't turn around to see her reaction; he just wanted to get out of Boston and back to the comfort of his silly Maine hick town. A day of driving, all for nothing.

Duncan was happily back in Lobster Claw and anticipating his evening with Charlotte. He glanced at his watch and found he still had half an hour before meeting her. He was showered and dressed and giving himself the once over in his bathroom mirror, intently looking at his reflection. He was 53, no wife, no family of his own. Time had passed so quickly, always so busy with work, traveling and dating scores of Boston's most eligible women. When he met Melinda, he thought that she was 'the one'. They talked of marriage and children and had been together for five years, but for some reason, neither one of them could pull the marriage trigger. When he was ready to settle down, Melinda would plead for extra time.

"Oh, Dunny, next year would be perfect—I have this huge job that's going to take all summer, and well, you know how much I just want us to have the perfect wedding."

And when next year came, her excuse was something else.

But Duncan also knew he couldn't lay all blame of hesitation on Melinda. Extreme relief flooded him whenever she postponed wedding plans, and they carried on life as usual, attending corporate parties, weekends away, and his extremely busy life designing the Boston waterfront, miraculously turning rundown warehouses into shining high-rise Boston Harbor front condominiums that every Bruin, Red Sox, and Celtic clamored for. They were both on top of the world professionally, and they looked fantastic with each other.

Duncan dipped his fingers into a container of pomade and fingered it through his hair, leaving it fuller and spiky. The evening breeze blew through the open bathroom and he ran a hand over his stubbled cheek.

"You know it wasn't meant to be," he said to his reflection. And truth be told, as much as he was angry with both Melinda and Eric, Eric had done him a favor. Duncan had been under the spell of Melinda—her beauty, her success—for so long, that he could no longer see that their relationship was on the path to nowhere. When he caught Eric and Melinda together, her spell was broken, and Duncan was whipped back into reality. The sudden need to leave and return to Lobster Claw hit him like a foul ball at Fenway Park, and he immediately retreated to the comfort of his childhood home.

And then Charlotte Templeton entered his life. The moment he saw her requesting cans of evaporated milk and a baby bottle at Elsie's, he knew that this was a real woman in every sense of the word—she was obviously on a mission and she seemed determined to accomplish it. And when he discovered she was caring for a sick dog, all thoughts of Melinda vanished.

But he was going to go slowly with Charlotte. Duncan wanted to get to know her—was she married? Widowed? Divorced? Children? Grandchildren? There was something he found so attractive about her when he saw her earlier that morning, that before he knew it, he asked her to dinner and she accepted.

Duncan smiled, running his hand through his hair one more time.

"Not bad, old man," he laughed as he grabbed his truck keys and headed out to what he hoped would be a most enchanting evening with an even more captivating woman.

CHAPTER TWENTY-SIX

"WHAT AN ABSOLUTELY GLORIOUS EVENING!" TATIANA WAS SERVING champagne on hand-painted trays to her Beach Block neighbors.

"Unbelievable—best opening day I can recall in years!" exclaimed Betsy from Take the Cake, helping herself not only to a glass of champagne, but to a generous scoop of pink cherry blossom ice cream courtesy of the LC Ice Cream Parlour.

"Champagne float!" she proclaimed, holding up the fizzy glass of champagne and ice cream.

"Oh, that's a wonderful idea!" Charlotte had just arrived, looking forward to not only the Beach Block festivities but to Duncan's dinner invitation. Not wanting to look overly eager, she kept her wardrobe and make up simple—a white cotton skirt, light green silk blouse, and a pair of green espadrilles that matched her blouse. She kept her makeup to a minimum with just a hint of amber shadow on her lids, and her favorite Rose Blush lipstick. She pulled the sides of her hair back with an antique pearl hair clip, letting the rest of her wavy hair fall gently on her neck and shoulders. Pearl drop earrings completed the look. Casual, but elegant.

Charlotte dropped a scoop of pink cherry blossom ice cream

into her own champagne glass as the bubbles tickled her nose and lips.

"This party is such a wonderful idea, Tatiana. Thank you so much for doing this and especially after this crazy busy day!"

"Impromptu parties are my specialty, Charlotte. Owning an art gallery has taught me a thing or two about last-minute soirees. Plus, I had a lot of help from our Beach Block buddies. It's all cake, cookies, and ice cream, but who cares!"

"I don't!" said Charlotte taking a sip of her champagne float, looking at the platter of beautifully arranged fruit, cookies and cake slices.

"Hm... what will I have next?" she murmured, trying to decide on either a coconut macaroon or a slice of the vanilla bourbon cake.

"How about one of everything, and we can share?"

Charlotte felt the hairs on the back of her neck prick up at the sound of Duncan's voice. A chill of excitement coursed through her blood, and she felt the goosebumps on her arms rise at the sound of his deep voice.

Keep your composure Char, she thought. She felt her cheeks flush and waited for the heat to cool before she faced him.

There, I think it's okay to turn around she thought, feeling the temperature of her cheeks return to normal. The goosebumps, however, remained. "Oh, when it comes to dessert, I don't like to share."

"Oh, one of those, are you?"

Charlotte spun around and faced Duncan, and almost didn't recognize him. Gone was the leather bomber jacket and work boots, now replaced by a red and blue plaid shirt, navy blue tie, tucked into a crisp pair of jeans. Instead of the boots he wore a pair of high-end black running shoes. He kept it casual, but quite elevated.

"Yes, I am," she replied. "Especially when it comes to Betsy's.

And to Bridget's Chocolate Box, which by the way, are almost gone."

"Well, next trip to Boston, I'll be happy to replenish."

"Champagne float?" was all Charlotte could respond, holding up her glass of champagne. She couldn't tell if it was a few sips of champagne on an empty stomach or Duncan's nearness that was causing her lightheadedness.

His ruddy and sunburned complexion was brightened by his smile.

"I'll pass. I don't like to indulge in alcohol when I drive. Even if it's a little glass of champagne. But," he said, reaching around her, his arm gently brushing hers, "I will help myself to one of these. And one of these." He then placed a macaroon and piece of vanilla cake onto a paper plate.

"You may not share, but I will," he said as he carefully took his fork and separated a mouthful of cake from the slice. Duncan held out the fork toward Charlotte's lips. She felt his gesture intimate but not intrusive. She took the fork from his hand, and savored the bite of cake, the rich creaminess of the frosting, and the flakiness of the cake, suddenly highlighted on her taste buds, and she could acutely taste the sweet vanilla and the caramel notes of the bourbon.

The intent stare of his hazel eyes, coupled with his dazzling smile left Charlotte momentarily numb, and for the first time in a very long time, she let herself be captivated by a man's charms.

"You approve?" he asked, and Charlotte was no longer spellbound. *Well, maybe a bit,* she thought, looking into his face, his friendly eyes and his amazing smile.

"I do," she said, smiling up at him.

"There," he whispered, as he reached his thumb to her cheek and she could feel him brush away a small cake crumb.

"Thank you." Charlotte started to feel extremely self-conscious at Duncan's nearness and by the touch of his hand on her face. She took her glass of champagne, now with the melted ice cream, and drank it like a shot.

"I think I need another one of these," she smiled, reaching out to Tatiana who was gracing the room with another tray of champagne.

"Duncan!" Tatiana exclaimed, leaning and kissing Duncan on his cheek. "So glad you could make it! Our Charlotte here has done an amazing job with the shop, but I'm sure she'll fill you in on all the details. I hope…"

"Hey Tatiana, can you come here for a sec?"

Tatiana was interrupted by the gravelly voice of Harry who had just poked his head through the gallery door.

"Oh, that Harry," Tatiana laughed, placing the tray on the counter. "He always has something up his sleeve. Would you please excuse me?"

Duncan and Charlotte watched as Tatiana waltzed over to Harry who was wildly gesticulating and laughing as he grabbed Tatiana by the arm and pulled her outside.

"Congratulations," said Duncan, stepping away from Charlotte. He took the fork from Charlotte and began to eat the cake.

"Thank you. I think it went well." Charlotte found herself tongue tied, which was especially unusual when it came to work. She always loved talking about Loch Ladies and now, if today was any indication, The Shop at Beach Rose Path had the potential of being just as successful. Words raced through her mind but she couldn't seem to manage to get them from her brain and out of her mouth.

"It's been a long time since I've lived in Lobster Claw, but I don't recall anything here like what you've done—coffee, cookies, books, souvenirs. It's a nice little niche business, Charlotte. Great work."

Charlotte felt her heart lighten by his kind and encouraging words, and her ability to speak returned.

"You're right—it is a niche. I really didn't think of it like that, but I think it provides a place of homeyness, and sometimes I think tourists like that. They want a feeling of being at home while not at home, and that's exactly what I want to provide. Thanks, Duncan. I couldn't articulate that before, but yes, that's exactly it!" She took a sip from her second glass of champagne, and felt the sparkling lightness of the bubbly wine shimmer through her body, giving her that extra push of confidence she needed at this moment.

"Maybe you can help me find my niche," Duncan said, pouring himself a glass of ginger ale from several bottles of soda that had been placed on the counter.

"What do you mean?" asked Charlotte, intrigued by his statement.

"Well, it's a long story, but I feel I'm in Lobster Claw to stay. I've been a contractor and architect pretty much all of my adult life, and now I think it's time for a change. I have something in mind, but I'm really only good at designing and building. Maybe you could help me?"

Charlotte thought she saw a tinge of sadness in his eyes. He obviously loved what he had done professionally, but she sensed that it no longer fulfilled him.

"I'd love to. We can discuss it over dinner if you like."

Duncan took a sip of his ginger ale and Charlotte watched as he looked around the room. He seemed to be taking in all the festivities, and she saw his shoulders slacken and his body relax as he leaned back against the counter.

"About dinner. Would you mind if we rescheduled?" He had stepped closer to her.

A smack of disappointment clutched Charlotte. Having dinner with Duncan was the cherry on top of the sundae she was savoring all day, as she was truly looking forward to spending time over a quiet dinner and getting to know him better. She tried hard to retain a poker face, as she didn't want him to know she felt let down. "We can reschedule," Charlotte said.

"Good. Because tonight I want to spend it here." Duncan nodded his head toward the growing crowd in The Blue Hydrangea.

"If Lobster Claw is going to be my home again, I want to start it with people who care, the people right here. And with you."

Charlotte locked eyes with Duncan's as her disappointment abated. She found she could not look away from him, as she felt his calloused hand gently caress her cheek, and felt his lips press a gentle kiss on her forehead. Charlotte trembled at his touch and by his heartfelt words.

"I'd like nothing more," she managed to say as she watched Duncan's smile widen across his handsome face.

"Hey, everyone!" Harry's excited cries suddenly filled the room.

"Elsie just delivered burgers! Bonfire on the beach in twenty minutes!" Cheers rose in The Blue Hydrangea as everyone headed outside to help Harry build his bonfire.

"I guess we'll be having dinner after all," Duncan said, taking Charlotte's hand and leading her outside for a bonfire on the beach.

CHAPTER TWENTY-SEVEN

"Time flies when you're having fun, doesn't it?"

Tatiana and Charlotte were walking down the creaky dock from The Shop at Beach Rose Path to Take the Cake, as Charlotte needed to pick up an order of cookies for the big Fourth of July weekend. Summer was in full swing and ever since Memorial Day weekend, Charlotte and the rest of the Beach Block were in full force, opening their establishments earlier and closing later. But Charlotte didn't mind. Her love for retail management was rekindled with The Shop at Beach Rose Path, as patrons who visited loved to sit on the couch, order coffee and cookies and always left with a memorable souvenir, much to Charlotte's delight. Customers always departed happy, letting Charlotte know they couldn't wait to return next summer, enthusiastically purchasing T-shirts or a book on the history of Lobster Claw. Charlotte even made time to teach herself how to string the seashells that Violet had lovingly tucked away, and sometimes Charlotte got the feeling that they were left just for her to find. The aprons, on the other hand, were still a mystery. She didn't want to sell or wear them, but at the same time they were too pretty to be left in a plastic box, and she was still using her retail management mind to figure out their purpose.

"Didn't I tell you on Memorial Day pretty soon we'll be saying it's the Fourth of July already?" asked Tatiana. Charlotte laughed as she could not believe how quickly midsummer had approached. There were still a lot of weeks left until Labor Day, but Charlotte knew the end of the summer would come all too quickly. And then what?

She was seeing Duncan on a regular basis, but he was busy trying to get himself up and running with his own boat business, which planned to launch on the Fourth of July. Little Lovey was now with her permanently, and the puppy had thrived under Ivy's expert care and was still growing. Charlotte loved the company of the dog, and she was an absolute hit with customers as well.

Charlotte watched as Little Lovey made her way just a little too close to the piping plover sanctuary.

"Come, Little Lovey," Charlotte called and loudly clapped her hands twice, a training technique she used with Peppe, which worked very well with Lovey, too. The yellow dog turned her head towards Charlotte, wagged her tail furiously and ran back to her mistress. Tatiana and Charlotte showered praise on the pup, and Charlotte reached into her pocket for a treat.

"Good girl," Charlotte cooed as Lovey gently took the treat from her mistress' hand.

"Very good girl," Tatiana said, giving Lovey a small treat from her own jacket pocket.

A light mist sprayed down upon the two women. Even though it was hazy and gray, Lobster Claw remained beautiful. The wild dune grass blew in the cool dewy breeze, and when Charlotte looked out to the sea, she could see Sea Star Lighthouse. Even on this dark and drizzly day, the lighthouse's bright white tower stood out, just as much of a beacon as its bold black lantern cap. She hadn't made her way out to the lighthouse's craggy shores, yet, but once the calmness of the autumn settled over Lobster Claw, she intended to hike the beach with Little Lovey and get a closer look. Charlotte cherished the view from her bedroom window toward the lighthouse, searching for the ever-present rays of this stalwart beacon, not only shining light, but shining hope. She loved to look out onto the ocean at night, and watch the spotlight illuminate the shore, shining over the coast as the sun would during the day.

"Wait until you see the lighthouse at Christmas time. It's decorated so beautifully," Tatiana said, pulling her scarf over her hair.

"Christmas?" laughed Charlotte. "Can we get through the summer first?"

Christmas? Charlotte thought, a tiny sensation of alarm spiking in her blood.

She sighed, blowing the air out of her cheeks.

"Christmas is spectacular in Lobster Claw, Charlotte. I can't wait for you to see it." Charlotte felt Tatiana's hand reassuringly caress her shoulder. Charlotte reached up to Tatiana's hand and gave it an affectionate squeeze. The two had become close over the last couple of months, Tatiana almost like a mother figure to Charlotte. Charlotte had lost both her parents when she was in her 30s. Her father passed from a stroke and Charlotte swore her mother followed due to a broken heart, almost one year after Charlotte's father died. They had been together for over thirty years, and when Charlotte's father passed so unexpectedly, her mother was never the same. Charlotte took comfort in knowing that they were together, and even death did not part them.

"It's hard to imagine Lobster Claw in the winter, Tatiana. The summer has been so amazing that I feel like it's never going to end. But I know that it will. It's just going be a different Christmas for me, that's all."

Tatiana extended her arm over Charlotte's shoulders and hugged her closer.

"It will be a great Christmas, Charlotte. Gets busy around here too, might surprise you a little."

Charlotte smiled at her friend.

"I have no doubt," she said. "But, first we have to get through the rest of the summer and this weekend!" Charlotte didn't want to talk about Christmas. It was too sad for her and she wanted to keep it as far away as possible. It was going to be her first Christmas away from Castle Loch. And away from Hamish.

"This weekend will be insanely crazy, but a lot of fun," Tatiana said, now pulling the hood of her jacket over her long silver locks.

"Mist is getting heavier," she said. "Let's get a move on."

Even though the morning was dreary, the forecast was sunny and hot for the Fourth of July weekend. Business was slow, so both ladies were able to close up their shops for a while to catch up and walk along the beach.

"How's Duncan?" Tatiana asked.

Charlotte couldn't help but smile at the sound of his name.

"He's good. Busy with getting the boat business up and running, but we talk every day."

"Wonderful." Tatiana smiled at her friend. "He's a good man, Charlotte. I know he's had his share of troubles, but then again we all have. I know I most certainly have."

"You? Oh, Tatiana, you seem like trouble just floats right off you, like water off a duck's back. You seem so resilient and that nothing would keep you down for long."

They had reached The Blue Hydrangea. Tatiana inserted the key into the lock and the three stepped inside. It was such a beautiful little gallery, and no big-city art museum could compare, in Charlotte's estimation.

"Oh, Charlotte," said Tatiana. She reached into her mini fridge and pulled out a bottle of water which she poured into her electric kettle.

"Tea time will do us some good," she said, bringing out some mugs she kept under the register counter, along with tea bags. Little Lovey had settled herself on the dog bed Tatiana kept for her in a little nook near the front door.

The water boiled quickly and Tatiana poured the scorching water into the mugs and over the teabags. She pushed a large yellow ceramic mug toward Charlotte.

"It may seem that way, but I have plenty of moments of melancholy. Of sadness. Just like you. I've loved and lost."

Charlotte followed Tatiana's gaze to the window, where a silhouette of the sun was now making an appearance in the lightening gray sky. But Tatiana was not looking out the window. Charlotte followed Tatiana's gaze and saw she was looking at one of the framed paintings near the window of a little girl. Charlotte also noticed that there was no caption or price under the frame as there was with all Tatiana's other art works, which meant it was not for sale.

The child was perhaps two years of age. She had chin-length sunshine yellow hair, with a slight curl, and bangs that rested softly on the child's forehead above two shiny bright blue eyes. She was looking out of a window, her chubby arms and hands extended on the panes of glass, pointing at something on the other side. There was a hint of a smile on the girl's rose-pink lips, and a look of pure wonderment graced the child's face. She wore a pink dress which was overlaid by a smock, which looked vaguely familiar to Charlotte for some reason. Then, like the proverbial ton of bricks, it hit Charlotte as to why it was so familiar. The smock the baby was wearing was exactly like one of the aprons she had discovered in Violet's boxes.

Charlotte quickly looked back at Tatiana, who continued to look at the child's painting, seemingly lost in a world of her own.

"I never noticed that painting," Charlotte said, breaking the moment of silence between the two women. "She's a beautiful child." Charlotte searched Tatiana's face for some kind of recognition, but she found none.

"Isn't she?" Tatiana smiled and sipped her tea.

"I was rummaging through my attic looking for something else when I found it. It was given to me many years ago, a gift. She's the daughter of a good friend."

Charlotte thought she caught a note of poignancy in Tatiana's voice, which now sounded so far away, as if she was reliving the moment the painting was given to her.

"Do you know what's become of her?" Charlotte asked, sipping her tea. She herself almost couldn't take her eyes off the painting. The colors were so vibrant—the pale sun reflecting through the square panes of glass; the sun's rays pinking the child's full cheeks, and tinting her hair the color of a spring daffodil; the simple wonderment shining in the blueberry-blue eyes with round black pupils, focusing intently on whatever it was on the other side of the window. She seemed fascinated, as a plump index finger was pressed on the glass, pointing at something. And then, of course, the smock, tied over a peony pink dress.

Tatiana put her mug on the counter and looked intently at Charlotte.

"She died a year after this painting was commissioned. She was two when this was painted and three when she passed."

"Oh, Tatiana, I'm so sorry to hear that. If you don't mind me asking, how did she die?"

"Fever. She had some kind of virus and no matter what the doctors tried, it never resolved."

Charlotte reached for her friend's hand as tears formed in Tatiana's eyes.

"I'm sorry, Charlotte. I brought the painting out because it's such a beautiful work of art. And she was such a sweet little girl. Her name was Annabelle."

Annabelle! The name on the box of aprons! Charlotte maintained a straight face, as she could see Annabelle meant a lot to Tatiana and she didn't want to upset her with news of a box of aprons with Annabelle's name on the label.

"Such a beautiful name," Charlotte said, gazing back at the picture. "And you're right, it's too beautiful to keep in storage."

"That's what I thought, too," Tatiana murmured, dabbing her eyes with the sleeve.

"This way she can be part of Lobster Claw again." Tatiana stood and drank the last of her tea.

"Enough melancholia for today," she said, her smile as bright as the rays of sun now streaming through the gallery's windows.

Tatiana had turned her back to collect the tea mugs and Charlotte quickly took the opportunity to snap a quick photo on her phone. There was still something vaguely familiar about Annabelle's face, and Charlotte wanted to examine it more closely at home. There obviously was a connection between Tatiana, Annabelle, and the aprons, and although Charlotte had no idea what that could be, she wanted to find out. She didn't want to pepper Tatiana with any more questions about the beautiful child Annabelle, and left it at that.

Charlotte walked and opened the gallery door as Little Lovey woke up from her cat nap.

"Well, back to business!" she declared, bending down and petting Little Lovey on the head. "Thanks for the much-needed break, Tatiana, but duty calls!"

"Yes, it does," said Tatiana, walking Charlotte and Little Lovey out toward the wooden dock that would take them back to Beach Rose Path.

"Don't forget those cookies," Tatiana reminded Charlotte, who abruptly turned in the opposite direction toward Take the Cake.

"Right!" Charlotte laughed. "Coffee without cookies is a definite no-no at The Shop at Beach Rose Path. I'll text you later." Charlotte hugged Tatiana perhaps a little tighter than she normally would, as she still sensed a great sadness in her friend.

"Thanks, Charlotte. Talk soon." Tatiana headed back inside of The Blue Hydrangea, and Charlotte walked toward Take the Cake, basking in the now warm sunshine. The gray sky had cleared and it was now a robin's egg blue, reflecting off of the calm ocean waves.

"I think we have a little bit of a mystery on our hands, girlfriend." Charlotte said to Little Lovey, bending down to pat the dog on her head. Lovey looked up at her mistress as if she knew exactly what she was saying, and she probably did, she was so intuitive to Charlotte.

"But we will tread very carefully. Something tells me Annabelle meant more to Tatiana than meets the eye, with her putting that painting up for a reason." She was more talking to herself with her assumptions about the beautiful child Annabelle. But as Charlotte was about to open the front door to the bakery, she pondered that there was something else familiar about the painting, and not just the smock. She couldn't quite put her finger on it but there *was* something else.

Charlotte put thoughts of Annabelle at the back of her mind, as Betsy rounded from the other side of the glass bakery counter with a massive box of cookies for another busy day at The Shop at Beach Rose Path.

CHAPTER TWENTY-EIGHT

Duncan Kirk was ready for the next adventure in his life, and spending time with Charlotte helped him realize that his life in Boston was a closed chapter, and a new one was about to open in Lobster Claw. Although he would still need to drive to Boston a few more times to tie up loose ends, a sense of purpose had overcome Duncan—one that he hadn't felt since his first designing job so many years ago.

If Charlotte can start over, so can I, he thought as he carefully docked his father's boat at the Lobster Claw pier. Duncan was going to embark on what his father had originally wanted to do with his boat, but sadly, waited too long.

Duncan fully understood the reasons why his father, Callum, put off his dream—it was because he was such a fantastic and responsible father, putting his two children through college, and when Ivy was accepted to veterinary school, his father was not going to let Ivy get herself into a mountain of debt. So with her scholarships and grants, and Callum's financial assistance, Ivy was able to graduate practically debt free. This was a sacrifice on so many levels, Duncan understood, on Callum's part, and he continued to work full time, but as long as his children were happy and on the path to their own financial independence and success, then Callum was happy.

Duncan stood on the deck of his father's boat that he christened *Callum's Pride*, named for his own pride and joy, his two children.

"This is for you, Dad," Duncan whispered into the ocean breeze that caressed his sunburned face.

"Ahoy, there mate!" Duncan's first customer shouted and waved from the dock.

Elsie McEverett was carrying a large cardboard box and was ready to board *Callum's Pride*.

"Ah, my first and hopefully not my last customer," laughed Duncan, stretching his arm and helping Elsie aboard. He took the box from Elsie and put it under the seat.

"Oh, don't you worry, Duncan. Once words gets out about your water taxi service, you will definitely need a bigger boat." She winked at Duncan who felt himself smile at Elsie's positivity.

"Sure hope so, Elsie. Ready?"

"I am more than ready for the debut ride on *Callum's Pride* from Lobster Claw to Camden. And thanks so much—this is going to be so much faster than having my son drive up here from Camden. Traffic is a horror show this time of the year!"

"It will be nice to see Mac," Duncan said, getting behind the wheel and starting the engine.

"Well, you can see him to say hi and bye because I'm not hanging around. He needs this junk of his, so I'm doing him a huge favor. He's meeting us at the dock, I'm handing over the box, and then we are hightailing it back to Lobster Claw. My sister can only handle the Everything for so long without me, don't you know."

Duncan saluted at his first customer.

"Aye aye, madam!" He then pulled the lines from the dock,

cautiously backed his way out of Lobster Claw Harbor, and within minutes, he and Elsie were headed out of the bay and toward Camden on *Callum's Pride*'s inaugural run.

CHAPTER TWENTY-NINE

THE SUN WAS BEGINNING TO SET ON LOBSTER CLAW HARBOR, AS brushstrokes of lavender, coral, and turquoise painted the evening sky. Duncan stood on the bow of *Callum's Pride*, mesmerized by how the colors of the sky were reflecting off the water, giving it an ethereal and almost heavenly beauty. He felt as if he was almost in another world, surrounded by the quickly changing colors of sunset that started to fade from bright to dim. Duncan looked at the wooden dock leading from the Beach Block to Charlotte's. She had set out some of the same Adirondack chairs that were in front of The Blue Hydrangea, but closer to shore and he could see a few customers still milling about the beach with bright pink The Shop at Beach Rose Path bags laying at their feet in the warm sand.

He glanced at his watch. 8 p.m.

Duncan made sure the boat was secured for the evening and found himself walking along the dock toward Beach Rose Path. So much had happened that day, and he was bursting with excitement over the possibility that his father's dream becoming a reality, and he could only think of one person he wanted to share it with, and that was Charlotte.

He ran his hands through his ocean sprayed hair and brushed off any boat debris that might be on his clothes. He peeked inside the window and saw Charlotte take two coffee pots from the store area back into her own house. She quickly returned with a towel and started wiping down the counter and the coffee table. Her long wavy chestnut hair was pulled in a ponytail and tied back with a red, white and blue silk scarf. She was wearing a red skirt with a white polo top and blue sneakers.

She would be dressed patriotically today. He smiled as he watched Charlotte who had turned toward Little Lovey, nestled in her bed by the door. The dog was chewing on a giant rawhide and contentedly watched her mistress.

Although they had been seeing each other often, Duncan still did not know exactly why Charlotte was in Lobster Claw, as most of their time was spent talking about work. She had given him the story of running Rory's place, which, of course, was true, but how did she know Rory? He knew she had been engaged, and that her fiancé had died in an accident, but that was all. But then again, she knew little of him as well, and the real reason he was in Lobster Claw. It still hurt to talk of Melinda's betrayal, so Duncan always kept it short—broken engagement, time to move on, that type of thing, so he was just as guilty about being closemouthed about his own reasons as she was with hers.

"Give it time, Dun," Ivy had told him last week when they had lunch together. "She'll open up when she's ready. Charlotte is not the type of woman to wear her heart on her sleeve. She's private and keeps things close to her chest. Not to mention she's incredibly busy and is probably so exhausted at the end of the day, talking about herself is the last thing she wants to do. Plus, you're one to talk, Mr. Don't Ask Me Any Questions."

Duncan knew Ivy was right, on both counts. Charlotte was mature, reserved, and poised, and Duncan didn't like to talk about himself. Ivy, of course, knew what transpired between he and Melinda, but she was the only one. While Melinda's betrayal still felt extremely raw and difficult to speak about, Duncan also didn't believe in sharing everything with the world; just with his sister, and even then, it could be a struggle. While Ivy was open and honest and was never afraid to ask for any sort of advice, Duncan was calmly confident, never boastful, and closed. His emotions were not for sale, and he preferred to quietly conquer his own demons in the privacy of his own head and heart. Duncan got the sense that Charlotte was like that too, something else that he found attractive about her. Charlotte was obviously courageous—starting over again at this stage in her life in an entirely new place—and also a survivor. She wasn't pretentious or arrogant, just a person trying to live life as best she could and on her own terms.

But tonight was different for Duncan. The day had been simply amazing. Elsie's delivery of junk to her son turned into an all-day excursion, as her son was coming back to Lobster Claw with a few friends for a Fourth of July party on the beach.

"You know, Duncan, you might be onto something," Mac, Elsie's son said, as they had pulled out of the calm bay waters of Camden, heading back to Lobster Claw.

"On to what, Mac?" Duncan steered the boat as Mac stood next to him.

"A ferry service. There is none from Lobster Claw to Camden. This time of the year traffic is a bear, and this is a pretty quick trip. Something to think about."

"Funny you say that Mac, because I have thought about it. It's something my father wanted to do but never had the chance." The strong summer sun shone down on *Callum's Pride*. The ocean was calm and there was not a cloud in the sky.

"Could be something you might do all year long—you don't have to go out on open ocean—you pretty much stay within the lanes of the bay and avoid the open waters."

"Not sure this little boat would do well in the winter, but I suppose it could be something to do maybe 6 to 8 months of the year. Something to think about," Duncan said, watching the waves lap upon the rocky shoreline of Maine.

Mac and his friends had hired Duncan to take them back to Camden the following afternoon, and Duncan found himself on the brink of possibly fulfilling Callum Kirk's family dream.

"What do you think, Dad?" he wondered, as he found himself gently opening the door of The Shop at Beach Rose Path. The familiar tinkle of bells lightened Duncan's mood, making him feel that this could be a very real possibility.

"I'm sorry, we're closed for the evening…" Charlotte's musical voice rose from behind the register as she suddenly popped up like a jack-in-the box.

"Duncan!" He heard the delight in her voice, as she rounded from the register and greeted him with a hug and a kiss on his cheek. A sudden wave of lightheadedness hit him, as the scent of rose and vanilla from Charlotte's hair literally made him weak in his knees.

"Nice to see you, too," he said, softly kissing her lips.

Duncan saw Charlotte's face turn the color of a blooming peony. She hugged him again and then pulled away, her smile lighting up the darkening store.

"Busy day, I presume?" He sat down on the couch as Little Lovey pranced toward him, hopping into his lap. She looked up at him with her big brown eyes, and then settled in contentedly, as his hand petted her silky head.

"An understatement," Charlotte said, plopping down next to him.

"I can't believe how fast the inventory is going. I had to place another order today, but that's a good thing, isn't it?"

"It's a great thing," he said, feeling a smile sweep across his face.

He could feel Charlotte studying his face, and smiling herself.

"You've got something up your sleeve, don't you Mr. Kirk?" She laughed, her hand gently kneading his shoulder. Her affectionate touch not only relaxed Duncan, but energized him as well.

"How about a walk on the beach?" Fireworks will be starting soon," he said. It was probably a ridiculous thing to ask after the day Charlotte had probably had, but Duncan wasn't ready for the day to end, and a romantic walk on the Maine beach on the Fourth of July would do them both good.

"I'd love it. Little Lovey loves her evening beach strolls. Just let me officially close up and then we can go."

"Sounds perfect," Duncan said. As if on cue, Little Lovey tumbled from his lap and headed toward the door.

"Don't worry, Lovey, we're going, we're going," Duncan laughed, watching Charlotte pull down the blinds and flip the sign on the door from open to closed.

"Yes, it does sound perfect," she whispered, standing on her tip toes and quietly kissing Duncan.

"I can't wait to hear all about your day," she whispered. He wrapped his arms around Charlotte, and they headed toward the darkening beach, with the beam of the Sea Star Lighthouse, lighting the shore on Beach Rose Path.

CHAPTER THIRTY

TIME FLIES WHEN YOU'RE HAVING FUN.

The words Tatiana spoke on the Fourth of July weekend echoed within Charlotte's mind, when the bright flares of fireworks that showered from the sky that night were now replaced by lightly falling leaves the color of bright gold and light crimson.

Autumn arrived in Lobster Claw a bit earlier than it did in Boston, and Charlotte already noticed the beautiful sunsets made their appearance a bit earlier and the glorious sunrises dawned a smidge later.

Charlotte was watching one of those sunrises, sipping her coffee while Little Lovey pranced around near the shore. She was sitting in one of the Adirondack chairs reserved for guests, but today, it was going to be her turn during this beautiful and peaceful part of the day, where the sun was breaking and the still warm breezes blew in from the ocean.

"Not too far, Lovey!" Charlotte commanded as Lovey scampered closer to the piping plover's restricted area. She was now four months old and healthy as could be. She responded to Charlotte's training extremely well—was still getting overexcited about rewards—and always listened when called. Lovey turned her yellow head toward Charlotte as if to say 'Okay, Mom!' and sprinted in the opposite direction, chasing the white caps on the lolling waves.

A sense of contentment settled over Charlotte like a comfortable old sweater. The Shop at Beach Rose Path was turning a profit this summer, and Charlotte's days were filled with thinking of ways of bringing in business, new merchandise, and other ways to entice more customers to the shop. Even some year-round residents of Lobster Claw found it a place to have a cup of coffee, sit for a while and chat with tourists about how special a place Lobster Claw was.

Charlotte found wonderful friends in the Beach Block, and especially with Tatiana, and Ivy made an appearance a couple of times a week for a Lovey check in.

And then there was Duncan.

As busy as he was getting his own business off the ground and into the water, they were still able to see each other almost every evening, either walking to the Beach Block for some dessert at Take the Cake, or just sitting peacefully on the beach, watching Lovey frolic by the shore. Lovey adored Duncan, and Charlotte was beginning to feel the same. Anytime he was near, Charlotte felt her heart accelerate and her body tremble. The attraction she felt for him was strong, and she knew that he felt it too, catching him on several occasions just gazing at her, brushing up close if he happened to come into her busy store, and the strong squeeze of his arms around her. Charlotte knew she was being cautious, and she sensed that he was too, never going too far, but at the same time, Charlotte wished that he would be bold enough to go a little further.

And then what? she would think. *Then, you'd be sorry that he did and that you relented. Things are fine the way they are now. It's only been a summer, and summer romances never last.*

That's what Charlotte believed, anyway. When it came to

affairs of the heart, summer wasn't real. It was fleeting, dreamy, and enchanting, just like the long and leisurely walks on the beach while watching the majestic and colorful sunsets near the lighthouse. Charlotte was under the spell of a magical summer trance, and now with the turning of the leaves, the coolness of the evenings, and the shortness of the days, the spell was about to break, and she would be hurtled back into a cold reality.

On the other hand, Charlotte couldn't ignore her growing feelings for Duncan. She knew she was falling in love with him, and although the chemistry between them was powerful, she got the sense that was something holding him back from taking that leap from like to love. True, Duncan had been engaged, and that he ended it because of his fiancée's infidelity, but she still wanted to know more. Did he still love her? Was he ever planning on seeing her again?

Charlotte sighed. When she accepted Hamish's proposal to start fresh in Lobster Claw, the last thing she was looking for was a romantic relationship. And here she was with not only the possibility of one, but a new dog, new friends, new business. She was crossing a threshold into a new life, with one foot over the threshold, but the other, still stubbornly fighting not to step onto the other side.

"Should I let him know how I feel?" she whispered, putting the cup to her lips and sipping the warm brew, hoping that an answer would be whispered from somewhere on this glorious morning.

"Silly girl," she laughed as she rose from the chair. She heard the vibration of her phone and grabbed it with an enthusiastic greeting.

"Hamish! How wonderful to hear your voice!"

"Oh, yours, too, Char. How've ya been?"

"Oh, there's so much, Hamish. So much. I wish I could just hop on a jet and fly to Scotland and have tea and scones and just chat." Charlotte was beyond thrilled at hearing her old friend's voice.

"Well, how about the other way around? That's why I'm calling. I'm actually in Halifax now visiting with Rory and am planning to stop down to Lobster Claw for Labor Day weekend —would that work with you? Maybe you can put this old man to work in the store?"

"Hamish! Are you kidding? That would be wonderful! Oh, I've missed you so much, and you can meet everyone, and…"

Hamish laughed. "Sounds like a plan then, Char." Hamish's cheerfulness warmed Charlotte's heart. She would actually be seeing Hamish in just a few days.

"I'll text you the details, Char. Sure am looking forward to some tea and scones with my old friend."

"Same here, Hamish. Yes, text me everything and I'll see you soon!"

"See you soon. Going to play a few rounds with Rory now, so I'll be signing off. Take care, Char."

"Come on, Lovey," Charlotte called, ready to tackle the day, and especially so now that Hamish Falconer would be paying her a visit.

CHAPTER THIRTY-ONE

TWHACK

Hamish watched as the golf ball arched high in the clear Canadian sky. It let off a sound like steam releasing from a pressure cooker as it sailed through the air, then gracefully landed a hair from the 9th hole.

"You've still got it, Hame!" Rory Ruskin grabbed his golf bag as Hamish put his iron back into his bag, ready to make the trek down the green to the 9th hole.

"Aye, I do still love this sport," he said, patting his old friend on the back.

"Say, you make that putt and we'll call it a day. Let's go to the clubhouse for a drink, how's that?"

"Sounds perfect to me." They reached the 9th hole and Hamish effortlessly putted the dimpled white ball straight into the hole. The two friends laughed, gathered their clubs and set on their way for their post-game drink.

"It's been so great to see you, Hamish," Rory said, ordering their favorite stout beers. The bartender presented Hamish and Rory with two large glasses filled with frothy coffee-colored beer with foam about two inches high. Hamish took a draught, delighted by the milky and rustic stout.

"Been great to see you as well, my friend. As much as I love being home, I do miss this side of the pond."

The two friends drank their beer, and Rory order two more.

"So, you're definitely headed down to Lobster Claw?" Rory asked sipping his beer.

Hamish slid his glass away on the shiny oak bar. Only Rory knew the truth.

"Aye, Rory, it's time to put things to rights."

"Things are right, Hamish. The best decisions were made at the time, I believe. I thought you did too."

Hamish nodded his head in agreement.

"Yes, yes, it was the best decision for me and Hannah. But was it for Tatiana?"

"She agreed to all your terms, Hamish," Rory said, looking his oldest friend right in the eye. "You should have no guilt about anything at all. None at all."

Hamish took the last sip of his beer. "I never thought that by sending Charlotte to Lobster Claw that these old memories would be dredged up again. Never even gave it a thought that Tati was even still in Lobster Claw. I had tried so hard to forget all about her and then Charlotte told me about her and their friendship. No, I was the one who gained, and Tati was the one who suffered. Ever since I found out she was in Lobster Claw, I've barely thought of anything else. She probably won't even want to see me, but I've got to try. I owe Charlotte an explanation as well. Here I am just appearing on her doorstep out of nowhere. It would seem a little suspicious to me if I were her."

Hamish felt Rory's reassuring hand squeeze his arm.

"In my book you owe nobody anything. Everything was legal and Tatiana made her choice."

"You're a good friend, Rory Ruskin. That you are. But no matter the outcome, I need to see her. Even though our years with Annabelle were few, well, there'd be no Annabelle without Tatiana."

"You do what you feel is right, Hame. I'm here for you."

"Thank you, Rory," Hamish said, grateful for his old friend's loyalty.

But as he was approaching his 75th birthday, Hamish knew he could no longer keep the past buried in his heart and in his soul. Would it do any good, righting old wrongs and opening old wounds? Wounds that cut so deep Hamish could still feel them decades later.

"I know people think that some things should stay in the past, but it has been tugging at me ever since Charlotte mentioned Tati and I can't get her out of my head. I've had trouble sleeping, even eating, if you can believe that," he laughed, as the bartender brought each man another glass of stout, "but I do think this is part of my past that needs to be revisited, and I think I might be the better for it."

"You might feel better, but what about Tati? Do you think she'll even see you?" Rory asked, wiping the foam from his chin with his sleeve.

"Aye, I've thought about that, too, Rory. It's just a chance I'll have to take."

"Here's to taking chances," Rory said, holding up his glass for a toast.

"To taking chances," Hamish said as the two friends clinked their glasses together, with Hamish, now, feeling more confident in his decision to see the woman from his past who had changed his life forever.

CHAPTER THIRTY-TWO

"So I FINALLY GET TO MEET THE GREAT AND POWERFUL HAMISH Falconer," Duncan said, pouring himself a cup of coffee in the shop. He stopped by the store as he was on his way to Boston to tie up the legal loose ends with his firm. He was selling his share to the other partners, and then he was off to meet with the realtor who sold his condo. His life in Boston was officially coming to a close, and his life in Lobster Claw was opening. He planned to reinvest his buy-out monies into his ferry business that was doing well, making deliveries and taking tourists up and down the Maine coast. He was thinking about potentially purchasing another boat, and he and Charlotte talked about the possibility of starting a sightseeing tour business with guests meeting at The Shop at Beach Rose Path. But those plans were still in the future. Duncan needed to deal with the here and now and he wanted it all done by the end of the day, so tomorrow could truly be the first day of the rest of his life. And that would hopefully include Charlotte.

"Oh, Duncan, you'll just adore him, and I can't wait for you to meet him. I know he'll feel the same about you."

It was an hour before opening, and Charlotte was scurrying

about the store, ensuring there were enough coffee cups, napkins, and everything else she would need for the busy day head. Hamish would be arriving around 7 p.m. after the store closed and then they would finally catch up on the last few months.

"I hope he likes what I've done with the place," Charlotte said, opening the back door to let Lovey out into the enclosed area in the back yard.

"He'll more than love it, Charlotte," Duncan said, pulling Charlotte by the arm and settling her on the couch.

He looked deeply into her shining golden-brown eyes, tiny lines forming every time she smiled, the dimples in each of her cheeks deepening. She always seemed to be glowing and positive, and he found her optimism rubbing off on him, which pleased him tremendously. He told Charlotte he was tying up the legal loose ends in Boston, but that wasn't the only reason for his going. There was something else that he needed to do.

"I wish you didn't have to go today," she said, taking his hand and bringing it to her lips, her kiss making his own heart beat faster. "I'll miss you."

Her words touched him deeply and he leaned in and kissed her, the softness of her lips never failing to trigger shooting stars behind his closed eyes.

"I'll miss you, too," he whispered. "But if I don't pull myself away from you now, I'll never leave," he laughed, rising from the couch.

"Come on. Walk me to my truck," he said, extending his hand. Charlotte slipped her hand into his and he squeezed it lovingly. He wrapped his arms around her as they walked out into the coolness of the early September Labor Day weekend.

"Drive carefully," Charlotte whispered. Duncan felt her arms tightening around his chest and her soft lips again on his.

Duncan opened the door of the truck and hopped into the cab and started the engine. Lovey's barking was then heard above the roar of the truck's engine.

"Oh, hold on a sec, Duncan, she wants to say goodbye." Charlotte ran into the yard, opened the gate, and Lovey dashed to the passenger side of the truck, where she was used to getting in.

Duncan leaned over and opened the door, the enthusiastic dog jumping into the passenger seat, lavishing him with her kisses.

"Okay, okay," Duncan said laughing. He adored Little Lovey and loved nothing more than spending time with the dog as well as her mistress.

"C'mon, sweetie. Duncan needs to go. He'll be back later."

Little Lovey looked at Charlotte, gave Duncan one last kiss and hopped out of the truck. She sniffed around at the tires and then trotted into the back yard.

"Text me when you get there," Charlotte said, kissing Duncan on the cheek.

"Will do." He put the car in reverse and pulled out onto Sand Dollar Drive and toward the bright lights of the big city of Boston.

"Okay, then," Charlotte said, making her way back to the house. She opened the gate to the yard where Lovey was lying on the grass, her paws furiously working on something.

"What do you have there, Lovey?" Charlotte asked, bending down to take what was an envelope from Lovey's paws.

"Oh, this must have fallen out of Duncan's truck when you hopped out. Don't chew this." She wiped a bit of slobber away and saw the envelope was addressed to Duncan. The penmanship was beautiful and flowery, and very feminine. Charlotte even thought she detected a hint of a scent, perhaps perfume? There was no return address, and the envelope was opened. A lilac-colored sheet of paper was folded inside of the envelope.

Don't do it, Charlotte, she silently commanded herself. But she didn't listen and found herself almost in a trance, slowly pulling the sheet of paper from the envelope. As she began to unfold the paper, the scent became stronger.

"It is perfume," she whispered. It smelled expensive, a perfume that could only be bought in a high-end store in a big city.

The letter was written in the same delicate and beautiful script that was on the envelope. Charlotte allowed her eyes to read the letter.

Dunny,

I made a mistake. If I have to apologize to you for the rest of my life, if that is what it truly takes, then I will, if it means you would come back to me. I am not sure why I did what I did, but I can and will promise you that Eric never meant anything to me. You know how you are when you get wrapped up in a project—nothing in the world exists except for that. Not even me. It was at a low time in our relationship, and Eric gave to me what you did not. I am not blaming you for my terrible indiscretion, but I am human, I am a woman, and I needed you, but you were not there for me. I was angry and I did something terribly, terribly stupid. Please remember how amazing we were together in every aspect of our lives. Every. My heart, my soul, and my body aches for you, Dunny. Please come back to me.

Forever yours, and with all of my love. M.

CHARLOTTE'S SHAKING HANDS TURNED OVER THE ENVELOPE. IT WAS postmarked August 27, Boston, MA a little more than a week ago.

He's had this and he never said a word, Charlotte thought as she could feel the hot tears sting behind her eyes. And now he was on his way to Boston. Was he really tying up loose ends or was he going to see her?

Charlotte heard the soft whimper of Lovey, who had sidled close to her leg, knowing that her mistress was in some type of distress.

She crouched down beside her dog and hugged her tightly. She kissed the top of her soft head, thankful for Little Lovey's caring presence.

"I'm okay, sweetie," she said, rising back up and walking toward the house. She had work to do and Hamish was arriving this evening. Now was not the time for tears. She quickly relived the last few moments she had spent with Duncan and chastised herself for her own stupidity.

Duncan's caresses, his kisses, his words of endearment. Was that all they were, just useless gestures and careless sentiments? She was so confused by everything at the moment, her head was spinning as fast as wheels on a speeding car, and her heart was racing just as fast, and she no had no idea how she was going to make it through the day. But Hamish would be here later, and they could sit over tea and cookies like they used to, and she knew Hamish would listen, console and advise. Knowing that Hamish would be here on the other end of the day would help Charlotte get through the day itself.

"Okay, Lovey, let's do this." She wiped away her tears, put on the coffee and opened her storefront door to the customers that were heading down the wooden dock, and put Duncan Kirk well at the back of her mind.

CHAPTER THIRTY-THREE

"Sure you won't reconsider, Duncan?"

William Dane and Alfred Grayson sat opposite Duncan at the cherrywood conference table in the main conference room on the 34th floor of 100 Federal Street in Boston. The view of the Boston Harbor stretching out into the Atlantic Ocean was breathtaking today, the water and sky both a brilliant blue. Duncan looked out the window watching the long queue of planes, lined up like obedient children, across the harbor at Logan International Airport. One by one, each taking their turn, the planes sped up on the runway and then ascended gracefully into the wide expanse of blue, late-summer sky.

Off into the great beyond, just like me, he thought, as the authoritative yet friendly voice of Alfred Grayson brought him back to the present.

William Dane and Alfred Grayson were cousins, and the original founders of Dane Grayson. When they hired an eager young architect over twenty-five years ago, Duncan Kirk lived up to their highest expectations, and ten years ago made him an official partner in the business, adding Duncan's name to the corporation, giving him all of the benefits, both positive and negative, as part owner of Boston's most famous architectural and design business.

Duncan sighed heavily.

"Believe me, Alfred, it's all that's been on my mind, and I've come close. But I know that my life is in Maine now and that is where I want to be. Where I need to be." He envisioned Charlotte's thick, russet, wavy hair blowing in the ocean breeze and her smiling brown eyes.

The cousins looked at each other, Alfred raised his bushy white eyebrows, and William's thin lips upturned into a smile.

"We're happy for you, Duncan, we truly are, and we also understand," Alfred said. "Your payout should be in order, and we believe you'll be happy with the results, but we do have one favor to ask."

"Anything," Duncan said. He had always been extremely grateful for these two gentlemen taking a chance on a cocky young graduate ready to make his mark on the world. They were father figures and friends, and Duncan would do anything for them.

"We would appreciate it, Duncan, if you would let us keep your name in the company. Dane Grayson Kirk has such a better ring to it than simply Dane and Grayson. It is an homage to you for bringing in some of our best and loyal clients. You also never know where the winds of life may blow you." He winked at Duncan.

"The winds are blowing me right back to Lobster Claw and my little boat," Duncan laughed.

"We understand and respect your decision. In fact, we are a little envious," William laughed, patting his cousin on his arm. "Duncan, if you ever need co-captains in the future, well, I hope we are the first ones you think of."

Duncan's heart swelled with love for the two cousins.

"I hope you know my decision was not an easy one to make, but…"

"But there's a woman in Lobster Claw who is keeping you there, I suspect," laughed Alfred. "And by the shade of red your face is turning right now, I also suspect I am correct."

Duncan laughed. "You are ever so correct, Alfred. Charlotte has changed my life in so many ways. If you told me I would be in love with this wonderful woman five months ago, I would never have believed you. But here we are."

"In love. Duncan. We are so happy for you. She's a lucky woman." William rose and rounded the table and wrapped his arms about Duncan in a fatherly hug.

And there it was. He just admitted to his two closest confidants he was in love with Charlotte Templeton.

Alfred shook his hand and brought out his best bottle of bourbon. He poured the amber liquid into three Irish crystal glasses, each man taking a glass and raising it.

"To love, to life, and to Lobster Claw. Best of luck to you, Duncan."

They clinked their glasses, and each downed the malty whiskey.

"And no worries. My plans include another boat, so you'll be hearing from me about co-captaining!"

William and Alfred escorted Duncan from the building. A sense of sadness and melancholy suddenly seized Duncan as the warm breeze blew in from Boston Harbor. He looked around at the skyscrapers, several of which he had designed and helped to erect, knowing that although this part of his life was now a closed chapter, the excitement of a new chapter with Charlotte was beginning. All he wanted to do was meet with the realtor, and make one more stop before heading north back to Lobster Claw and back to Charlotte Templeton.

CHAPTER THIRTY-FOUR

Duncan steered his truck into the parking spot right in front of David Charles jewelers, Boston's premier jewelry store, and also a building which Duncan had designed. He hopped out of the coolness of the cab and into the warm humidity of the late summer Boston afternoon. He paid for the parking at the meter, and opened the jewelry store's door and was met by a cold blast of air conditioning, which sent shivers through his blood.

"Duncan! Good to see you!" David Charles greeted his long-time friend. They had become fast friends when David requested Dane Grayson Kirk to work on plans to expand David's generations-owned family business.

Duncan vigorously shook David's hand in greeting.

"Great to see you, Dave. How's the family?"

"All good, Duncan. No complaints. How's life in the hinterlands?"

"All good, Dave. No complaints."

"Fantastic. Let me go into the back office and get you the box. I think you'll be very pleased with what we've done for you."

"Thanks, Dave. I'm sure it's amazing."

David disappeared behind a black door and Duncan looked at

the glass case full of the most expensive rings, necklaces, watches, and bracelets in the city of Boston.

"Well, well, look what the cat dragged in."

Duncan's heart almost stopped not only at the words that were just spoken, but from the voice that had spoken them.

He lifted his head from the case and turned to see Melinda in all her glory—a figure-hugging orange silk dress, black stiletto shoes, and a white leather jacket topped over her shoulders. Her honey-colored hair was curled on top of her head into a bun while diamond earrings dripped from her earlobes. She was still gorgeous, and still deadly, as the thought of the letter entered his mind.

"Melinda," was all he could muster. Duncan couldn't believe Melinda was standing in front of him, and of all places, the jewelry store where he'd bought her engagement ring.

"Hello, Dunny." Her red lipsticked mouth revealed pearl white teeth, and Duncan suddenly had the image of a vampire who had a thirst for his blood.

Melinda sauntered closer to Duncan, her manicured claws matched her lips and they incessantly tapped on the glass case, putting his nerves instantly on edge.

"You've blocked my calls, blocked my texts, and you didn't even have the common decency to answer my letter. I know you got it, Dunny."

"I want no contact with you, Melinda. We are over. End of discussion."

He could feel the anger rising in his voice, but out of respect to David and to the reason why he was even in the store, Duncan kept his cool, as he knew his stillness would send Melinda over the edge as well.

"Well, in case you did not read my letter, it was a letter of apology. I am sorry. I was wrong." She put her hand gently on Duncan's cheek. He grabbed her hand away, but she quickly pulled his hand to her full lips and seductively kissed it. She looked at him with her big violet eyes under heavily mascaraed black lashes, putting on her most coy and flirtatious act she could produce.

Duncan instinctively heaved his hand away as if it had just touched a hot stove.

"That's enough, Melinda. Time for you to move on."

"Melinda! Come on. We're supposed to be there now!"

A man, about Duncan's age, had poked his head in the door of the store. He looked vaguely familiar, but Duncan couldn't place him. He stepped inside and Duncan saw he was wearing an expensive suit and shoes.

Melinda immediately pulled away from Duncan as if she had been caught. Which she had been. Again.

"Oh, Paul, I just ran into an old friend. Paul Beardsley meet Duncan Kirk. Duncan, I'm sure you recognize Paul from Rise and Shine Boston."

Duncan nodded his head.

Paul's face contorted in frustration and reddened with impatience.

"Melinda, let's go. We don't have time to be reminiscing with old friends."

"Paul and I are off to the Boston Critics Television Awards. He just won a huge award for his commentating on the plight of the right whale."

"Congratulations," Duncan laughed.

Paul grunted and left, Melinda sidled up close to Duncan. He smelled her signature scent of Coco Chanel and could feel her breath on his face.

"And you never mind about that letter, Dunny," Melinda whispered.

Duncan barely stifled a laugh full well knowing that Melinda knew she had been caught by her current man of the month with her former fiancé. and that there was no way she was going to let the champion of the right whale escape her malignant clutches.

Melinda strutted toward the door, turned around, puckered her red lips and blew Duncan a kiss.

The door shut as David appeared from the back office.

"Oh, sorry, Duncan, but I just wanted to shine it up before I brought it out to you. Let's have a look."

David dramatically opened the chocolate brown velvet box, lifting it up for Duncan to behold.

"David, this is absolutely perfect. Even better than I could have hoped for. I know I can always count on you."

"Let me tie it with one of our signature emerald green satin ribbons. Just give me a moment, and you'll be all set."

David once again quickly disappeared through the door behind the counter, giving Duncan a moment to digest what had just transpired with Melinda.

She probably saw my truck parked out front and just had to make an appearance, he reflected, laughing at the sheer audacity of Melinda not only flirting with him, apologizing to him, but having another man right outside of the door.

Duncan shook his head in bewilderment. Any doubts he had about their breakup, were now hammered from his mind, and only thoughts of Charlotte filled his head. Seeing Melinda for the final time made Duncan realize his future was with Charlotte, and he sensed that Charlotte felt the same. He wanted to give Charlotte something special to mark their summer together, and with Ivy's help, he found the perfect gift. He hoped she would like his gift, as he felt it was the perfect reflection of their relationship thus far. Charlotte had a keen mind for business, and this not only showed with her own success with The Shop at Beach Rose Path, but for his boat business as well. Without Charlotte, he never would have the little ferry business, and they had discussed plans for Duncan's expansion for next summer. He was excited for the possibilities of next year, but Duncan was also looking forward to the quietness of winter, still taking long walks on the beach to Sea Star Lighthouse with his 'two girls', cozy winter evenings by the fire, and simply being with the woman he loved and that sweet dog.

I love you, Charlotte, that I know, and now I want to make sure that you know it too, he thought as David appeared again from his magical back room.

"That should do it." A satin ribbon as green as an Irish shamrock was expertly tied about the velvet box.

"Let me know how she likes it," David said extending his hand in friendship and gratitude.

"I certainly will. Thanks for everything, Dave." The two men shook hands and Duncan walked from the store back to his truck. He felt the heat in his body and his heart racing, but it was not from the late summer humidity of the city. He just wanted to drive for the next few hours, north to Lobster Claw, Maine, north to home and to the woman he loved.

CHAPTER THIRTY-FIVE

Charlotte shut the door to the shop and flipped the sign to the closed side. The Saturday of Labor Day weekend wasn't as busy as she had prepared for, and she was grateful. The store was running at a profit, and any financial gains made after September were all gravy. The success of The Shop at Beach Rose Path was all due to Charlotte's retail experience, excellent business sense, and just plain hard work. She was eager to talk to Hamish about the profits and was looking forward to letting Rory know as well, hoping she had a permanent home in Lobster Claw if she wanted it.

She loved being by the sea, with Little Lovey by her side, her new friends at the Beach Block, and she had come to love her bungalow and Beach Rose Path more than she ever thought. Charlotte created a website and had planned to expand during the winter months, with potential online sales during the slower season. She delighted in the emails from guests, all letting her know they couldn't wait to return to Lobster Claw. Charlotte had risen like the proverbial phoenix from the ashes and was thrilled with the results.

And then there was Duncan. Up until earlier, Charlotte was

giddy with anticipation of seeing him at the end of the day and attending the summer wrap up party on the beach on Labor Day evening. As hard as she tried to push the lingering doubts in her mind after finding the letter, Charlotte couldn't help but feel she had been made a fool of.

"I knew I shouldn't have let my guard down," she said to Lovey, sitting on the couch, who wagged her tail happily at the sound of Charlotte's voice. Lovey plopped down beside her mistress, and buried her face in Charlotte's neck, who now felt free to let the tears flow. Charlotte tried to choke back the sobs so she wouldn't upset Lovey, but she couldn't stop herself. For the first time all day, she could finally unleash her emotions after having to keep them pent up throughout the workday.

The release felt cathartic, and her little puppy lapped the tears from Charlotte's cheeks.

"I knew it was too good to be true. But I only have myself to blame."

She was startled by a loud hard knock on the door. Charlotte dragged herself from the couch and found Hamish on the other side, a smile as big as the moon on his face.

"Char! What's wrong, lass?" Hamish asked, concern filling his voice, as Charlotte's tear-stained face greeted him at the door.

Charlotte was so overcome with emotion at seeing her beloved friend that the crying started again, and she let herself fall into the fatherly arms of Hamish Falconer.

"Here, this will make you feel better."

The hot toddy filled the room with the scents of chai tea, cinnamon and honey. Charlotte gratefully took the steaming cup from Hamish's large hands and sipped it, and smiled.

"And the few shots of bourbon won't hurt either," she said, savoring each comforting sip.

"Aye, Char, that's the magic ingredient. Glad to see you had some in your cupboard."

"I didn't even know it was there," Charlotte said, taking

another swallow of the hot amber tea. The chai, cinnamon, honey, and lemon were absolutely delicious and calming, but the added bourbon warmed her body and calmed her nerves.

"Could all be very innocent, Charlotte," Hamish said. He was sitting opposite her in one of the chintz chairs, with Little Lovey at his feet. The dog took an immediate liking to Hamish, and for the past hour, as the two discussed Charlotte's dilemma, Little Lovey did not leave Hamish's side.

Charlotte sighed. "You're right, Hamish, it could. But he's had the letter for over a week and acted as if it was nothing out of the ordinary—a love letter from his former fiancée. What if it dredged up old feelings, what if..."

Hamish interrupted her. "What if Duncan did go down to Boston to see her, but to let her know it was over. Did that cross your mind?"

Charlotte looked at her old friend, as a small smile started to form on his face. He looked exactly the same as he had when they each departed Castle Loch, except that Hamish looked much more relaxed and happier, unlike herself, feeling like an emotional mess.

"It actually didn't, and I think you know that." Charlotte could feel the hot blush of embarrassment sear her cheeks, as Hamish was always a step ahead of her in matters of the heart.

"He's a busy man, Charlotte. He probably tossed the letter aside and forgot all about it. You did say he had some business dealings in Boston he had to attend to, and I'm sure that's all it was. From what you have told me about him, he seems like a reputable and honorable man, and I think you need to give him the benefit of the doubt, for now, at least, and let him explain when he returns."

"Always the voice of reason. Exactly what I need now, Hamish. And your timing is impeccable. But I haven't been much of a host, crying on your shoulder the very second you arrived. I'm sorry for that."

Hamish rose and sat next to his old friend, putting a comforting arm around Charlotte's shoulders.

"Now, there, Char. I was there with you when you lost Landon and Peppe, and I know how terrible that was for you. I don't blame you one bit for your sadness or your distrust in Duncan. But as I said, let's hear his side of the story, and I'm sure it's as innocent as this Little Lovey, here."

Charlotte grasped his massive hand and squeezed it affectionately.

"I've missed you so much, Hamish. Thank you for everything," she said gazing into his dark blue eyes. Hamish held her gaze, and then it hit her. Why Annabelle's painting seemed so familiar—Annabelle's eyes were the same color of summer blueberries, and with the black irises as round as pennies. Hamish's cheeks also had the same fullness and roundness. His nose was small and slightly upturned and the cupid's bow of his lips was exactly the same as the child's. Hamish had the masculine face of Annabelle. But how could that be?

"Char, you okay? You look like you've seen a ghost."

I think I have, she thought to herself.

A fierce knock on the front door caused Charlotte to jump.

"You sit there, Char. Finish up that toddy. I'll get that."

"Thanks, Hamish," was all Charlotte could say, trying to disguise the shock at the resemblance of the little girl Annabelle to her old friend Hamish.

Hamish opened the door and Charlotte saw Duncan standing on the doorstep.

"I'm sorry, I'm looking for Charlotte."

"Duncan, come on in," Hamish greeted. He held his hand to Duncan and introduced himself.

"Hamish Falconer. Old friend of Charlotte's. I suspect she may have told you I was planning on visiting."

Hamish escorted Duncan into the living room. Charlotte

knew she looked like a slobbering fright, but at the moment, she didn't care.

"She did," Duncan said, gripping Hamish's hand.

"A good strong handshake, Duncan. You're a man of great character. Charlotte, your Duncan is here."

Duncan walked quickly toward Charlotte, and then stopped. She could feel her eyes begin to well up at the way Hamish said 'your Duncan'.

Is he, Hamish? I don't know anymore.

"Charlotte, what happened?" Duncan quietly asked, his hands flying to her cheeks in a gentle caress.

Hamish stood behind Duncan as Charlotte felt his arms sweep her into his embrace.

"I'm going to leave you to it," Hamish said quietly.

"No, Hamish. What I need to say to Duncan can be said in your presence." She pulled away from Duncan, rose from the couch, and stepped closer to Hamish, who had one foot out of the door.

"No, Char. This is between the two of you. Get it all sorted out. I'm sure it will all be fine." He kissed Charlotte on the cheek. "It's been so long since I've been in Lobster Claw, a nice walk down to that Beach Block will do me nicely. Might even stop for some of that ice cream you rave about."

"All the shops are open late for the weekend, and I'm sure there's plenty of ice cream for you." Charlotte hugged Hamish. She watched him walk leisurely down the rickety wooden dock toward the Beach Block. Tomorrow she would talk to him about Annabelle. It was time to talk to Duncan now.

"It's time for Lovey's evening walk. We can talk on the beach." She knew she sounded curt, but she couldn't help it, as her feelings had been crushed by the letter.

"Charlotte, I don't understand." Charlotte heard the hurt in Duncan's voice, but she was hurting too, and angry. She abruptly turned around and walked to the dining room table where she had tossed the letter after having read it to Hamish.

"Maybe this might jog your memory and help you understand," Charlotte said, turning away from Duncan and grabbing Lovey's collar and leash.

She looked at Duncan and saw his face redden with what she hoped was embarrassment.

"Of course I can explain this, but how did you get it?"

"Let's walk. We have a lot to talk about."

Charlotte heard a sigh of what she thought was exasperation escape from Duncan's lungs, as the two headed out into the evening. She could feel his nearness and the pull of his being, and she wanted nothing more than to turn around and forgive him for any indiscretion because she knew at this moment, that she truly loved Duncan Kirk and wanted and needed him. But even though her feelings were intense and she knew without a doubt she had fallen in love with him, he still needed to prove to her that the letter, and his former fiancée, meant nothing to him, and she silently prayed that would be his explanation as they headed toward Sea Star Lighthouse.

CHAPTER THIRTY-SIX

HAMISH STROLLED DOWN THE OLD WOODEN DOCK, WATCHING THE blinking light of Sea Star Lighthouse beam over the Atlantic Ocean. He hadn't been out of the States for so long that he didn't remember that the days ended earlier, and even though it was only 7:00, the sun was almost down as the dark purple horizon settled over the ocean.

He looked toward the Beach Block and immediately noticed that the buildings were brightly lit with the warm glow of lights emanating from the windows, and the streetlights radiated like lanterns in the evening. There were still plenty of people milling around the block, as outdoor seating was provided and families ambled about with ice cream cones and baked goods. He could see the first building—the blue one—was lighted, and from what he could tell, the front door was open.

"She must be there," he said, walking toward the beckoning light of The Blue Hydrangea.

Hamish had no idea what he was walking into but he knew he had to see Tati, even if it was for one last time. It was no coincidence that he was here in Lobster Claw, as she was, and he was not going to let the opportunity to speak to her escape. No matter what had happened in their long lives and no matter the decades they had been apart, they were still, and would always be, bound by their daughter.

In the window of The Blue Hydrangea a slender silhouette appeared and Tatiana's youthful beauty flashed before Hamish's eyes, as he remembered the first time he had seen her so many years ago.

$\approx$

HAMISH AND HANNAH WERE ENGAGED TO BE MARRIED WHEN HE accepted the Castle Loch offer. Their plan was for Hamish to live and work in the States for one year, return to Scotland to marry and bring Hannah to America. Although he knew Hannah was not keen to move from her beloved Scotland, she had promised Hamish she would, once he had established himself professionally and financially.

"Please, Hannah, just come with me. You can stay with your aunt in South Boston. She's already said she'd love nothing more than to have you."

"Hamish, please, we've been over this. I will join you when we're married. I'm not ready to leave, but once we are married, I will be, I promise."

Hamish didn't want to pressure Hannah, knowing she could be very obstinate, and he didn't want to cause a case for any arguments before he left, so he said no more.

Hamish immersed himself as the Assistant General Manager at Castle Loch, never taking a moment off and always striving to be the best as he could possibly be at his job. He couldn't wait to return to Scotland, marry Hannah and bring her back to Winchester, where they could live in the beautiful club's housing and start their life in America together.

Soon, my darling, we shall be married and living in this beautiful country of America. As much as I miss Scotland (and you!!), I must tell you this was the best decision of my life. The opportunities are boundless, and I believe they will be for you as well. Besides, the course will remind you of the rolling green hills of home, as you can see from the photos I am enclosing.

IT WAS A BEAUTIFUL DAY AT THE END OF JULY WHEN HAMISH signed off on his letter to Hannah.

I just hope she will love it here as much as I do, he thought as he slipped the envelope into the clubhouse's mailbox.

"Hamish, this call's for you," said the clubhouse receptionist.

"Thank you," Hamish said, taking the forest green receiver from the receptionist.

"Hame! Rory here. Violet has been relentless. She wants you to visit ASAP. What do you say? I'm sure the club can do without you for a weekend. You may not think so, but please, if not for me, then for Violet."

Hamish heard the laugh in his old friend's voice. Hamish was working every day and all day, but it didn't even feel like work, as he loved it so much. He knew he had to be careful; too much of a good thing could quickly turn bad.

Hamish knew Rory was right. He was working non-stop, always making sure he was proving to Castle Loch and to himself that they had made the right decision in hiring him. But he sorely needed a break. He missed Hannah, and her letters seemed distant lately, and he was getting concerned, as each day that passed brought them closer to their wedding, and that meant Hannah leaving Scotland. He was beginning to fear she would not be able to leave. The pressures of working all the time and the nagging feeling that Hannah was unhappy were beginning to become of great concern to Hamish, and he had to agree with Rory that he needed a break—both physically and mentally.

"Well, you tell Violet I will definitely make some time for a visit." He quickly calculated in his head that he was certainly due a few days off, and that his General Manager would not give him any problems about it whatsoever.

"Well, how about this weekend? You can drive up Thursday night, and leave on Monday—would that work?" asked Rory.

"I'll make it work, Rory. And I'll see you on Thursday night."

"Wonderful! Violet will make you her famous shepherd's pie, so bring an appetite. Oh, and your clubs!"

"See you soon, my friend," said Hamish, realizing now that what he truly needed was an escape from the worries of his present everyday life.

When Hamish arrived, he was certainly ready for the promised meal.

"I think it's high time you two get a move on outta here."

Violet Ruskin wiped her hands on her apron. She had just finished cooking and baking food enough for a month, and now was headed back to the kitchen for the clean up.

"Why don't you tell us how you really feel, Vi." Rory got up from the dining room table and wrapped his arms around his wife. Violet was five months pregnant with their first child, but that didn't stop her from not only cooking and cleaning, but with helping Rory run their souvenir business. She combed the beach several times a week for the most beautiful shells she could find so she could string them into garlands. She would insert small chimes within the shells, and when the wind blew through the shell garlands, it as was if a symphony of fairies dwelled within the shells, creating a musical and magical sound. The tinkling of the bells was soothing and calming and had a mystical effect on the customers who clamored to buy them every summer.

"I'm going to do my clean up, and put some food away for

you, Hamish, to take back with you, and then I'm going to put my feet up and work on my shells. But I'd like to do that in peace and quiet, so you two, vamoose!" she laughed, shuttling the two men out the back door.

"Violet, I can't thank you enough," Hamish said, planting a friendly kiss on Violet's chubby pink cheek.

"Oh, anything for you Hame," she smiled. "But as for that other one..."

"You don't know what you'd do without me, love," said Rory, kissing his wife passionately on her rosy lips.

"Oh, get out of here," Violet laughed, the blush rising higher on her cheeks as she headed back into the kitchen.

"Hamish, let's head down to McGilvery's. Sad to say it's going to close next month. Seems like the town council of Lobster Claw wants to clean up the joint, make it more attractive to tourists."

"What is this world coming to?" Hamish laughed as he and Rory hopped into Rory's old truck to make the trek down to the block of buildings down at the other end of the driftwood dock.

"We could walk, Rory. Beautiful evening."

"That we could, and that we should," Rory said, as they got out of the truck and started to walk down the old dock.

"Might not be the best idea gettin' behind the wheel of the truck after a pint or two."

Hamish laughed. "Or three or four, knowing you, my friend."

"T'is true, t'is true."

The two men made their way down the dock as the sun began to set on Lobster Claw. McGilvery's was the first building in a block of four—a bakery, hardware store, and a general store.

"Are all the buildings closing?" asked Hamish as they found a seat at the bar. "Seems a shame if they do."

"Not quite sure. I only know about Arlan McEverett who runs the general store. He bought a place a few miles down on Sand Dollar Drive that has a storefront and one of those fake lighthouses attached to it. I think the bakery will stay and the hardware store's been sold. Will be interesting to see what happens, but as long as it brings in the tourists, it's okay with me."

Hamish felt the ocean breeze blow through the restaurant's open windows and the scent of the sea sailed in with it, as Hamish immediately felt the tight muscles in his body loosen. All the anxiety about Hannah and work vanished, and it was as if he was in another world, far away from the pressures of managing the golf club and a fiancée who was possibly getting cold feet.

The two men spent the next couple of hours reminiscing over pints of lager and sharing an order of McGilvery's famous fish and chips.

"Can I get you two anything else?"

Both Hamish and Rory were knocked out of their laughter and conversation by the sound of a young woman's voice.

Hamish turned toward the bar and for a moment forgot where he was, as he found himself staring into the bluest eyes of what he could only refer to as an angel. Her long blonde hair cascaded like honey dripping from a honeycomb upon her slender shoulders. Her cheeks were as pink as newly bloomed cherry blossoms, with full lips to match. Light blonde eyebrows were arched over her luminescent blue eyes and a black apron was tied around her graceful figure.

"One more round, Tatiana," Rory answered. "Oh, where are my manners. Tatiana, pleased to introduce you to my old friend Hamish Falconer. Hamish, this is Tatiana. She's McGilvery's niece."

"Good to see you, Rory." Tatiana extended her delicate white hand toward Hamish. He shook it and it was as soft as the wings of an angel.

Hamish couldn't believe that for the first time, he found himself tongue tied. Tatiana's sweetness and beauty almost rendered Hamish mute. He then felt a sharp kick under the bar.

"Nice to meet you, Tatiana, is it?" *Stupid sounding idiot* he silently scolded himself.

Tatiana slowly pulled her hand away from Hamish's.

"Yes." Her smile was like starlight that illuminated the darkening restaurant.

"Tatiana, when you heading back to school?" asked Rory, as she pulled the levers behind the bar and filled two large glasses of the amber-colored lager.

"Chasing me away already, Rory?" Tatiana laughed as she placed the two mugs on the counter.

"Classes don't start until the end of September. So you're stuck with me. How's Violet? I heard you are having a baby—that's wonderful. Congratulations!"

Hamish heard no words that Rory spoke. He was so transfixed by not only Tatiana's obvious beauty, but by her friendly and easy manner, which made her all the more enchanting. Her blonde wavy hair bounced with every step she took behind the bar, as her supple figure moved like a dancer, and he thought her absolutely breathtaking. Hamish found himself not wanting to leave, and as Tatiana became busy with other customers, he let his eyes wander to wherever her angelic presence was in the restaurant.

"Tatiana certainly is a beauty, but you're taken, Hamish." It was the truth in Rory's words that brought Hamish back to his senses.

"You are correct on both counts, Rory," Hamish whispered. He had not confided in his friend the issues he was having with Hannah and her refusal to join him in the States before they were married. Hamish was confident this would pass, but Hannah's resistance was putting pressure on their relationship, and the words of her letters were just that—words. There was no loving feeling in them of late, no mention of missing him, just how things were going in the village they were from. He loved

Hannah and wanted nothing more than to marry her, but her letters had cast doubts which concerned Hamish.

"Trouble in paradise, Hame?" Hamish heard the concern in his friend's voice, but Hamish could not bring himself to confide in Rory. He saw how loving he and Violet were with each other, and it made Hamish envious and sad at the same time.

"No trouble, We'll be married, and Hannah can't wait to live in the States." He hoped his white lie would suffice.

"Ready to head back?" Rory asked and Hamish nodded his head.

"Oh, this is on me," Hamish said, taking the bill from Rory's hands.

"I knew you were going to do that. You settle up. Just going to hop into the restroom."

Hamish was grateful for the moment alone. He wanted one more chance to speak to Tatiana, and settling the tab was the perfect opportunity.

"All set for this evening?" Tatiana's voice, like a choir of angels, hypnotized Hamish once again, albeit briefly.

"You can put your money away because my uncle says it's on him tonight."

"Oh, no I can't do that. I'm here visiting up from Boston this weekend, and...."

"Boston! I live in Boston. I go to school at Art College of Boston. I'll be graduating in May. Where in Boston do you live?"

"Well, technically not in Boston, but Winchester."

"Oh, close enough," said Tatiana, wiping down the counter. "I babysit for a family in Winchester every now and again. Do you work in Boston?"

Tatiana's friendly demeanor no longer left Hamish tongue tied, and her amiable presence put him at ease. It was as if he had known her forever, as he began talking about Castle Loch and just coming from Scotland.

"Hamish, I'm going to head back, but feel free to lag behind if you like." Hamish felt the grip of Rory's strong hand on his shoulder.

"Just want to make sure Violet is okay, but like I said, it's your vacation, so you don't need to follow me back like a chick after a hen. Stay and enjoy your time off."

As much as Hamish wanted to stay and talk with Tatiana, he knew he shouldn't. He was engaged and was getting married, and to be in the presence of another woman was not how Hamish operated.

"Right with you, Rory," Hamish said, watching his friend leave the restaurant. Hamish turned toward Tatiana.

"Thank you and your uncle for a wonderful evening." Hamish thought he detected a faint of look disappointment cloud Tatiana's face, but her effervescent smile brightened not only her face, but his heart.

"I will. It was a pleasure meeting you and I hope I see you again soon."

Hamish's eyes were locked with Tatiana's and feelings of guilt and immense attraction flooded his body as he turned to leave not only the restaurant, but a woman who was like no other. So leave he did, full well knowing his life was with Hannah and at Castle Loch.

Hamish was loading his rental car with his golf bag, as Monday, of course arrived all too soon. He had a wonderful weekend with his old friends, and being in Lobster Claw was just the medicine Hamish needed. He was ready to get back to work.

"Can I tear you away for one last drink before I hit the road, Rory?"

"I'd love to, Hame, but Violet's at a doctor's appointment and well, I've got to tend to the store." Rory shut the trunk of Hamish's car.

"Of course." Hamish said. He had said his goodbyes earlier in the day to Violet.

"Hamish, you know you're welcome anytime, old friend,"

Rory said as he hugged him. "Drive careful, and we'll be in touch for another visit. Violet's not due until November, so they'll be plenty of time for more visits."

"I'll let you know when I can get the time off again, Rory. Thanks for everything."

"Safe travels, my friend," Rory waved as he headed back into the store.

Hamish got behind the wheel of the car and headed down the main road, but suddenly stopped. He put the car in reverse and turned in the opposite direction and parked in McGilvery's empty parking lot. He wasn't due back at Castle Loch until Tuesday morning, so if Rory didn't have time for a drink, Hamish certainly did. He also knew he wanted to see the alluring Tatiana one last time.

There were a few customers inside sitting at the tables having lunch, and Hamish saw her immediately on the other side of the bar straightening up menus. She looked up, saw him and waved him to the bar, her incandescent smile lighting up the room.

"Hamish! I thought you left for Boston." Hamish thought she seemed as happy to see him as he was to see her.

"On my way now. Just wanted to stop in and thank you once again for dinner. It was very gracious of you."

Tatiana's long yellow hair was loose and it flowed around her like spun gold described in a fairy tale. If it was possible, she looked even more radiant today than when they first met.

"Our pleasure," she said. He felt as if his heart was going to beat right out of his chest and decided to take a seat at the bar. His mind was no longer his own; Tatiana had seized it.

"Can I get you anything?" Hamish barely heard Tatiana's musical voice as it escaped her lips in a whisper.

Their attraction was palpable, and whatever was happening between the two of them was happening at the speed of a freight train roaring down the tracks—fast, furious, and impossible to stop. He didn't feel he was himself in this woman's presence. He didn't know who he was or what he was doing, but he knew one thing—this woman had bewitched him, and he couldn't let her go.

"Tati...." It was all he could say, as he felt the softness of her hand laid upon his. Electricity as he never experienced bolted through his body, and he was jolted to his core. He wanted nothing more than for her to keep her velvety hand upon his.

"I know." He watched her lick her pink lips as her grip on his hand grew tighter.

"It's crazy but I haven't been able to think of anything else except you, Hamish. When I first saw you, I thought you were the most handsome man I had ever seen. You were like a knight in shining armor who hopped out right from the pages of a fairy tale, I felt this instant connection to you, as if we met in another life."

Hamish couldn't help but smile because, although he couldn't convey his feelings, even to himself, that was exactly how he felt about her.

Tatiana smiled. "I know. It sounds so silly, and I don't even know what you'd call it—kismet, serendipity. Love at first sight. It's like out of an old romance novel or movie, but I feel it, and I think you do, too."

A sudden flush of warmth rose in Hamish's cheeks, and he put his strong hand on top of hers, caressing her soft hand with his thumb.

"I do feel it, Tatiana. That's why I came back. I wasn't going to but when I drove away from Rory's I turned the car right around and back here. It was almost as if I had no control over my own actions. The car turned and then I was here. I couldn't leave without seeing you again."

"Do you have to go? So soon?"

"I have to be back at work tomorrow morning, but, no, I don't have to go so soon."

"I'm off in an hour. Could you wait?" Tatiana's blue eyes held Hamish captive. He would wait forever for her.

"I can wait," he whispered.

Tatiana leaned over the bar with her hands still enclosed within his, and gently kissed his cheek. He could have been knocked over by a feather with her sudden and affectionate gesture.

They drove down to Camden and parked in the lot of a restaurant. They spent the next several hours talking about their lives, how Tatiana, once she graduated, planned on going to New York to work in an art gallery. How much she loved Lobster Claw. Hamish spoke of his newness to America, and how much he loved his new country. He could sit in this car forever and just talk to Tatiana.

Day quickly turned into evening when Hamish drove Tatiana back to Lobster Claw. He still could not pull himself away from her, nor she from him.

It was 10 p.m. and Hamish knew he had to get back on the road to make it back to Castle Loch in time for work in the morning.

"I'll come back next weekend," he whispered into Tatiana's ear as he walked her to the door of her home.

"I'll find any excuse," he said, wrapping his arms around her body, pulling her as close to him as he could. He could feel Tatiana's arms tighten around him and felt her face snuggle into his chest.

I know this is wrong, he thought to himself as a sudden vision of Hannah appeared behind his closed eyes. Was it possible for him to fall in love so fast with a woman he just met? Was it even love that he felt for Hannah or just simply the affection of a man and a woman who had known each other their entire lives? Could he love both of them in very different ways? He couldn't answer any of these questions with Tatiana gently caressing his neck, as her lips found their way to his.

"Hamish," she whispered and he could hold back no longer as he kissed her more passionately than he had ever kissed anyone before. She returned his kiss with such fervency that nothing in the world existed at this moment except for him and this incredible woman that was in his arms.

Hamish never made it to work the next day. Instead of checking employee schedules and lunch and dinner menus, he and Tatiana were watching the sun rise at Sea Star Lighthouse. The sky was a magnificent kaleidoscope of colors—the horizon was the golden yellow of the sun just rising as the clouds and sky were reflected pink, cantaloupe and azure. The jagged wall of rocks caught the dusky coral shadows as the calm bay was a rainbow of salmon, cerulean and silvery tones.

A mild breeze blew Tatiana's shining hair onto Hamish's cheeks. He could feel its softness, like the downy feathers of a swan, tickle his face and his lips. He felt her pull away from him, as she ran her hands through his own thick black hair, and when he turned to look at her, she was gazing into his eyes.

"It felt like the night would never end, but it has, Hamish." He could feel the softness of her fingers outline his lips.

"Aye. It has, my sweet Tati." It was all he could say. So much had happened in just one night, and he wasn't ready to return to the life he had known before meeting Tatiana. He wanted more time, but time was a luxury he did not have.

Hamish hugged Tatiana as tight and as close to him as he possibly could, and he could feel her arms close around him. He knew this could very well be the last time they watched the sun rise together, and he then felt her soft lips on his own.

"I appreciate your honesty last night, Hamish, and perhaps one day, we will find each other again, but now is not our time. After you told me about your fiancée, I should have let you get in that car and drive back to Massachusetts. But I couldn't. Even just one night with you would be enough and then I knew I would have to let you go. But I also want you to know that I am not sorry, and I will never tell a soul, for as long as I live, about our one enchanted night together. It is something that is my very own, not to be shared with anyone, but you, of course, and last night will live with me forever. But it's time for you to go, my Hamish."

Hamish felt his heart break with each word Tatiana spoke, but he also knew she was right.

"Tati..."

His words were cut off by her lips on his, ardently and lovingly kissing him for one last time. Hamish returned her kiss passionately, pulling her soft body as close to his as he possibly could, also for one last time.

He felt Tatiana's lips pull away from his, as her arms around him loosened. She stood up and put her hand out for his. He took it and stood as they walked hand-in-hand back to his car.

Tatiana stood next to Hamish, her beautiful long blonde hair billowing in the cool morning sea breeze. Her blue eyes shone with happiness, not sadness, as she put her arms about his neck. He breathed in her scent—the essence of the ocean—sparkling, clean, light— the perfect combination of the sunshine and the sea. He inhaled this perfume so he could always remember, and anytime later in his life that he was on a beach, his thoughts always brought him back to that moment in time with Tatiana.

"Goodbye, my Hamish," she whispered, gently kissing him on the cheek. "I shall never forget you."

"Tati, there must be some way." He was desperate at the thought that this would be it—that she had made the decision for both of them that their brief affair was at an end.

She shook her head, her hair gently falling over her face.

"No, my Hamish. We both know it must end here. Please get into your car and drive away from me before I change my mind."

Hamish now saw sadness cloud over those incredible blue eyes, blue eyes that were seared into his psyche.

"Change your mind," he whispered, taking her into his arms once again. As he tightened his embrace, she slowly pulled away from him.

"Goodbye, my Hamish." Tatiana turned from him and walked away onto the shores of Sea Star Lighthouse.

"Goodbye, Tati," he whispered, and he swore he could feel his heart breaking.

Hamish and Hannah married, beginning their lives as newlyweds at Castle Loch. Hamish was busy with his ever-growing responsibilities at work and there was word floating around the club he could soon be promoted to General Manager. Hannah was hired as the club's gardener, something she enjoyed immensely. But one thing eluded their contentment—a child. Hannah could not wait to become a mother, but after several months of not becoming pregnant, Hannah fell into a deep depression.

"Hannah, please," said Hamish one evening after a particularly long day at work. "We've only been married for a short time, there's nothing to be upset about."

"Oh, Hamish, I just know something is not right. All of my sisters got pregnant on their honeymoons. And they keep getting pregnant! I thought by now I'd be half-way through my first pregnancy. But nothing. Why?"

"I can't say, darling," Hamish tenderly said to his wife. He caressed her long black hair and her pale white cheeks as her brown eyes welled with tears of desperation. He loved her dearly and he hated to see her so upset.

"Let's give it time, sweetheart," he murmured, kissing her tear-stained face gently. "Our time will come."

Hamish tenderly tucked his sleeping wife into bed. He turned off the light in their bedroom and padded into the living room. He sat down on the couch, head in his hands, and prayed that his wife be given a child.

Although Hamish was not a religious man, Hannah was very devout, and he took it upon himself, for his wife's sake, to ask the Lord for help.

Hamish was at a loss. All of Hannah's five sisters had big families of their own, and all pretty much giving birth exactly nine months after they were married. He thought, too, Hannah would be pregnant by now, and was looking forward to the quintessential patter of little feet scurrying about the house. He had dreams of teaching a son or daughter the finesse of the game of golf, and returning someday to show them the beautiful shores of Scotland where they came from. But it was not in his hands, nor was it in Hannah's. They would simply have to be patient, and when the good Lord thought it was time, then they would be blessed with a child.

Hamish glanced at the clock on the wall. 9:00. He generally didn't get into bed before midnight, but he was restless and no TV show or book could distract his overloaded mind, so he decided to take a walk on the grounds. Hannah slept like the proverbial log, and he knew she would not wake until morning, so he made sure the door was locked and headed out into the spring evening.

The newly opened lilac buds perfumed the night air, and the scent blew through the cool night breeze. Hamish got as far as the mailbox and saw that the flag was down, so he opened it and found a huge pile of flyers and bills.

"Aye," Hamish sighed. He took the large pile into both his hands and headed back to his house. Hannah was so good in retrieving the daily mail and sorting through it for him, but her sadness got the better of her, and she must have forgotten. No longer in the mood for a walk, he opened the front door and tossed the pile onto the coffee table.

Yup, he thought. Store flyers and glossy pamphlets littered his coffee table. He picked through the mess to gather the bills when he noticed what looked like a card. The envelope was the same color of the newly-blooming lilacs and his name was on the front written in a very delicate script.

The word "Mrs." was not in front of Hamish, so this was not one of Hannah's sisters from home, sending the never-ending supply of cards and letters.

Hamish opened the envelope and pulled out a card that had a drawing of a lighthouse on it. His hands started to tremble as he saw in tiny script, below one of the jagged rocks *"Sea Star Lighthouse, Lobster Claw, Maine."*

He slowly opened the card and read what was written.

My Hamish,

Well, I have broken my promise to myself. As I told you that morning last August, I would never forget our night together, and I have never told anyone. That promise I could easily keep. But as you can see, I have contacted you, something that I did not want to do, but for this reason, I wanted to break my promise. I did not "have" to break it. I wanted to, as I could not go on with the rest of my life with you not knowing that from our one night together, we created a new life.

I was beyond shocked at finding out I was pregnant, but not for one moment was I scared or regretful. This was a life force that could not have been stopped. My family has been very supportive of me, and I am beyond grateful for their love.

The baby is due at the end of May. I have decided to give the baby up for adoption and then continue with my final year of school. I did not come to this decision lightly. The baby deserves a home with two parents who will love and take care of him or her, something that I am unable to do. My parents also believe that this is the best decision for not only the baby, but for me. And I do agree.

I cannot tell you how many times I have wrestled with the idea of whether or not I should let you know, but it would be cruel of me not to let you know that you had brought a child into this world. Or maybe it is cruel of me to let you know. I pray not, but please rest assured the baby will be adopted into a loving home and will be wanted and taken care of.

My Hamish. I have never forgotten you and I never will.

Tati

"A BABY." HAMISH READ THE CARD AT LEAST FOUR TIMES BEFORE HE fully understood what he was holding in his hands. One magnificent night of romance, passion, and love that resulted in a baby.

Everything that night had been so spontaneous, that neither of them thought of or mentioned the possibility of a baby, but it had happened.

Hamish picked up the envelope and looked at it.

"Oh, thank God," he said as he saw there was a return address. He also did a quick calculation in his head.

The baby is due at the end of May. He looked at his watch. The date was May 8.

"There's time," he said. He put on a pot of coffee, and with one of the club's note pads made a list of everything that he wanted to say to Tati and that he needed to do. Hamish knew that he would not be able to sleep one wink, and he spent the night formulating a plan that he would present to Tatiana.

After enduring a sleepless night of careful plotting and planning, morning finally arrived. Hamish explained to Hannah that Castle Loch needed his assistance at their other property in Maine, and that he would return later that evening. He kissed his wife goodbye, and started his journey to Lobster Claw, hoping he could persuade Tatiana from making the mistake of a lifetime.

Hamish was sitting at Rory and Violet's kitchen table. Violet had made breakfast for the three of them and was now feeding their baby, James. "I think you're doing the right thing, Hamish," said Violet, spooning applesauce into James' little mouth.

Rory and Violet were the two people who Hamish could trust and he laid out his plan to them.

"Now I just need to convince Tati. I have her address, so I was hoping you could point me in the direction, Rory."

Rory wrote the directions and handed them to Hamish.

"Not too far, just about ten miles. When you return, I hope it is with good news, Hame."

"I hope as well, Rory." He hugged his friend and kissed Violet and the baby and with Rory's directions, headed toward what he had hoped was the beginning of a new life for he and Hannah.

Twenty minutes later Hamish found himself sitting in front of Tatiana's home.

Feeling as if his heart was ready to beat out of his chest, Hamish rang the doorbell. Several minutes passed and no one answered.

Damned. No one must be home, he thought.

He pushed the doorbell again, harder, as if his forcefulness would bring someone to answer the door.

"Coming!" He heard Tatiana's voice on the other side of the door. When it was flung open, Hamish felt she was even more beautiful than when he last saw her. Her blonde hair was hanging loosely around her shoulders and she held a protective arm over her belly.

"Hamish! My God, what are you doing here?"

She threw her arms around his neck, as the scent of a clean ocean breeze filled his nostrils. That scent brought him immediately back to so many months ago to the night that now put them in this situation.

"Come in." She took Hamish's hand, again, so soft and comforting, and led him into her living room.

"I'm sorry, Hamish, but you were the last person I expected to see on the other side of the door. I presume you received my letter."

Tatiana sat down next to Hamish. He trembled at her nearness, and could not keep his eyes from her belly, knowing that the baby they created was soon to be born.

"Tati, you should have told me sooner," was all he could say. Her smile lit up her beautiful face, and Hamish felt his heart skip a beat.

"Would it have changed anything, Hamish? I knew full well that night that you were a taken man. I knew that. And as I said to you then, that night would be enough for me. We had to go our separate ways, back to our lives, and what we had that night I would never forget. And then, when I realized I was pregnant, I knew that I could not give this special child what it needs—a home with two parents who could take care of him or her. That was not a difficult decision for me, Hamish. What was difficult was whether or not I should tell you."

Tatiana sighed heavily, and Hamish felt it was a great weight lifted from her in letting him know how she felt.

Hamish took both of Tatiana's hands into his own, and brought them to his lips where he placed a gentle kiss.

"I knew you were an amazing woman, Tati. What you are proposing is completely selfless. I am not surprised that you put the welfare of this child before your own. And that's what I want to talk to you about."

"The decision has been made, Hamish. The adoption agency is one of the most reputable in the country, and I have the utmost trust that the baby will be placed in a wonderful home."

Hamish felt Tatiana's grip loosen from his hands, as she pulled them away. She rested both her arms on her burgeoning belly.

"I have no doubt about that, Tati. But I believe there is another option. Can you hear me out?"

Tatiana once again took hold of Hamish's hands and smiled.

"I will hear you, Hamish," she whispered.

And then Hamish began his story.

"My wife, Hannah, well, it's been difficult for her to conceive for some reason. There doesn't seem to be any medical explanation for it, but well, it's just not happening, and this has sent her into a depressive state of sorts."

Hamish could barely believe the words of his and Hannah's situation were actually coming from his mouth, but with Tatiana, he knew he could tell her everything, honestly and openly.

"Well, we thought she'd be expecting by now, but she's not. Anyway, what I am trying to say is, Tati, let me and Hannah adopt the baby."

"Hamish!" Tatiana stood and walked over toward the bay window in her living room. Large lilac bushes ensconced the front and when she opened the window, their beautiful scent flooded the room. He watched as Tatiana, her back to him, looked out the window. He then heard quiet sobs and watched her shoulders shake from crying.

"Tati," he whispered, gently caressing her trembling shoulders. She turned toward him, tears falling from her beautiful blue eyes, as she buried her face into his neck and wrapped her arms around him.

"I am trying to be brave, Hamish," she said, quietly pulling back and gazing up into his own eyes. "I put on a brave and confident face for my parents, assuring them that I am fine with my decision. And I am, but sometimes, I am terrified by it. I don't think I can explain, but if or when the day comes when our baby discovers he or she is adopted, I don't want them to think that I just casually made a decision not to keep him or her. I didn't! I love this baby so much and I want nothing more for her or him to have a beautiful life. The thought of knowing I will never see this child have the life that I want is unbearable. Oh, Hamish, I know my emotions are all over the place, and I don't expect you to understand…"

"Oh, Tati," Hamish whispered, pulling her back into his arms.

"You are so brave. So strong, I wish I could have helped you before this. But when I read your letter, I thought the same thing —how can I let my child be raised by strangers, as loving and caring as they will be? This is our child, Tati. Ours. I can provide for our child, Tati. Hannah and I will adopt the baby, and you will never, ever have to worry about the child's welfare. Never."

Hamish gently caressed Tati's tear-stained face, and saw what he thought was a glimmer of hope in her blue eyes.

"How could this be possible, Hamish?" she whispered. She reached up and stroked his cheek, the softness of her hand on his face, shattering his heart. "Your wife. What would you tell her?"

Hamish pulled Tatiana back to the couch and they sat down.

"On the drive up here, I've had time to think about it, and a million different scenarios ran through my head, but I would simply tell her that a daughter of friend of Rory's fell pregnant. The family wants to keep it as private as possible, that they don't trust adoption agencies, and that they would want to see the baby with someone they knew. I know it sounds convoluted, but Hannah is in such a state, I know that she wouldn't question anything—she'd only want to help, and if meant bringing a baby into her life, then, she would agree."

Tatiana took her hands from Hamish and clasped them in her lap. She closed her eyes and breathed deeply. When she opened them, she looked at Hamish, registering no emotion at all.

"Yes, Hamish. I want the baby with its father. But there is to be a condition, Hamish."

"Anything, Tati. Anything."

"When the baby is born, please be here. And also please make sure that I am able to see the baby. I've heard that mothers who are giving up their children for adoption are not allowed to see their babies, but I want to see ours. Even if it is just once for a few moments. That's all I ask."

"I promise, Tati," murmured Hamish, taking Tatiana into his arms again.

Three weeks later, on Memorial Day weekend, Tatiana gave birth to a beautiful baby girl. She was perfect in every way. Hamish hired a family lawyer who took care of all the legalities for a private adoption.

Hamish and Hannah drove to Maine as soon as they got word Tatiana was in labor. Hannah was beyond delighted and could not wait to hold their baby. As Hamish suspected, Hannah questioned nothing. She was thrilled with the simple fact that she was going to be a mother, and that was all that mattered to her.

When they arrived at the hospital, the lawyer took Hamish and Hannah into a conference room where papers were signed and notarized, making baby Annabelle Hannah Falconer their legal daughter.

"The baby is healthy and will be ready to go home with you tomorrow. Mrs. Falconer, the nurse outside this room will show you to the nursery to see the baby, but Mr. Falconer, I will need a word with you privately," said the lawyer as he placed all the legal documents into his briefcase.

"Of course. I'll come back here right after I bring Hannah to the nursery."

"Oh, Hamish," Violet whispered, grabbing on to her husband's arm. "It's a dream come true. We have a baby!"

"Oh, Hannah, we do," he said quietly, wiping the tears of joy from his wife's eyes.

"I cannot wait to see her."

They walked to the nursery and looked in the large window where several newborns were swaddled inside of bassinets. And then they saw the bassinet marked Baby Girl Falconer.

"My God, Hamish, there she is. She's perfect, Hamish. Just perfect."

Hamish wrapped his arms around his wife and gazed at the beautiful little girl who was the exact replica of her mother, already with golden yellow hair, like newly grown wheat, on top of her pink head, with a tiny button nose and lips as pink as early blooming roses. Hamish knew her looks would change as she grew, but right now, when he looked at his daughter, he was looking at Tati.

"Hannah, you stay here. Let me go finish up with the lawyer." He kissed her on the forehead and chuckled as Hannah couldn't take her eyes from the little baby on the other side of the nursery window.

"You needed to see me, Mr. Bradford?" Hamish closed the door to the conference room quietly, where the lawyer was buckling his briefcase.

"Everything is all set, Mr. Falconer. I just wanted to let you know that the child's mother requested to see you. I said, of course, I'd leave that up to you and it's totally your decision."

"I would like to see her, Mr. Bradford."

"She's in room 527. As everything is complete, I'll be leaving you now. I won't be needed tomorrow when you bring the baby home. I wish you and your wife the best of luck. I will send all documentation to you for your own records, but if you do happen to need me, please contact me."

"Thank you, Mr. Bradford, for everything," Hamish said, extending his hand to the lawyer, who kept everything professional and most importantly, private.

The lawyer left and Hamish took a deep breath as he pushed the elevator button to the fifth floor.

The maternity nurse escorted him to room 527. Tatiana lay in a hospital bed, a radiant look on her face, sleeping soundly. He didn't want to disturb her, but her eyes fluttered opened, as if she knew he was here.

"Hamish," she whispered. "She's beautiful, isn't she?"

"Aye, Tati. Even more beautiful than you," he laughed and saw that incredible smile light up her fatigued face.

"What does your wife think?" she asked tiredly.

"Well, she's no longer in love with me, as that little girl has won her heart right over."

Tatiana laughed. "I'm so happy, Hamish. I know our daughter will have a wonderful life."

Tatiana reached a hand toward Hamish, who took it, and again, pressed it to his lips.

"I can't thank you, Tati, for giving me and Hannah the best gift we could ever ask for. You'll never have to worry about her. Never."

"Goodbye, my Hamish," she whispered, and then closed her eyes and fell asleep.

Hamish stood over the sleeping Tatiana. His heart swelled with love for her. If it were not for that one fateful night, there would be no Annabelle, and no daughter for him or Hannah.

Hamish bent down and gently kissed Tatiana on the forehead and he swore he could smell the scent of that August evening on the shore at Sea Star Lighthouse.

"Goodbye, Tati," he whispered as he gazed upon her exquisite sleeping face for one last time.

THE YEARS PASSED SWIFTLY AND HAMISH WAS NOW A MAN IN HIS 70s. As he watched the colors of the sunset over Sea Star Lighthouse transform from light to dark lavender, pink to scarlet, and coral to dark orange, Hamish Falconer, after all these decades, was ready to see the mother of his daughter, Annabelle. Tatiana Dulka. He hoped she would be ready to see him, too.

CHAPTER THIRTY-SEVEN

Charlotte decided that she would let Duncan be the first to speak. After all, it was his letter. She knew she was being childish, but she didn't care as envy consumed her and shrouded any common sense. The letter was romantic, sad, and was imploring for forgiveness. Duncan had the letter for over a week, and then he had a trip to Boston to "tie up loose ends." Did this include seeing her as well? Charlotte wanted to interrogate Duncan, but not until he spoke first.

"It's nothing, Charlotte, if you would let me explain," said Duncan. They were walking along the shoreline, the sun sinking lower in the sky as the bright light of Sea Star Lighthouse flashed from the lantern room.

"You can explain, Duncan," Charlotte said curtly. "The floor's been all yours, or the beach, I should say." She watched as Lovey darted in and out of the calm surf, trying to catch those forever unattainable white caps.

"I can explain, Charlotte, but will you believe me?"

"Oh, so this is how it's going to be? It's on me to believe you? Duncan, that letter was heart rendering. It was from your fiancée begging for forgiveness. Didn't this touch you somehow? Didn't it dredge up old feelings for her?" She knew she was triggering an argument, but if that's what it took to get the truth out of him, then so be it. It was very uncharacteristic of her to act like this, but then again, she had almost forgotten what it was like to love someone and feel the sharp pangs of jealousy.

Soften up, Charlotte. Don't be like this. Let him explain, she reprimanded herself as she turned to face him. *You shouldn't have read it anyway.* His salt and pepper hair waved gently in the evening breeze, his usually bright hazel eyes looking dark and somber in the dimming evening. He was wearing his leather bomber jacket, and Charlotte longed for him to wrap his arms around her so she could feel the comfort of the buttery softness of the leather enveloping her body. Disappointment flooded her as Duncan made no such move.

"I'm not going to argue with you, Charlotte," Duncan said, reaching his hand to Charlotte's shoulder. She felt his tender squeeze making some of her hurt melt away.

"And that's *former* fiancée, by the way," he chuckled.

Charlotte put her hand over his, clasping it tightly.

"I don't want to argue, either, Duncan, and I'm sorry," she whispered. "And I should not have read the letter…"

Duncan laughed, now wrapping those bomber jacket covered arms about her, and she felt herself melt into him.

"The letter," he whispered into her hair. Charlotte slowly pulled away, as she detected a hint of amusement in his voice.

"C'mon, let's sit," he said, guiding her to one of the Adirondack chairs further down on the beach.

"In all honesty, Charlotte, I barely looked at the letter. I only opened it because I was shocked that it even found its way up here, and I will admit I was curious about what she had to say. Melinda did her due diligence in digging up where I am, obviously. I blocked all her calls and texts, and well, short of driving up here herself, which she wouldn't be bothered doing, she wrote me a letter. A very unconvincing one, at that."

Duncan reached over the wide arm of the bright green Adirondack chair Charlotte was sitting in and took her hand. Lovey edged in next to him and gently nosed his other hand, and he began patting her soft blonde head.

"I'm not going to lie, Charlotte. I didn't know if I was over her or not when I first got up here. I spent many sleepless nights trying to decide if I should go back to Boston and to Melinda. And I almost did. I was ready to hightail it back to Boston in May when I lost my electricity in a storm. And then I stopped in Elsie's and this woman, her gorgeous wavy chestnut hair flying wildly in the sea breeze asking Elsie for God knows what. I watched you follow Elsie up and down the store. You seemed so distressed, but still in control—you needed to get something done and nothing was going to stop you. And nothing was going to stop me from helping you, so I paid, hoping that I would see those big brown eyes again soon. You left, and I headed right back to my powerless home. And then I come to find out you were helping this little lady," he said, lovingly petting Lovey.

"Melinda never would have done anything like that. You knocked me right back to my senses, and I never looked back. Whether it was luck, fate, call it whatever you want... and then, when I saw you in my sister's office, I knew I had to get to know you. You are everything Melinda is not—you're kind, caring, with a beautiful spirit, and I knew I wanted to know you more. This summer has been incredible with you, Charlotte. I went to Boston to sell my part of the company to the other co-owners, finalized the sale on my condo, which I'm putting into the boat and the business. I know I'm rambling, but...."

Charlotte leaned over the chair and kissed Duncan intensely, stopping his sincere words, as they tugged at her own heart.

"Duncan," Charlotte softly whispered, "I'm sorry I doubted you. I'm so sorry." She suddenly felt ashamed and embarrassed by her ridiculous jealousy.

"Charlotte, don't apologize. If I found a letter like that from an old boyfriend of yours, I would have acted the same way. Maybe worse," Duncan laughed. Charlotte felt his calloused hands cup her face as he kissed her once more.

"Besides, there was one other thing I needed to do in Boston," he said.

"What's that?" Charlotte smiled looking at Duncan as a very sly grin appeared on his weather-beaten face.

"This." He reached inside of his leather jacket and pulled out a rectangular velvet box tied with a bright green ribbon.

"I hope you like it," he said, handing the box to Charlotte.

"David Charles!" exclaimed Charlotte in absolute surprise, running her finger over the jeweler's name on the embroidered ribbon. She knew the jeweler was not only famous in Boston, but world-wide as well.

"Only the best for the best," he said. "Open it."

Charlotte's hands wobbled as she slowly untied the ribbon. She opened the box, and gasped at what she saw inside.

"Oh, Duncan," was all she could say, as the sterling silver bracelet lit up the darkening evening. It was a chain-link charm bracelet, with three charms attached—a lobster, the silhouette of a Labrador retriever's profile, and a lighthouse. Charlotte lifted the elegant piece of jewelry as it shimmered in the sunset.

"It's magnificent, Duncan." She turned to him, tears starting to form in her eyes.

"Here, let me help you put it on," Duncan said, taking the bracelet from Charlotte's shaking hands. She extended her right arm, and Duncan fastened it upon her wrist. She watched the silver charms dangle in the dimming light of the late summer evening.

"It's beautiful, Duncan," Charlotte murmured. She was beyond touched at his thoughtfulness, not only for the bracelet itself, but for the charms, which signified their summer together.

"This is just the start, Charlotte," Duncan said, clasping her hands again. "I intend to fill that bracelet with so many charms, it will feel like a heavy weight on your wrist."

They both laughed, and Charlotte was still overcome with emotion.

"I want that too, Duncan," she said. "I can't believe how much my life has changed over the course of one summer. It's been beyond incredible."

"Like I said, call it what you want. I believe we were meant to meet. We were meant to find each other. We were meant to fall in love." Duncan stood, extending his hand to Charlotte. She grasped his hand, feeling his strength, feeling security and tenderness all at the same time.

"I just hope you feel the same," he said, as he kissed her. His kiss was like his hands—strong yet gentle, passionate, and caring. It was the kiss of love.

Charlotte could feel the bracelet slide on her wrist as she reached her arms around Duncan's neck. His eyes no longer looked sad and mournful—they were the sparkling hazel that had dazzled her when they first met.

"I do," she whispered, and returned her pledge of love with a tender kiss of her own.

CHAPTER THIRTY-EIGHT

"Finally." Tatiana sighed as she locked the door of The Blue Hydrangea and turned the sign in the shape of the flower from open to closed. It had been a long and busy day, not to mention profitable, as the last of the summer tourists purchased almost every summertime Lobster Claw framed print she had in stock. She would have to venture to her basement storeroom to find the few she had left of the sunrise at Sea Star Lighthouse, but her feet refused to budge. Instead, she sat down on an old, battered armchair, pulled up a stool and propped her feet up, gratefully sighing at the relief of sitting down. She had plenty of time to get in the basement to rummage for the prints. She had planned on opening the store early tomorrow, as it was Labor Day and the last push until the leaf peepers appeared around Columbus Day.

"I could use a cup of tea," she sighed, hoisting herself up and plugging in her electric kettle. She glanced at the bare spots on the gallery walls, thinking that it didn't look very good, but also realizing those bare spots were profitable, and she would be able to spend the winter comfortably, and with enough money left to invest in some new pieces.

As she muddled over her bare walls her eyes shifted and landed on the painting of Annabelle. Her baby girl.

It was Charlotte's mention of Hamish Falconer that prompted Tatiana to bring the portrait out of storage, and had found that it no longer pained her to look at it. She could now appreciate what a beautiful painting it truly was and was angry at herself for keeping it in storage for so long. Listening to Charlotte expound on her own grief about her personal losses made Tatiana rethink displaying the portrait of Annabelle. Tatiana, although 20 some odd years older than Charlotte, found a kindred spirit in her new friend, and if Charlotte could deal with her own grief, so could Tatiana. Tatiana found that having Annabelle's portrait hung in the gallery now provided her comfort, even after all these years. But there were times when she asked herself *did I even have the right to grieve after giving up my baby?*

"Don't go there, Tati," she scolded herself, pouring the boiling water over her chai teabag, immediately filling the gallery with the warming scents of clove, cinnamon, cardamom, ginger, and star anise.

Her spirits were lifted by the warming cup of tea and her guilt assuaged somewhat knowing that Annabelle, even for her short life, was loved by her adoptive mother and her biological father. But sometimes in the deepest part of night, the 'what ifs' plagued her mind—what if I kept her, would she still be alive? What if I let her be adopted the way I had originally planned, would she still be alive? Tatiana suffered many sleepless nights upon hearing of her daughter's death, and those 'what ifs' almost drove her insane. It wasn't until about a year after Annabelle's death, when Hamish sent her the portrait, that Tatiana was finally able to put to rest the what ifs. She knew as soon as she unwrapped the painting, and saw the contented look of her beautiful daughter—the rosy chubby cheeks, the brightness in her blueberry eyes, the plumpness of her toddler fingers pointing out of the window, reflected that Annabelle was loved and well cared for, and some things, such as an illness or death, could never have been prevented. But at that time, Tatiana found it heart wrenching to look at the portrait, and put it away, only looking at it on Annabelle's birthday and on a very special date in August when she knew Annabelle was conceived. Tatiana took comfort in knowing that Annabelle was an angel in the garden of Heaven, and that they would meet someday again.

With hot tea steeping on her lap, Tatiana was shaken from her daydream as a knock on her door made her jump almost off of her chair and caused her to spill her tea.

"Shoot," she whispered, annoyed that whoever was knocking was totally ignoring the closed sign on the door. She grabbed a roll of paper towels and dried herself off as she put her hand on the doorknob.

"I'm sorry but..." Tatiana was struck speechless at who she saw on the other side of the door.

"Hello, Tati."

Hamish Falconer stood on her doorstep.

Tatiana was suddenly whisked back in time, to all those decades ago, when she had first met the handsome Scot. Although most of his jet-black hair was now as silver as her own, he was still as handsome as when they first met at McGilvery's, where they stood now. He had a mustache and beard that matched his hair perfectly, and the lines on his face were deeper, but his eyes were still as blue and as mischievous — they were the eyes of Annabelle. He was still as lean as he was all those years ago, and with the exception of the decades wearing across his face, he looked the same, and she would know him in a heartbeat.

"Hamish," she whispered. It was almost like seeing a ghost. She then momentarily questioned herself to whether or not he was actually standing here, or was her gazing at Annabelle's portrait playing some kind of trick on her exhausted mind?

Tatiana felt herself tremble, watching him smile as she said his name. But she was struck dumb, and couldn't take her eyes from the father of her only child.

"May I come in?" he quietly asked.

"I'm sorry! Of course, yes, please come in. I just didn't expect…"

She shut the door behind him still shocked that he was actually in Lobster Claw. In her gallery.

"You just didn't expect to see me." Hamish finished Tatiana's sentence. "I didn't expect to see me, either," he laughed. "Well, what I mean is, I didn't expect to be here."

Tatiana still could not believe Hamish was here in the flesh.

"I'm sorry, Hamish. Please, won't you sit down?" She motioned to the two chairs that were normally reserved for she and Charlotte. He nodded and took a seat.

"Can I get you anything? A cup of tea?" was all Tatiana could say.

"Aye, tea would be lovely. If it's not too much trouble."

Tatiana shook her head. "No, of course it's no trouble. I was actually just having some, but it ended up on my lap…". She stopped talking as she knew she sounded silly and wasn't making sense. But how could she when the father of her child just breezed into her gallery after all these years? She had no anger with Hamish, and she never did. Not communicating was part of their promise, but the shock of seeing him was doing things to her that she could not control. Like blathering and shaking so hard she was sure he noticed.

The water in the electric kettle was still hot, so she found the cup that Charlotte usually used, took a chai bag from the box and poured the still steaming water over the bag.

"Oh, that smells like chai," Hamish said, a thankful smile on his face.

"I don't have any cream or sugar, if that's okay," Tatiana said, taking the mugs over to the chairs and handing Hamish a hot cup of tea.

"Exactly the way I like it. Thank you, Tati."

"No one has called me that in years, Hamish. In fact, you were the only person who ever called me Tati." She watched as he sipped the tea and thought she saw a faint blush rise on his cheeks. It could have been from the hot tea, the steam almost masking his face, but Tatiana didn't think so.

An awkward silence settled between the two of them, Tatiana not being able to touch her tea, as her hands still trembled and she didn't want hot tea all over her lap again.

Hamish set the mug on the small table next to the chair. He looked straight at her, and she felt as if he was looking into her soul, making her feel vulnerable and exposed.

"It was Charlotte who mentioned you, Tati. When I told her I was visiting Rory and that I was going to come down for a visit, she wanted me to meet her friends, and especially her friend Tatiana. That's when I nearly dropped the phone. I couldn't believe my ears when she first mentioned your name, nor could I believe it could truly be you. So I had to come see for myself, and here you are. Still as beautiful as that day we met at McGilvery's. Even more so."

Now it was Tatiana's turn to feel the heat in her body rush up to her face. But she didn't care. He still had the power to mesmerize her even after all these years, and she always knew she never stopped loving him, and her love for him and for their daughter was never more evident to her than at this moment.

"My Hamish," Tatiana whispered.

Hamish rose slowly from his chair and stepped toward Tatiana. He bent down on one knee and took her still soft-as-angel wings hands within his. Tatiana's mind flew back in time, feeling his loving touch just as she did that summer night, and she tightened her own grasp on his still strong hands.

"Tati, I'm so sorry. I'm so sorry."

Tatiana saw a vale of tears form over his blueberry eyes. The mischievousness of a few moments ago had now turned to sadness. She took her hand from his and caressed his bearded cheek.

"My Hamish, there's nothing to be sorry for. Nothing at all."

"But our daughter died, Tati, and there was nothing I could do to stop it. I was her father and I couldn't protect her. The one precious thing in my life I let slip away." Tatiana felt his head fall into her lap, his body now heaving with sobs that she knew he had contained for decades.

"My Hamish," she repeated, running her hands through his thick silver and black hair, trying to provide this grieving man comfort.

Tatiana bent down and kissed the top of his head.

"Hamish, there was nothing you could do. I have no doubt you did everything in your power to keep Annabelle safe, but we cannot control everything. Sometimes it is simply out of our hands and there is nothing we can do. Nothing."

Hamish raised his head, his tears falling onto her lap. His face was red with grief, and the pain from all those years ago seemed to have caught up with him.

"I never stopped loving you, Tati. Never. You were so selfless, so courageous."

Tatiana looked into his sad blue eyes. "As I told you so many years ago, Hamish, I knew you were not mine to keep. I had you for a brief moment in time, we created a life together, and you gave our child the best possible life. It wasn't that I was selfless or courageous, Hamish. I only wanted the best for Annabelle, and you could give that to her. I knew you had a fiancée, and if you had been mine from the beginning, I never would have let you go. Never. But you belonged to someone else, and I wasn't going to do that to your fiancée. What we had was brief and it was beautiful, and I never forgot it. I could never forget the only man that I ever truly loved. Never, my Hamish," she said stroking his tear-stained face.

"For so many years after Annabelle died I felt I was being

punished," Hamish said. "I was never honest with Hannah about Annabelle, and if she ever suspected, she never said anything. She loved that little girl so fiercely and she was broken when Annabelle died." Hamish returned to his chair, which he pulled closer to Tatiana, once again, taking her hands within his.

"But someone was looking over that woman," Hamish started. When Hannah was thirty-seven she became pregnant. Something we never thought would happen, and we had a son."

"Hamish," said Tatiana, her grip tightening around Hamish's hands. "You have a son? How wonderful."

"Aye, and now a grandson as well. He, Colin, brought so much joy into our lives, it was as if Hannah was born all over again. But she never forgot Annabelle, and she always told me she could feel her daughter's presence with her everywhere, especially when Colin was born. She would be watching Colin play in our backyard and she always had a wistful look in her eyes and she'd say to me, 'Hamish, Annabelle is here, playing with her brother.' Hannah became very ill herself when Colin was 18. He was away at college and he rushed back as quickly as he could before his mother passed. And right before she died, as Colin held his mother in his arms, she said, 'My two babies are here with me now. But I must go with Annabelle.' She closed her eyes, sighed, and I swear a smile passed across her face and then she was gone."

Tatiana could feel her own eyes fill with tears as Hamish spoke, his words so evidenced with the love he had for his wife and for his daughter and son.

"I'm so sorry, Hamish. Hannah was a good woman and even now is taking care of our daughter."

Tatiana stood up and reached her hand to Hamish, who accepted it. She guided him over to the other side of the gallery where Annabelle's picture hung. She could feel Hamish's strong arm wrap around her shoulder and he pulled her close to him as they looked at the painting of their beautiful Annabelle.

Tatiana let herself lean in closer to Hamish, feeling the connection between herself, Hamish and their daughter, and all the years and the distance between them quickly vanished.

"I had this painting in storage for so long," she said. "But when Charlotte mentioned her friend, Hamish Falconer, I knew it was time for Annabelle to be here in the gallery with me. You see, you weren't the only one filled with guilt. As much as I knew she was with her father and a woman who would raise her as her own, I still had given up my child. I tortured myself thinking that if I had only kept her, she would still be with us today. But I don't know that to be true, Hamish. It's impossible to know. But I take great comfort now when I look at this portrait of a beautiful and happy child that no matter how brief her time on this Earth may have been, she was greatly loved. She gave you and Hannah hope and happiness, and there was a reason she was born. She was ours, Hamish. And she always will be."

Tatiana felt Hamish try to stifle his tears, and she wrapped her arms around his waist and hugged him tightly.

"So many years, Tati. It almost seems impossible I'm in my 70s. But I could live to be one hundred and seventy and I'd still never forget what we had."

Tatiana felt Hamish's gentle kiss on the top of her head, sending her back to all those years ago when they first met, and she was that young woman once again in the arms of the man she loved.

Tatiana felt tears prickle at the back of her eyes. She took a deep breath and looked up at Hamish's still handsome face.

"Neither will I, my Hamish," she smiled. "Now enough sadness, let's make some more tea and sit and catch up. I think we have a lot to talk about."

CHAPTER THIRTY-NINE

"It's nice to finally have some time for just us, Hamish," said Charlotte. There had been no time yesterday or earlier in the day for the two friends to chat, as Hamish was true to his word, and helped loads of customers at The Shop at Beach Rose Path find the perfect T-shirt and tote bag, along with pouring endless cups of coffee and serving cookies and cupcakes, and managing to sneak one or two himself. Charlotte was brimming with curiosity about Hamish's rendezvous with Tatiana and she wanted to tell him about Duncan. The Beach Block was throwing an end-of-summer party on the beach later, complete with bonfire and a barbecue, and Charlotte knew she and Hamish would be knocked back into the grasp of the Lobster Claw crew, but she wanted and needed time for her and Hamish to be alone.

"Aye, Char," Hamish said, as she locked the door and put on the tea kettle.

"I even had Betsy bake you a batch of those cinnamon scones you love so much," Charlotte laughed, reaching under the counter for the Take the Cake bakery box. She opened the box and the delectable scent of cinnamon filled the air.

"Oh, Char, they smell amazing. Thank you for thinking of me, sweetheart."

Charlotte set the scones on a plate and brought them over to the coffee table in the bungalow. Hamish had settled into the wing chair and it was as if they were back in his executive suite at Castle Loch.

"So," Charlotte smiled, taking a sip of the hot tea. "You and Tatiana. I think I could guess, but…"

"But nothing, Charlotte." Hamish bit into his scone and washed it down with a large gulp of tea.

"Absolutely delicious, Char." He put the tea on the saucer and looked at his old friend. "I could guess with you and Duncan as well, but I won't. You seem very happy, Charlotte. Very happy."

"I am, Hamish. But age before beauty," she laughed. "What's your story with Tatiana?"

Hamish quietly relayed to Charlotte his love story with Tatiana, Hannah, and Annabelle.

"Hamish, why didn't you ever tell me?" Charlotte asked, tears in her eyes listening to the love and the guilt that Hamish reserved within himself for all these years.

"Oh, Char, it happened so long ago, and in all honesty, I wasn't proud of myself. Even though it was before Hannah and I were married, we had entered a very dark part of our relationship, but I always knew she was the woman I was going to marry. And then Tatiana came along, and I can't even begin to describe how instantly enamored I became of her. It was as if some great force of nature knocked me over when I first laid eyes on her and I was paralyzed to do anything else. Aye, she was beautiful, but Tati was more than a physically beautiful woman. She had a beautiful soul—she was kind, giving, confident, genuine. She made me feel safe and at peace. It's impossible to describe how it all happened so quickly, and for such a short period of time, but it happened, and the result was Annabelle."

"Do you think Hannah ever suspected you were Annabelle's

biological father?" Charlotte only knew Hannah as Colin's mother, and she never suspected there was a child before Colin.

"If she did, Char, she never told me. Hannah would kid me every now and again that it was amazing that Annabelle reminded her so much of me—the way she squinted her blue eyes when she laughed, and the little dimples in each of our cheeks."

"Dimples!" Charlotte laughed. "I've never seen you without a beard!"

"No, you haven't. I've pretty much had a beard since Annabelle came to live with us. I grew it intentionally, to try to mask any other similarities between us, silly as that may sound."

Hamish looked down into his now empty cup. "I think that Hannah knew, but I was too much of a coward to talk to her about it."

"You are not a coward, Hamish," Charlotte said quietly, now moving closer to her old friend and taking his hand.

"What you did was noble and it was evidence of your greatness of character that allowed you to do such an unselfish thing. You were able to give Hannah what she wanted most, and I'm sure a huge burden was lifted from Tatiana as well, knowing that her daughter would be raised by her very own father instead of strangers. You were no coward, Hamish Falconer."

"Thank you, Char," Hamish softly said, as Charlotte could see the clear film of tears in his eyes.

"I have something for you," she said, getting up. Charlotte descended the basement stairs and retrieved the plastic container labeled *Annabelle*.

She sat on the chair next to Hamish who removed the top and pulled out the aprons. The one that Annabelle was wearing in the portrait was carefully folded on top. He pulled it out, and Charlotte saw a look of grief in his eyes.

Charlotte watched as Hamish gently touched the soft cotton of Annabelle's smock, his finger carefully gliding over the silk pink ribbon still tied in the center part of the chest.

"I found these in the basement, with some of Violet's other things. I thought they were hers, and that she and Rory may have lost a child, as there are matching ones in an adult size. But when Tatiana put the portrait of Annabelle up in The Blue Hydrangea, I thought there was something so familiar about the painting. I realized it was the smock, but there was something else familiar about her that I could not put my finger on. And now I know— you and your daughter have the same exact eyes, Hamish."

Hamish brought the smock up to his nose.

"I can still smell her, Char. The clean scent of her soap and shampoo that Hannah was always bathing her with. It's still here."

"Oh, Hamish." Charlotte gripped her friend's hand tighter.

"Hannah made me promise to donate everything of Annabelle's to charity when she died. She couldn't live with the constant reminders, but I couldn't part with these. Hannah made them herself, and it always warmed my heart when I came home and saw the two of them wearing their matching frocks. I sent these up to Rory and asked him to save them."

"No wonder we were such kindred spirits, Hamish. You knew what it was like to lose someone you cherished with all of your heart. You knew exactly what I was going through when I lost Landon. But you never made it about you—it was just me you were concerned about—and my wellbeing. But you knew." Charlotte was overwhelmed with emotion at the selflessness of her friend and father figure. Hamish was the only one who could reach her during those dark, dark days in the aftermath of Landon's and Peppe's deaths. And now she understood how he was able to do that.

"We've had ourselves quite the lives, haven't we, Char? We've both loved and lost, and made it through the storms of life. We both have faith that our lives still hold hope for better days, which we have certainly seen, and I think we are at the point where our lives are only going to get better. What do you say?"

Charlotte smiled at Hamish, thinking that he was absolutely

right—the best days of their lives were right around the corner, and Charlotte couldn't wait to see what these days would bring.

"Who would have thought that little Lobster Claw, Maine held the keys to your past, and now to my future? Thank you, Hamish. If it weren't for you and Rory, I don't know where I'd be."

"That's another thing I wanted to talk to you about, Charlotte. Rory." said Hamish.

"Oh, no," Charlotte said, a sudden panic now filling her stomach. "I hope he's happy with what I've done. The store's been very profitable and…"

Hamish's generous laugh interrupted her. "That's another thing I haven't been honest about, Charlotte. The shop."

"I don't understand, Hamish." Now Charlotte could feel true panic rise, making her heart beat faster.

"The property doesn't belong to Rory. It belongs to me."

"Okay, Hamish, now I really don't understand what's going on. This is yours?"

"Rory did originally own the place," Hamish began. "But he and Violet were having financial issues, which Rory didn't want her to know about. A year after Annabelle was born, Rory asked if I would buy into the store at 50%. I agreed as he was a good friend, and I didn't want to see his young family experience financial ruin. But I also bought into the store so I could have a piece of Lobster Claw always with me. It was where Tatiana was from and Annabelle too. Anyway, when Rory decided to move to Halifax, I bought him out and by this point in time, I wasn't sure what I wanted to do. I knew I wanted to return to Scotland, and when Castle Loch went under new management, this became the perfect situation for you. And it looks like I was right!"

"Why didn't you just tell me it was yours?"

"I was afraid if I did, and knowing you as well as you know I do, you'd think I was just trying to take care of you—instead of you taking care of yourself. I knew your perspective would be different if I told you it was a friend's and not mine. Am I correct?"

Charlotte shook her head in amazement at Hamish's uncanny ability at knowing her. "You are ever so correct, Hamish. I guess I would have felt it was more charitable than me achieving something on my own and helping a friend."

"I knew you'd pull off another miracle, Charlotte. Wait here." Hamish got up and went into the dining room where his suitcase was. He opened it and pulled out another colored folder—this time a blue one.

He sat back down in the chair with a thud.

"No one has ever known this is mine. Not Hannah, not even Colin. This was my special connection to Lobster Claw. My connection to Tatiana and Annabelle. But I no longer need that connection, and I have signed the deed over to you." He handed Charlotte the blue folder which contained all the legal documents making her the lawful and official owner of The Shop at Beach Rose Path.

"I don't understand, Hamish. Why?" Charlotte felt tears in her eyes that she was unable to stop.

"You deserve to be happy, Charlotte, and from what I can see, you are," he said quietly, taking Charlotte's hands in his own.

"You've done a magnificent job here, and on your own. You've earned it, Charlotte. And the plain fact is that I want this little piece of paradise to be yours. It's that simple."

"I don't know what to say, Hamish," Charlotte whispered, the folder trembling in her hands. "Thank you."

"You're very welcome, Char. We can go over all the details tomorrow. I'm not leaving for Scotland until the end of the week. I moved my flight back so I could have more time here."

"That makes me just as happy, Hamish." Charlotte got up, as did Hamish and she felt his fatherly embrace about her shoulders.

"I think we have a party to get to as well, don't we? And you need to fill me in more on that Duncan of yours. I am done talking about me."

"Duncan," Charlotte whispered. "You'll have all the time you like with him at the party. I think it's going to be a Labor Day party like no other."

"Aye, Char, that's for sure." Hamish laughed as they cleared their tea things into the kitchen and got ready for the last official night of summer.

CHAPTER FORTY

A SURGE OF HAPPINESS AND CONTENTMENT FILLED CHARLOTTE AS she and Hamish walked along the dock toward the Beach Block. She didn't think she ever saw a sunset as beautiful as tonight. The evening sky was the color of cobalt, with crevices of fuchsia and rose winking in the twilight. The silhouette of sailboats peacefully floated on the late summer sea, tranquilly gliding toward the bay to be docked for the evening. Charlotte was especially comforted by the beacon of Sea Star Lighthouse, as she now considered it a dependable friend—it became a vestige of safety for her, especially on those sleepless nights, when all she needed to do was look out of her window and the light would be shining across the ocean, her own guiding light of optimism and faith.

Little Lovey trotted ahead of them, once again, curiosity getting the better of her, scampering a little too close to the piping plover sanctuary.

"Come, Lovey," was all Charlotte needed to say, and her best friend was quickly by her side.

"That's a good dog you have there, Charlotte," Hamish said, reaching into his pocket for a little treat.

"I don't know what I'd do without her, Hamish," Charlotte smiled. "And I don't know what I'd do without you."

"You'd do just fine, and you have, Char."

"Thanks to you, Hamish." Charlotte would be forever grateful to her friend and benefactor.

"You're welcome. Now, enough of the sentimentalities. Let's party," he grinned, as the laughter of the crowd on the beach grew louder with every step they took.

Lovey ran ahead and sat stock still in front of The Blue Hydrangea, her head going back and forth as she watched the movement within the store.

"Tatiana has her favorite treats—she bakes them herself, pumpkin cookies" explained Charlotte as they joined Lovey outside of the store.

"Not surprising," Hamish quietly said. Charlotte followed his gaze watching the lissome movements of Tatiana gathering up a tub of ice with champagne bottles.

"You pretty much pulled an all-nighter, Hamish. As you are a guest in my home, I think an explanation is necessary," laughed Charlotte, full well knowing where he was and who he was with.

"Aye, Char, haven't done that in decades." He turned to his friend, a smile of joy widening across his sunburnt face.

"We had a lot to catch up on, as you can imagine. And it was a wonderful evening," he concluded, turning his head back toward the door and waving at Tatiana, who now had a smile just as happy and as big as Hamish's.

Tatiana put the bucket down and waved them in, grabbing a cookie from her special cookie jar for Lovey, who gratefully took it from her.

"Might we be of service, madam?" Hamish laughed, as he loaded more bottles of champagne into the overflowing bucket.

"Thank you, kind sir," Tatiana answered, and kissed Hamish gently on the cheek.

Charlotte watched as Tatiana pulled a trolley from the back of the gallery, and the two of them loaded several buckets onto it, as if they had been a couple for their entire lives. To Charlotte it was pure magic to see both of her friends happy and wondered what the future had in store for them.

Charlotte then turned as she felt the cool night air upon her back as the door to The Blue Hydrangea opened.

"Duncan!" exclaimed Charlotte as she walked toward him and greeted him with a kiss of her own.

"I thought I might find you in here," he said, caressing Charlotte's cheeks. Lovey had sidled up to him, her wet nose nudging for a hug herself.

"And, you too, Lovey," Duncan quietly said bending and scratching the dog behind her soft yellow ears.

"Duncan!" exclaimed Hamish, walking toward Duncan.

"Good to see the other man in Charlotte's life again," he said, extending his large hand which Duncan happily accepted.

"I told you, Charlotte, a good strong handshake is the sign of a good man," Hamish said, releasing his hand from Duncan's grip.

Duncan kissed Tatiana on the cheek as she brought the trolley closer to the front door.

"These will have to do," said Tatiana as she went behind her counter and pulled out paper cups and placed them on the counter.

"Perfect," Hamish whispered, kissing Tatiana on the cheek. Charlotte's heart filled with happiness watching the affection Hamish and Tatiana had for each other.

"Everyone ready?" Tatiana asked, grabbing Hamish by his arm, ready to escort him to the party.

"Not quite yet, if you don't mind, Tati," Hamish said quietly. Charlotte detected a note of melancholy in his voice, and she couldn't understand why, as he seemed to be so happy to be reunited not only with her, but with Tatiana as well.

"Before we head down to the party," he said, taking one of the magnums of champagne from the ice bucket, "I'd like to say a few words."

"Charlotte," he began quietly, "you've been like a daughter to me all these years, and I don't know what I would do without you. We've been through so much together—love, loss," and he nodded toward Duncan, "and love again, I'm grateful to have you in my life, Char."

"Hamish," whispered Charlotte, as tears formed in her eyes. She felt the strong arms of Duncan enfold about her, providing her comfort and happiness.

"You are Beach Rose Path, my dear."

Hamish then turned toward Tatiana.

"Tati, to find you again is one of my life's greatest gifts. And this time, I won't let you go." He pulled Tatiana close to him, and tenderly kissed her blushing lips.

"My Hamish," she whispered and kissed her old love once again.

"And last but not least," Hamish continued, his own face now the color of crimson, "Duncan. I entrust Char and Lovey to you. I believe I'm a pretty good judge of character, and I know you'll take good care of both of them."

Charlotte beamed at Duncan as he lovingly looked at her and tightened his arms about her.

"I give you my word, Hamish. They are my girls, now."

"Cheers to us!" Hamish announced as the cork from the bottle caused a loud pop, and champagne overflowed into the paper cups.

CHAPTER FORTY-ONE

"I HOPE YOU KNOW I MEANT WHAT I SAID."

The party had ended and Charlotte, Lovey and Duncan had made their way back to the beach in front of The Shop at Beach Rose Path, sitting in their Adirondack chairs, the warm waves lolling in over their bare feet. It had been a wonderful evening spent with friends, food, and the satisfaction of knowing that Charlotte was now in the comfort of Duncan's love.

Hamish and Tatiana left the party early, heading back to The Blue Hydrangea to discuss plans for Tatiana traveling to Scotland during Christmas and New Year's. Charlotte could not have been happier for her two friends and their rekindled love for each other.

Charlotte took Duncan's hand and held it to her lips, softly kissing it, the roughness and strength making her happy with every touch.

"You said a lot, Duncan," she smiled. "You said you've never been as happy since being back in Lobster Claw. You said you couldn't wait for next spring to get the boat back on trips. You said you liked my idea of starting a sightseeing business..."

"Okay, okay, yes, I did say a lot of things, and I meant every one you just mentioned." He rose from his chair and pulled Charlotte from hers, walking her down closer to the shoreline.

He held her in his arms and kissed her passionately, and Charlotte knew, with that kiss, their lives in Lobster Claw would never be the same.

"But I was talking about when I said that you and Lovey were mine. I meant that more than anything, Charlotte. Because without you, I don't know where I'd be now. Thank you for giving me a second chance at life. At love."

Charlotte gazed into his hazel eyes, the lines in his sunburnt face making him even more handsome than she ever thought any man could be. Charlotte's heart surged with love for him, with his arms firmly enveloping her, and she knew their future together would be nothing but brilliant.

"Thank you for *my* second chance, Duncan. I love you."

Duncan's kiss was ardent, passionate and the kiss of love, and that was all Charlotte needed. She knew Beach Rose Path in Lobster Claw, Maine, would be her home for the rest of her life, as the ever-guiding beacon of Sea Star Lighthouse shone over their world that would never be dark again.

RATE AND REVIEW

We hope you enjoyed *Beach Rose Path* by Barbara Matteson. If you did, we would ask that you please rate and review this title. Every review helps our authors.

Rate and Review: Beach Rose Path

ABOUT THE AUTHOR

Barbara Matteson is a life-long New Englander. She lives right outside of Boston with her husband, son, black Labrador retriever and a leopard gecko.

Barbara's first novel, The Perfect Mrs. Claus, was published in November 2022, and she has also had an essay published in Victoria Magazine in January 2022.

Beach Rose Path is her second novel, set in one of her favorite places, Maine.

OTHER TITLES FROM 5 PRINCE PUBLISHING

9 781631 123726